# ALIENS, SMITH AND JONES

## A PRIMROSE FILES NOVEL

# ALIENS, SMITH AND JONES

## A PRIMROSE FILES NOVEL

## BLAINE D. ARDEN

To my friends, for taking me as I am

I love you all

# 1

THE DROSS WOODS, FOUR-BLOODY-SOMETHING IN THE morning, hunting for six-armed, two-legged white creatures.

Agent Connor Smith, personal assistant of Chief Security Lieutenant Natalie Tallis of Primrose UK, yawned. The lingering mist clung to his ankles as he tightened the straps of his field gear. He took his tranq out of its holster and flicked his torch on. The dense, tall trees hampered visibility, and the smattering of shrubs didn't help, either. The path, at least, was wide enough for two.

"How many were there again?" Agent Simpson, team Alpha's leader, asked. His dark, bald head gleamed in the early dawn as he moved to stand next to Connor.

"Ten, I think." Or eleven. Connor hadn't been awake enough to pick up everything during the interview with the Cleaton brothers, two aging sheep farmers, who had called it in. Why have a sheep farm so close to this vast and dense piece of forest? It was asking for trouble.

"They kept them in the stables, right? So, what happened?"

"Broke out," Connor said as he trailed into the woods after Simpson. Though Connor outranked the stocky but agile team leader, Simpson had at least a decade of field experience on him. Simpson's torch lit up the uneven, knobby-rooted ground, and Connor used his to search the shrubbery next to the path. He wished he'd brought an extra coffee, because he was not awake enough for this. Hopefully, the pale colour of the creatures made them easier to spot.

"So, *broke out?*"

"Have you seen the thing they called stables? It's nothing more than a rickety old shed. Even one-armed creatures would have had no problem breaking out, let alone these... Noren, I think the brothers called them."

"All I understood was that we're here to catch us some aliens." Simpson veered left, following the whimsical bend in the path, and looked back. "It was a late night."

"Right, you were chasing another missing artefact. Lieutenant Tallis filled me in. File's probably making its way to my desk as we speak." Connor squinted, aiming his torch at the shrubbery to his left. A mix of red, yellow, and purple flowers brought some colour to the otherwise dreary looking forest. "It's the eighth time this has happened. It's becoming a problem."

"Don't I know it. So, did they say how big these fellas are?"

"Chest height or about. Why? Spot something?" Connor pointed his torch along Simpson's.

The shrubs shuddered and shook until Simpson stepped forward. A twig snapped, followed by meowing. A cat. Just a cat.

Connor shrugged at Simpson and they moved forward again.

Somewhere a shout rang out: a high-pitched screech that caused goose bumps.

"One down!" someone called through the commlink—team Bravo's Forente or Briers, Connor guessed. "There are at least two others here."

"That way," Simpson said, pointing to their right, onto a

narrow path overgrown with creepers.

Connor nodded, but Simpson had already turned away.

Step by step, they followed the narrow path, the darkness only broken by the light of their torches. They were hampered by the creepers as they moved along—listening, stopping, and listening again—as well as having to push low branches out of their way every other step.

One by one, more teams called in their catches.

"They seem to like sheep," Forente commented after his first catch. "I heard one bleat, and the next thing we know, one of those Noren is coming right at us."

"Good to know," Simpson said. "Keep up the good work."

"How many is that now?" Connor eyed the shrubbery in front of him, squinting as he pointed the torch at it. Eerie how dark a forest could be at daybreak. He preferred the smell of fresh moss to the damp, woodsy smell that now hung around him.

"Seven. I think."

So, three to go, and he and Simpson had yet to run into any.

Something rustled behind them, and Connor turned, aiming his tranq. He hoped it wasn't another cat. More rustling, but no movement in the shrubs. The foliage was denser here—they must have reached the middle of the woods by now.

Satisfied a Noren wasn't stalking them, Connor went to catch up with Simpson. when a sudden crunching of leaves to his right stopped him again. Something whitish moved behind a tree, too large to be a rabbit. He wished he'd paid more attention when Tallis had told them what to look for. Not that she'd been any more awake than he was. Simpson wasn't the only one who'd been working late. The—

Another crunch, nowhere near, though. If there were two Noren around, he'd need Simpson. He tapped the commlink.

"Simpson?"

"That was me. The path circles back onto itself."

That was a relief. "There's one behind a tree in front of me."

"Right. Want me to move around it?"

"Good idea." Then he remembered the comment about the sheep. "Wait. You don't have to. Draw it out, bleat if you have to. All I need is a clear shot. I can't take a shot as long as it's hiding behind that tree," Connor said, keeping an eye on the tree the Noren hid behind. He hoped it was just the one, even though they didn't seem violent towards humans.

Simpson's imitation of a sheep sounded nothing like the real thing, yet the Noren thought it genuine enough, since it came out from behind the tree, straight into the dense shrubbery next to it.

"Bugger." Connor tracked the movement, but the shrubbery blocked his view. "I don't have a shot. It fled right into the bushes."

Simpson didn't reply. Instead, he made his way around Connor, judging from the flashes of torchlight jumping around, and repeated his sheep imitation.

The leaves shuddered, and Connor narrowed his eyes, hoping to get a clear shot.

Simpson bleated again, and this time the Noren came running out of the shrubbery. Connor aimed and pulled the trigger. The Noren went down hard. Hit in one. He knelt next to the creature, taking the cuffs out.

"Nice shot, Smith," Simpson said when he reached them.

"Thanks." Connor cuffed all three sets of arms. It seemed like overkill, but he knew better than to take any risks. He was about to activate his earpiece to ask how many were still on the loose when a shrill whistle sounded, calling them back.

"Well," Simpson said as he helped Connor pick the Noren up, "I guess that's that."

"All in a day's work, Simpson, all in a day's work." At least, for a personal assistant at Primrose.

"CONNOR, COME ON, HURRY UP OR WE'LL MISS THE TRAIN."

Connor rolled his eyes as he warmed some hair gel in his hands. Why had he agreed to join Isa to the pub straight from work? Sure, he always had a spare set of clothes in the office—you never knew what might happen in this job—but he'd much rather have gone home and taken a shower first. Actually, as wonderful as that sounded, after the long days he'd had this week—tracking a missing Noren—he'd rather lounge on his sofa with a cold beer and some soothing music.

At least, they assumed the Noren was missing. After returning to the shed and locking them all up, they'd done a recount and had ended up being one Noren short, according to the brothers. The Cleatons swore they had counted them several times. There should have been ten, but they'd only caught nine. So, either one had escaped, or the brothers couldn't count.

Now, one seemingly harmless missing alien wasn't worth the effort, but adding that in with all the artefacts that had gone missing in the past two years, it seemed suspicious. Enough for Tallis to make finding it a priority, and have Connor put a search out for it. Three days had passed and nothing had turned up yet. No odd sightings, no disturbances, no spooked sheep, nothing.

"Connor."

Bloody hell, Isa sounded annoying when she was impatient. He almost *heard* her pouting.

"I'm coming, I'm coming." He ran his hands through his hair, messing it up with style—as shown by his hairdresser—

and cast one last glance in the mirror. That would have to do. He washed his hands, grabbed the hanger with his suit, and exited the toilet.

Isa waited for him in the hall, arms crossed, as he walked back into his office to hang up his suit. "You don't look half bad," she said, looking him up and down with piercing, cognac-brown eyes. "I guess I can forgive you for taking so long."

Isa Griffin, personal assistant of Chief Security Lieutenant Clark Matthews, was Connor's colleague and best friend. She was wiry and about half a foot shorter than him, but deceptively strong. Her short, thick auburn hair didn't even need any product to look stylish—according to Connor at least. Isa never stopped complaining about her unruly hair.

He snorted as he hung the suit on the coat rack in the corner of his office, right next to the giant stainless-steel filing cabinet. He hadn't been in the toilet for more than five minutes, including the time it had taken him to change clothes. "Where were we going again?"

"Clyde's. Unless you prefer some place quieter."

He hadn't been to Clyde's in ages. Not since Zack. "Are you trying to tell me something?"

"No." Isa didn't even need to look at him—the slight change of pitch in her voice said enough.

Bloody hell, she was trying to set him up...again. He rubbed his forehead. She knew he hated being set up, but she wouldn't stop. What was it about Isa, his *best* friend, that made her go out of her way to find him a new bloke? He stared at his desk, frantically looking for a reason not to join her—a missed report, a last-minute delivery—but, as usual, there was nothing, not even a misplaced scrap of paper.

He shook his head and followed her out of his office. It might be better if he pretended not to know what she'd done, even though they both knew better.

They'd barely reached the corridor when Tallis rounded the corner. She pushed her long blond hair behind her ear, revealing her sharp jaw line, and held out a file. "Connor, oh, good. You're still here. I scheduled a meeting with Parker tomorrow at ten, but I need to reschedule and I can't seem to reach him. Can you call him first thing and make sure he gets this file?"

Connor took the file and nodded. "Of course, Lieutenant, first thing. Do you need me to stay?" Any excuse would do.

"No, no. I have everything I need, thank you. Enjoy your night out. You, too Agent Griffin."

"Thank you, Lieutenant," Connor and Isa said simultaneously, even though Tallis was already walking away, obviously deep in thought.

Connor tried not to show his disappointment, ran back to his office to put the file on his desk, and followed Isa towards the lifts.

"You know, I still can't believe you got her."

Connor raised his eyebrow. "Thank you for that vote of confidence."

Isa shook her head. "No, not that. You're good, the best around here, probably, not counting me, of course. It's just..." Isa shrugged, waving her hands in the air.

Connor knew exactly what she meant. Tallis was rather particular in choosing her personal assistant. His predecessor had been a somewhat stern-looking lady, right down to the grey bun and reading glasses, who could no doubt outrun him. If she hadn't decided to retire after one bullet wound too many, she'd probably still be working.

No one had been more surprised than Connor when Chief Research Lieutenant Rupert Holloway, his then-boss, had recommended him to her. He'd not even been here a year, and Tallis was one of the most revered lieutenants at Primrose. One trial week had been all she'd needed to hire him as her personal assistant almost a year and a half ago. He shuddered to think how green he'd been when he'd started working at Primrose.

They were almost out of the building when one of the guards stopped them. "Agent Smith?"

Connor nodded.

"I'm sorry, sir, but Lieutenant Tallis needs you to come back in."

Isa cursed.

"Tell her I'm on my way."

"Yes, sir."

Connor turned to face Isa and shrugged. "I'm sorry. I guess we'll have to do this another time." He tried to keep his face blank. He really didn't want her grumbling about how ungrateful he was.

Isa's expression showed a thunderstorm on the horizon, but all she did was sigh. "Yeah. It's not like we have a nine to five, is it? Any idea what it might be about?"

"After Simpson's report and the Noren, I wouldn't be surprised if it has something to do with the missing artefacts."

"I guess you'd better go up. Call me later, all right?"

"I'll text you."

"You'd better." Isa leaned in and kissed his cheek. "Who knows, you might be done in half an hour, and you can still make it to Clyde's tonight."

Connor nodded, even though he had no intention of going. Whoever she had lined up for him would have to find his own entertainment tonight.

TAKING A DEEP BREATH, CONNOR PUSHED THE DOOR OPEN WITH HIS elbow and entered the meeting with a full tray. Tallis mouthed a 'thank you' when he put a steaming cup in front of her.

She turned to the burly bloke next to her. "That's absurd, Andrew. I can't believe you still think it's a coincidence."

"What else *can* it be?" Commander Andrew Kittler, head of Primrose UK, asked. "No one but us knew about those artefacts, no other organisation or person even has the ability to locate them—"

Tallis clicked her fingers, interrupting him. "Connor, please enlighten Commander Kittler."

Connor nodded at her, put the tray down near the door, and took his own coffee with him as he ambled over to Tallis' desk, set up to one side of the oval table, to commandeer her keyboard. This was what they'd been working on relentlessly for the past hour and a half, and the reason she'd decided to call this emergency meeting.

Connor opened the file—a map and timeline of A-Watch findings and the fire at Lieutenant Langham's house—on the big screen hanging in front of the teal-coloured wall opposite Tallis' desk. "A-Watch, the system we use to trace artefacts of alien origin all over the country by scouring for certain alien materials, was developed for us by our former Chief Development Lieutenant, Wilfred Langham. After his retirement, Lieutenant Langham retained ownership of the programme and took the original first test CDs with him, storing them in his own personal safe at his home at Grantham Park."

Commander Kittler straightened up in his seat. "But...his house burnt down almost two years ago."

"Yes, it did." Connor showed a photo of a burnt computer tower, and melted CD. "The contents of his safe were retrieved intact except for one test CD, which was later found partly melted inside Lieutenant Langham's computer. Or so we believed." He paused to give Tallis the chance to take charge of the conversation again.

"We now have doubts,"—Tallis rose from her chair—"about the authenticity of the CD we rescued from that fire. We think what we have in our possession is not the actual test CD, which included a fully working prototype version of A-Watch. We think the test CD was removed before the fire."

Commander Kittler frowned as he watched the screen. "Natalie, have you been holding out on me?"

"We only have a partially melted CD and a strong hunch. Rupert called me less than two hours ago about the results of his initial tests, and he'll need to conduct further tests before we'll have any definitive proof."

"What does this have to do with the missing artefacts?"

That was the question Tallis had been waiting for. Connor smiled at her pleased expression.

"In the two years since the fire," she pointed at the timeline on-screen, "our agents have ended up empty-handed *eight* times after A-Watch located alien artefacts. That is *no* coincidence. Somehow, someone knows how to get there before our agents do."

Commander Kittler studied the timeline with a frown. "You think they have the programme."

He seemed at least half-convinced. That was good news, because further testing would eat up a large part of the research budget, which Commander Kittler would have to sign for. Connor handed out the papers containing the estimated costs for the research needed and crossed his fingers as the commander winced at the numbers.

"I think they do, but we can't be certain until Rupert finishes his research."

"Can these tests really determine whether or not the CD you have is a fake?"

"Rupert says they can, but we'll need to get our hands on the other test CDs as well, and they're still in Lieutenant

Langham's possession."

"You don't think old Wilfred's involved, do you?

"No. He was asleep in the next room and barely even woke when the firefighters found him. Besides, Langham wouldn't have had to steal the prototype, let alone plan such an elaborate ruse. It's his programme, he knows exactly how to create a working copy."

"Good." Commander Kittler said. "After putting so much of his life into the company and the welfare of our alien guests, he would never do anything to hurt either."

"He wouldn't. Nevertheless…," Tallis blew a stray strand of hair out of her eyes. "Marcel will contact the lieutenant for a follow-up interview, and to ask if we can borrow the remaining CDs. They still play golf together, and he thinks it will sound better coming from him." She placed her hands flat on the table. "That is, if you approve, Andrew."

"How can I not?" Commander Kittler sighed. "We can't allow someone to get away with this. We *cannot* risk anyone getting their hands on what they don't understand—what *we* barely understand. So, yes. You have my permission. But, please, tell Rupert to keep it as low-cost as he can."

"I will." She sank back into her chair, looking as relieved as Connor felt. "Thank you, Andrew."

While Commander Kittler and Tallis discussed some of the plans in more detail, Connor cleared up and checked his watch.

Nearly ten o'clock. Isa would no doubt still be at Clyde's, and after the evening he'd had, he was tempted to join her. He could do with a drink right now. What he did not need, however, was Isa springing her blind date on him.

When he was done, he grabbed his backpack and headed for the train. He'd send Isa a text message once he was close to home.

He hoped he still had some beer in the fridge.

# 2

I T WAS CHILLY ON THE PLATFORM AS CONNOR WAITED FOR THE train to Eastworth, despite the clear blue sky above the arched glass and steel roof. A faint rainbow lingered in the air, miles across the city. He hoped it wouldn't rain; he hated arriving at work soggy. He pushed off from the concrete pillar he'd been leaning against and crossed the drab grey tiles, closer to where the middle section of the train should be. Five more minutes, unless it was delayed...again.

An odd tingling at the base of his spine made him turn...and he was lost. He stood frozen, fists clenched, amongst the hustle and bustle on the platform. People brushed against him as they passed him by, as if he didn't exist. Their chatter seemed to come from miles away. There was nothing but grey all surrounding him; the cloudy grey of stormy weather that kept him rooted to the spot. He was unable to move, scream, or even close his unseeing eyes.

Some creepy-crawly must have stung or bitten him. Any moment now, someone would notice. Time passed excruciatingly slowly as Connor waited for someone to free him from this stormy grey world that made him light-headed and turned his legs to jelly. Was he even standing? Or was he lying on the ground, unconscious?

When he tried to move, it was as if tiny needles jabbed into every nerve ending he possessed, faster and faster, until his body screamed and his stomach didn't know which way was up. Sensations flared with every pinprick: elation, warmth, loneliness, longing, hunger, desperation, joy, cold. It was too much, too fast, too intense. He screamed, even though he couldn't hear himself.

The flow of sensations slowed but didn't stop.

Connor wanted it to stop, wanted it all to stop, wanted control over his body back, wanted to see properly again. Sweat trickled down his face, yet he tasted blood. Had he hit his head?

The blue and yellow blur of an arriving train forced the grey out of his vision. He blinked and wobbled on his feet, surprised to find he was still standing. He would have gladly let himself slide to the ground if the people around him weren't crowding him towards the waiting train.

With his blurry vision, Connor didn't care whether it was his train or not. He let them herd him towards it, gladly accepting the strong hand at his elbow, guiding him inside.

As soon as he found himself sitting down, he leaned his head back and closed his eyes. Sleep had never seemed this welcome before.

Someone slapped his cheek, and Connor opened his eyes to find a blurry face in front of him.

"Are you all right?"

Was he? Connor frowned. "Tired," he said, though he had no idea why. At least—

"Here," the face said, pushing something into his hand: a wad of tissues.

"Thanks, but..."

"You have a nosebleed."

Did he? Connor pushed the tissues against his nose. They came away red, and he pressed them back again. "Oh."

"I think your tie and shirt are ruined. Your suit jacket seems fine, but it's quite a dark colour, so the blood doesn't really show."

*Bugger!* It was his favourite tie, too. One-handed, he took his tie off and stuffed it into his jacket pocket. He blinked to clear his vision, glad to see the friendly face of his aide.

She started at him with large eyes as she worried her lip. "What happened to you?" she asked, holding a packet of tissues within reach.

Her face seemed awfully close. "Sorry? What did you say?"

"What happened to you?" She rested a hand on his knee.

Connor frowned. "I think something stung me. It's all a bit hazy."

"You should go to the A and E, have someone check you out."

"Yes, maybe I should. Thank you."

She blushed and smiled as she leaned back. "Oh, it's nothing."

Connor smiled back, though it no doubt looked awkward with the tissues hiding half his face, and closed his eyes.

TWO SECONDS OF THE SLIGHTEST TINGLE WERE ENOUGH TO DRAG Noah back a century or two ago. Memories so fresh in his mind, it seemed as if they had happened only yesterday. Like sweet Dafydd lying in the grass, smiling up at him—

No! Focus. No time to wallow. He needed to find the source, and he needed to find it before—

Too late. It was gone as fast as it had appeared. He turned, scanning the station booking hall filled with restlessly pacing humans looking for the right platform. It could have been anyone.

Noah cursed himself for reacting too slowly. He'd let his memories get in the way. He would never be able to find the source now, not in this crowd.

No matter how long it had been since he'd been close to one, he should have been more alert, should have been ready. He clenched his fists and made his way to the escalator, hoping he would get another chance.

The moment he stepped onto the platform, it was back, that same tingle at the base of his spine. As he locked onto sky blue eyes across the tracks, a sudden, hot spike of bright, pure energy surged through him, and wave after wave of raw, unguarded emotion assaulted him. He took it all in, let it wash over him and through him, even when his own emotions flowed into the mix. He didn't care when the intensity of it all made his knees buckle, didn't care how greedy he was. He needed this, craved this, had missed this so much.

He was out of practice, and almost missed the sharp sting of overloading the source. He immediately put up a block—something he should have done from the beginning—to filter the force of his own flow. Mumbled words of apology wouldn't soothe the source's pain. He should break contact entirely, should leave well enough alone, but he didn't want to stop now, couldn't give it up. He'd take everything the source would give him. It was too late to push deeper, to reach the core, to find out who his source was—

A train passed between Noah and the source, and he was cut off. His heart pounded in his throat, and he fought hard to get his breathing back under control as his core cried at the sudden loss. Searching the platform on the other side of the tracks as soon as the train had passed brought him nothing. The tingling at the base of his spine had gone. His source had disappeared.

He leaned his head back against a concrete pillar, cursing himself for not identifying his source first, for being unprepared, for being greedy. He should *not* have forgotten. The source's wellbeing was more important than his momentary bliss, even after such a long time.

BY THE TIME CONNOR REACHED THE EASTWORTH BUILDING WHERE Primrose was housed, his head had cleared considerably, but he was still unsure about what had happened. With the way his head hurt, he decided a check-up would be a good idea. He took the lift to the Medical Department on the third floor, greeted the nurse behind the desk, and handed her his ID. "Does the doctor have time for me this morning?" He took his jacket off and almost missed the nurse looking him up and down in disdain.

"We don't do brawls, Agent...," she looked at the ID, "...Smith."

Connor stared at the blood on his shirt. The woman on the train hadn't exaggerated when she'd said it was ruined. He sighed. "I had a nosebleed on the way here. I also suffered a dizzy spell and some nausea. I don't think I got stung or bitten, but I'd like a check-up...if that's not too much trouble." He kept his voice as calm as possible, though he couldn't keep his irritation out of it entirely. He knew there was a problem with agents showing up after a bar fight or two, but she could at least ask before judging.

The nurse had the decency to look embarrassed. "I apologise, Agent Smith. I'll see if the doctor has a few minutes to spare before her fist appointment."

She gave him his ID back and disappeared through a door to her right, coming back out almost immediately. "Doctor Quiggins will see you now."

Connor remembered Doctor Quiggins from his last

check-up, barely three months ago, and greeted the tall woman with a smile. Her light brown skin looked warm against the sterile white of her lab coat and the walls, despite the fluorescent lamps.

"Agent Smith. An unexpected pleasure."

"I'm not certain about the pleasure, Doctor."

"Yes, Ursula mentioned a dizzy spell, a nosebleed, and some nausea. This happened on the way here?"

"Yes. Also, some haziness and blurry vision. I saw nothing but grey spots for a while," Connor added as he hopped onto the exam table. It wasn't quite what he'd seen, but he didn't think she needed to know exactly everything. He could always elaborate, should anything inexplicable turn up.

"Right then. Let me check your nose first." Doctor Quiggins stepped forward and hissed. "You have a hint of a bruise on your left cheek. Any idea how that got there?"

"A bruise?" Connor asked. He didn't... Oh, of course. "Someone slapped me to keep me awake on the train. She was the one who told me I had a nosebleed." He hadn't realised she'd slapped him hard enough to bruise.

"I guess we can add disorientation to your symptoms," Doctor Quiggins said while shining a tiny light up his nose.

She straightened up and pocketed the light. "No damage, but judging from the amount of blood on your shirt, I'd say you had a severe bleed. Any idea how long it lasted?"

Connor shrugged. "I don't know when it started, exactly. Probably before I got on the train, and it didn't let up until I reached my stop. That's at least fifteen minutes, I think."

She nodded and moved behind him. "I take it you don't have a history of them?"

Connor shook his head, stilling when he felt her hands on his neck. She pushed the collar of his shirt down. "No bites here."

Nor anywhere else, as it turned out. Not that Connor

thought she'd find anything, not now that his memory was returning, but he felt better for having it checked out. He got off the exam table and straightened his shirt. "Will you send a copy of your report up to my office?" That way he could file it away with his own report of the incident.

"I'm not done yet," Doctor Quiggins said as she held up a small scanner meant to check for alien residue and technology.

Connor flinched. "You don't think...?"

She shrugged. "Better to be safe than sorry. Besides, it's protocol, even with your nosebleed."

He suppressed a shudder as he held himself still, hoping nothing alien would turn up while Doctor Quiggins ran the scanner over his body.

Three beeps later, she was done. "All clear."

No parasites or alien invasion, then. That was something, at least. Connor let out a huge breath.

"You'll have the report before lunch."

Connor thanked her, but ignored the nurse on his way out. He was late. He was never late.

Already formulating the report in his head as he entered his office, Connor almost bumped into Tallis dressed in field gear.

"Good morning, Lieutenant," he greeted her. "Sorry I'm late, I..."

She held her hand up to silence him and handed him his tranq, earpiece, and various sets of handcuffs. She frowned as she stared at his cheek, no doubt wondering about the bruise Doctor Quiggins had mentioned. She turned away from him. "Renegade Noren on the loose near Presly Green. Team

Alpha's waiting for us in the garage."

Connor suppressed the urge to groan. This was not his morning. He exchanged his suit jacket for his field jacket, put his earpiece in, and followed her into the lift. "Noren? Is this the missing one?"

"More than one have been sighted, but it is possible."

"You think the Cleaton brothers kept a few?"

Tallis shook her head. "No. Team Delta reported the Noren sighting when they were investigating an unknown residue in the ground that A-Watch picked up. They think the Noren might have landed in Presly Green."

"Landed? They found a ship?"

"I wish. No. Whatever it was seemed to have disintegrated and only left an oily residue behind."

"We were called because…?" Team Delta was one of Matthews' teams.

"Lieutenant Matthews took Team Charlie up north to check out suspicious sightings."

Isa would be so annoyed when she got back from visiting her mother. She loved field assignments even more than he did.

"So, assuming they did land near Presly Green, how did they get all the way to the Dross Woods?"

Tallis' steel heels echoed through the garage as they made their way to where the SUVs were parked. "Research is on it already, but for now, we have no idea. They don't seem the sort to split up, seeing as we found so many of them in the Dross Woods."

Connor spotted Simpson and Flanigan—team Alpha's hulking strawberry blond and freckled driver—standing next to one of the SUVs and nodded at them. "How many did they spot this time?"

"At least two. Not as much forest to hide in at Presly Green—better visibility and access, with all the farmland and fields surrounding it. Luckily, there are acres of land and only a few farms on that side of the village. I'd hate to have to assemble a clean-up crew."

Connor climbed into the SUV and greeted the rest of the team.

"Right," Tallis said as she sat next to Connor. "Two Noren, possibly more, have been sighted at Presly Green. Caution is the key word. We don't want to spook the farmers..." She paused and put her finger to her ear. With a frown, she added, "Apparently, they killed a sheep, but the owners are convinced they saw a rabid dog."

Connor snorted. If anything, Noren looked like monkeys, albeit white monkeys with two sets of extra arms and mean, sharp teeth. The only good thing about the Noren was that they had no appetite for humans.

"Normal procedure. Teams of two, dropped at locations surrounding the sighting and working our way to the middle. We close them in as fast as possible and tranq them. Commlink on at all times. Clear?"

"Clear, Lieutenant!" they said as one.

Connor leaned back. Presly Green, a rural village with a lively farmer's market, was at least a forty-minute drive, so he could rest a little. He really should have drunk some coffee before going up to his office.

Someone pressed a warm cup into his hand. The smell of coffee hit him and he opened his eyes to see Italian-born Ornella Amato leaning over the back of her seat, trademark eternal smile on her heart-shaped face.

"Lieutenant told me you might need this."

Connor inhaled and sighed as he smiled at her. "Just the way I like it. Thanks."

Noah's hand shook, and he tipped his bottle to the floor, causing water to splash everywhere. He barely paid attention to it. All that mattered was finding Blue Eyes.

He tried to hold on to the fading sensations of the connection, but soon even the tiniest trace would be gone.

It was his own fault. He hadn't been prepared, had been distracted.

Noah cursed loudly enough for it to echo through the empty room. He *would* be prepared next time. There would *be* a next time. No matter how long it took him, he *would* find the source again, even if he had to go back to the station day after day.

Next time he would have his shields, and he would ignore the memories of Dafydd until the connection was made.

He *had* to find his source again. He needed more.

# 3

"I can't believe I missed going up north." Isa laughed. "Ghost sightings. All those people panicking because of one boy playing ghost."

"You know how it is, three sightings in the same area and we check it out."

"Pity, I missed it. And you? Noren hunting. Again. I visit my mum for a couple of days, and you guys have all the fun."

It hadn't been that much fun. A good result, but if Connor never saw those white, monkey-like creatures again, it would be too soon. At least they'd found something useful buried in the ground.

The owner of the land had been less than happy with them rooting around, but the Noren had started digging before they'd even arrived. In between the trees, deep into the ground and across the field from where Team Delta had found the residue, they recovered metallic slivers of what was now rumoured to have been part of a space ship. Connor preferred waiting for Research to investigate it to listening to rumours.

"I missed out on hunting those Noren twice now."

Connor rolled his eyes and looked behind him. "You make it sound like we're always out when you're not here."

From the moment they'd exited the train station, walking arm in arm towards the pub, Connor had the uneasy feeling someone was following them. The incident five days ago still played with his mind, and he couldn't stop checking out every sound. He'd nearly jumped when someone brushed past him on the train. Yesterday, for a mere second, he'd sensed that same odd tingle at the base of his spine, so slight he'd tried to convince himself he'd imagined it.

No tingle now, but there was something that made him look. Isa didn't seem to notice.

"Last time you were out hunting those Noren was when... where was I?"

"Home with the flu," Connor reminded her. "And it was two weeks ago."

"Huh," Isa said, "I could have sworn..."

"Flu," Connor repeated. "You texted me at lunch, insisting on me bringing you chicken soup from the canteen."

Isa frowned as she counted something on her fingers and sighed. "I hate it when you're right."

The pub was packed, even if the tiny dance floor was nearly empty. Their mistake for going on a Saturday night. They took the only available stools, right at the end of the bar.

"So, how was dear old mum?" Connor asked, trying to appear casual instead of paranoid as he scanned the room. There was already too much of that in their line of work.

"Mum was brilliant," she said, gazing at him as if trying to figure something out. "Not sure I like the new boyfriend, though. He's so clingy it's sickening. Still, he's got taste. Mum's house looks a lot classier with his furniture in it."

"He moved in already?"

Isa rolled her eyes. "Something to do with his flat being sold, or whatever. I didn't dare ask."

Connor shook his head. "As long as she knows what she's getting into."

"I wonder if *he* does. Mum knows how to deal with men."

"It's a wonder she's never been arrested, considering she chased number seven out with a baseball bat."

"It's probably because they're too macho to admit a woman bested them."

They laughed, and Connor scanned the bar again. Something definitely felt off, and not because they were waiting for that blind date Isa had arranged. No matter how many times he'd told her not to do it, she wouldn't listen. Yet, fool that he was, Connor had agreed to go through with it. Still, anything was better than staying at home, alone, mulling about the nosebleed incident. That would only end in another sleepless night. "So, who is he?"

Isa didn't look at him. Instead, she fiddled with her drink. "I met him at Ellen's."

Seriously? "Ellen's?" Connor cried out. "As in dating-anything-that-moves Ellen?"

Isa nodded, still not looking at him.

"You thought it was a good idea to set me up with another one of her friends?"

"He seemed quite nice when I met him a couple of weeks ago."

Connor groaned. Isa was a good friend, his best friend, but a lousy judge of character. Her choice in boyfriends was terrible. Her matchmaking skills were even worse. For some reason, she thought he needed a boyfriend who was exactly like him, or rather, who she *thought* was exactly like him. Because they never were. Not to mention that one of him was enough in a relationship.

He suppressed the urge to ask her more about the bloke, knowing that if he did, she would tell him every little detail she knew, from hobbies to job to family and all the strange little quirks she remembered. She was as compulsive about collecting facts as he was, after all. She never understood that part of the fun of dating was the discovering.

With a sigh, he turned and looked around again, hoping against all odds that this one would not be as bad as the last few she'd tried to set him up with. He steered the subject safely away from his blind date and asked Isa more about spending time with her mum and the new boyfriend.

He looked up when the door opened for the umpteenth time. He more than regretted their choice of seats. From this end of the dark, red-lacquered bar, they had a perfect view of the entrance. Connor couldn't resist glancing at the red-painted door every time it opened. Any random bloke entering could be his date, after all.

When the next to enter were a group of women, he shook his head at his foolishness and turned his attention back to Isa. She talked about her week, managing flawlessly to keep it as generic as possible, considering where they worked.

With one ear on the conversation, he scanned the crowd again. Something still made his skin crawl, as if someone was watching him, but no one seemed to be paying him much attention. At least, not until a blond across the bar caught his eyes. Nice eyes. Warm, smiling eyes.

He hadn't planned on pulling, but if he found someone interesting himself, he wouldn't have to go through the whole blind date thing...again. Unfortunately, the blond turned away and the only other bloke watching him wasn't his type at all—if "too eager" was even a type. He focussed on Isa again.

"Anyway, Mum's coming over for my birthday, *sans* boyfriend, and I thought you, me, her, a film, a restaurant, a little dancing maybe—"

A sudden sharp tingle surged up Connor's spine. He turned and froze as he was caught in a haze of cloudy grey. He couldn't move, just like last time, yet the sensations seemed different. Still a mix of emotions, but muted, less erratic.

*What do you want?* He didn't bother trying to speak. The

hold on him loosened, just a bit, and he was off his bar stool, inching towards the dance floor. Whoever, or whatever, rooted around in his mind failed to control him. He still had trouble coordinating his feet or even making them move, but he pushed through and wormed his way through the crowd.

Isa called out to him, but without a working voice, he couldn't reply, and he wasn't going to let them get away this time. Connor barely made it to the edge of the tiny dance floor, panting as if he'd been running a marathon. He didn't let it stop him. He *had* to catch them, *had* to know what they were doing to him, *had* to know what this meant.

Before he reached his destination—and he really should have known—a dancing couple knocked him sideways, breaking whatever spell he'd been under.

When he got back to his feet again, they were gone and so was the tingle. He was left standing on the dance floor, trying to catch his breath. He cursed and closed his eyes for a minute, taking deep breaths to calm himself and lose the sense of uneasiness.

He didn't like the situation one bit. The first time might have been a coincidence, but this time...this time, he'd been followed. He had to have been. How else had they known where to find him?

He jumped when a hand landed on his shoulder.

It was only Isa. "Sorry," she said. "You were pretty far away there."

Connor shrugged. "I thought I saw someone I knew." Telling her what had happened would only lead to more questions than he was willing to answer, not to mention ruin a good night out, despite the blind date.

"So, Jason arrived..."

Jason? Who was Jason? Oh, right, his date. Connor sighed and followed Isa back to the bar.

Jason was a tall blond stud wearing a hoody, and trousers

that clung to his hips. He seemed the complete opposite of all the dates Isa had ever introduced Connor to. He wasn't shy, either, because the moment Connor shook his hand, he started talking. This must be why Isa had liked Jason so much: they both talked up a storm. He had a nice voice, too, deep and resonating. Connor could imagine himself listening to that voice for hours.

The date might have gone a little better if Connor hadn't been so preoccupied. He kept zoning out and mulling over what had happened, ignoring both Jason and Isa and missing large chunks of what Jason was telling him.

In the end, Connor barely even noticed Jason leaving. By the time he finally had, Isa was glaring at him. She did hand him Jason's business card, though, so not all was lost.

No apologies changed her prickly mood, however, and Connor knew it was time to call it a night. He apologised again, even knowing it would fall on deaf ears. He should buy her a bouquet of roses tomorrow to make it up to her. Isa loved roses.

NOAH LEANED AGAINST THE WALL, SIPPING HIS WATER AS HE watched the dance floor, feeling the thrum of the bass under his feet while gazing at the couples swaying. He loved watching them dance, watching their bodies move to the music. He was itching to grab the first available body and drag them onto the dance floor, but that wasn't what he was here for. He risked a glance towards the end of the bar, where his source, Blue Eyes, sat drinking a beer.

After spending many a morning hanging around at various train stations without even the slightest tingle, Noah had tried a different approach. Blue Eyes had boarded the train at Templin Station, going east. That ruled out the University on the west side of the city. He most likely worked in the centre of Kinnon or one of the business areas. With a bit of luck, Noah only had to check out two stations, Kinnon Central and Eastworth Station. Unless Blue Eyes didn't work *in* Kinnon. Noah would *really* be looking for a needle in a haystack then.

Over the past few days, he had checked out both stations without any luck. Today had seemed another fruitless day, until he was about to walk home and sensed him, Blue Eyes. Noah tried to stay on the edge of his range as he searched the crowd, and there he was, walking arm in arm into the busy centre with some woman, laughing, and chatting.

Noah couldn't believe luck. He'd found him, he'd finally found him.

Unwilling to alert Blue Eyes to his presence, Noah had stuck to the shadows, keeping far back as he followed the pair. It took a lot of manoeuvring to stay within range but out of sight, with Blue Eyes constantly looking over his shoulder. He was either highly sensitive or extremely paranoid. Whichever it was, Noah hoped they'd reach their destination soon—preferably somewhere the woman could be easily ditched.

Noah didn't like the look of Clyde's. It was too small and far too crowded, although that might be to his advantage. Easier to stay hidden in a crowd.

Standing at the edge of a tiny dance floor, Noah checked out Blue Eyes. He was young, gorgeous, tall, and well built. A looker, as they said, with black hair, sky blue eyes, and a stylish goatee that suited him. Noah took another sip of his water. The size of the place made it difficult to stay at a safe distance. He had a feeling Blue Eyes knew he was here, the way he was still looking around as if he sensed Noah.

Noah knew he was taking a risk, but he couldn't leave, not after spending so much time and effort to find Blue Eyes. He needed to know who his source was.

Someone bumped into him, pushing him into the dancing mass. The tingle at the base of his spine flared up immediately. Noah ignored the muttered apology behind him, focussing instead on moving towards the safe side of the perimeter. He chanced a glance towards the bar, hoping Blue Eyes hadn't sensed him, only to find those sky blue eyes staring at him. The tentative connection between them activated, and Noah froze, caught out by his own foolishness.

He stepped back to temper the flow, but it was as if Blue Eyes was in control, not he. At least, Noah managed to reduce the incoming energy. He didn't want Blue Eyes keeling over— better to spread it out, let him recharge in between, and make it last longer.

*Connor Smith.* Blue Eyes' name echoed through his mind. Connor Smith, barely twenty-four, only child of elderly, deceased parents, liked cricket, played even, enjoyed...

"Connor!" someone at the bar called out at the same time as Noah sensed Connor sliding from his bar stool.

Stunned, Noah watched Connor struggle towards him when he shouldn't have been able to.

"Connor!"

Connor inched closer and closer, increasing the flow, and Noah desperately tried to regain control over his own body and move out of range. When he couldn't regulate the flow, he tried to shut the connection down completely...and failed.

This wasn't supposed to happen. He was supposed to play it safe this time. Why was Connor resisting? He shouldn't be able to. This was impossible.

Powerless to do anything, Noah waited, watching Connor walk towards him step by step, until...

The connection was gone, just like that.

Noah didn't waste time trying to find out what had happened. He crossed the dance floor and left the bar as fast as he could, not stopping until he was at least three blocks away.

He smiled, catching his breath. Despite the unforeseen struggle, he had him. He had his source. His name was Connor Smith.

**4**

A FTER A MORNING FILLED WITH NOTHING BUT PROCESSING crates for the Archive Department, Connor cursed slow days. Normally, they'd be a blessing, especially after a busy week, but for some reason, he was wired for action. At least lunch with Isa had been fun, as always.

He sighed and looked at the stack of crates still standing next to his desk. He really wanted to work on his report of the incident at Clyde's. He had been working on it all Sunday. But first, he needed to get through this lot.

He grabbed the next crate. *Maroon sphere*, the label read. Connor snorted. He doubted it came close to its actual name, but Primrose had never been very original in naming things. There were no warnings on the label, so he picked it up and twirled the small sphere around in his hands. It was warm to the touch, but didn't react to warm or cold, according to the report from Research.

The ringing of his mobile startled him. No one ever called his personal phone during working hours. He fished it out of his backpack and looked at the caller ID, which was decidedly blank. Probably someone who'd mistyped the number. He put the mobile in his backpack and turned his attention back to the sphere.

Which was glowing.

He frowned and browsed the report, but there was nothing in there about glowing. Connor was not surprised to find it hadn't been tested with sound waves.

He put the sphere back into the crate and closed it. Then he rang Research. Lieutenant Holloway's direct line.

"Holloway."

"Hello, Lieutenant. Connor Smith here."

"What are you sending back this time, Connor?"

"I prefer a quick pick up, actually." Connor rattled off the registration code for the maroon sphere. "It glowed when my mobile rang. Report doesn't mention glowing, or testing with sound waves."

Holloway must have put his hand over the phone, but Connor still heard him curse. "Apologies, Connor. It never should have been sent up. A new researcher with sensitive ears and an inability to remember her right from her left. I'll send someone up right away."

Connor winced at Holloway's tone, even if it wasn't directed at him. "I'll be waiting."

He put the phone down with a shake of his head. That researcher was not going to like their assignments for the next week. Holloway was a strict boss, and merciless when you made a mistake. In fact, when Connor had first met Holloway, he'd mistaken him for a Security Lieutenant because of his imposing, broad build and bellowing voice. Still, that tough exterior hid a keen intelligence, and belied the graceful deftness with which he handled even the tiniest implements. Connor had learned a lot from him, when he'd still worked at Research.

He didn't have to wait long for a shame-faced researcher to turn up with an even bigger crate.

"I'm so sorry, sir," she mumbled as she put the crate containing the maroon sphere into the larger one and sealed it. Her face turned an even brighter shade of red when she faced him again. "It won't happen again."

She, at least, wouldn't make that same mistake again. Connor handed her the accompanying forms when Tallis' voice came through the intercom. "Connor?"

"Excuse me," he told the researcher. He pressed the button on the intercom. "Yes, Lieutenant?"

"I'm expecting our police liaison in ten minutes. I'll need a copy of the Noren report, the modified version."

Connor grinned. Modified meant more nonsense about rabid dogs or monkeys to keep the local police happy. This was the fun part of working for a government-sanctioned secret organisation: making stuff up.

"Oh, and Connor?"

"Yes, Lieutenant?"

"I could kill for a coffee."

"One black, no sugar coming up."

"You're a lifesaver, Connor."

He turned to check on the researcher, but his office was empty. *No manners.* He shook his head and rose to get Tallis her coffee.

His mobile rang again. He grabbed it out of his backpack and frowned. Again, no caller ID. He hadn't given his number to someone recently, had he? Whoever it was would have to wait. He put his mobile away and left his office to get coffee.

Tallis was on the phone when he entered her office a few minutes later, a pissed off expression on her face, and her voice sharp. "What do you mean, you didn't realise? ... I don't care if nothing was found, it should have been reported."

Connor set the coffee cup on her desk and turned to leave, but she motioned him to stay.

"It's not your decision, Agent Hughes. This is not acceptable. I want that report on my desk within the hour." Tallis slammed her phone on her desk and sank back into her chair. "Can you believe that?"

"I'm sorry, Lieutenant, I only caught half that conversation."

"It seems the A-Watch had been steadily detecting traces of an unknown alloy at Presly Green for three weeks straight before team Delta was sent to check it out." Tallis sighed. "Team Echo was sent out after the first alarm, but since they only found miniscule traces on a cultivator working the terrain, all consequent alarms were ignored. Not even a false alarm report was filed."

"What about that oily substance on the field team Delta found? And those metallic slivers we found? I'm assuming they're connected?"

"Apparently, A-Watch picked up a second, larger trace of the residue some time yesterday."

Connor shook his head. "That's odd."

"I hope the report will clear it up. Please bring it in as soon as it arrives?"

"I will. Anything else, Lieutenant?"

Tallis shook her head and sighed. "No, not right now. Thank you."

With a nod, Connor turned and left her office.

As he waited for the report to be brought in, he processed three more artefacts for Archive. During that time his mobile rang twice more, and it was starting to drive him bonkers.

The report finally arrived—ten minutes late—but Tallis merely shook her head in exasperation when he brought it in.

With all the crates sorted, he opened his bottom drawer to fish his incident report out when his mobile rang for the fifth time. Beyond annoyed now, Connor picked up. "Yes?" He doubted he could sound less irritated if he tried.

"Connor Smith?"

At least the caller knew his name. "Who's this?"

"Jason. Jason Powell. We met at Clyde's the other night.

Isa gave me your number."

Oh. Hell. The blind date. He cringed. He really needed to talk to Isa about giving his number to strangers. He took a deep breath. "Yeah. I remember. Hello, Jason."

"You want to go for a drink after work?"

Was this guy for real? He still wanted to see Connor after Saturday's disaster? "I..." Hold on. Was he nuts? Who was he to decline a drink from a hot guy? Blond, curly, tight jeans, *gorgeous*. "Sure. Why not?" He could certainly use the distraction, not to mention make up for that lousy first impression.

"Good. Good. What time are you off?"

"Half six-ish." On a good day, at least.

"Meet up at Clyde's around seven, then?"

"I could make that," Connor said, crossing his fingers for nothing to ruin it. The day may have been slow, but that was never a guarantee.

"Good. See you there then."

Clyde's was blessedly quiet when Connor entered. He had no trouble locating Jason. Dressed in suit and tie, his half-long wavy locks neatly tucked behind his ears, he was more gorgeous than Connor remembered. Even if he'd barely taken notice then, he *did* remember.

Spotting Jason's almost empty glass of beer, Connor ordered two pints at the bar. After he'd had to cancel their date last night, he'd been surprised when Jason had texted about postponing to today. Connor should have known he wouldn't make their date the day before—it was dangerous to think he'd be out of the office in time. Of course, the results of the Presly Green metallic slivers had come in as he was about to leave.

The slivers, alloy traces, and oily residue all matched. The theory that the Noren had landed in some sort of space ship was becoming more and more likely. The question was, where was that space ship?

Jason smiled as Connor put the pints on the table and sat down opposite him. "Only a day and half an hour late." Jason raised his glass and took a sip.

He didn't seem at all put out, which was refreshing, considering Connor's demanding job messed up his schedule regularly. Connor shrugged in apology. "It's been busy." He had barely escaped in time today, either, after receiving a last-minute panic call from Archive.

They hadn't received Connor email about the maroon sphere, and thought they'd lost it. Sometimes he feared more for his sanity having to cope with Archive than he did facing aliens.

A hand waved in front of his face. He blinked.

Jason stared at him, a hint of a smile on his face. "You're not going to zone out again, are you?"

"Sorry. Thinking about work."

"Well, stop it. No talking or even thinking shop while we're here."

"Right, no use asking you what you do, then?" Connor countered.

"Actually, I told you that last time."

*Insert foot in mouth.* Connor opened his mouth to apologise again, but closed it when Jason held up his hand and shook his head.

"Look," Jason said, "let's pretend last time didn't happen and start over." He held out his hand, and Connor instinctively shook it. "Hi, I'm Jason Powell. I'm twenty-seven and an antique dealer."

Connor answered Jason's charming smile with one of his

own, enjoying the warmth of Jason's hand in his. "Connor Smith, twenty-four, personal assistant at Ironclad Security." The name of the cover company rolled of his tongue easily now, as opposed to when he'd started out as Tallis' PA. It had taken him weeks to stop giggling. Not that Ogilvy Research and Development had been any better—just less obviously picked from a classic science fiction book.

"Nice to meet you, Connor."

Connor returned the sentiment, even if he felt a bit foolish doing it, still holding Jason's hand. Which he had to let go of when Jason leaned back and took a swig from his pint.

"Good. Now that we have that out of the way, Isa said you like progressive metal?"

Just like that, the ice was broken, even though Connor felt out of his depth at first. Jason knew so much about him already, from his taste in music to his favourite place to shop, while Connor barely remembered a thing from their first meeting, except that Jason had looked bloody gorgeous in his tight jeans. If Jason and Isa hadn't been chatting up a storm, because that was what Isa did, Connor would have been suspicious about him knowing so much,

Jason didn't seem to mind telling Connor things he'd no doubt told him already, and he stayed true to his word and not even once mentioned work.

"Isa thinks I watch far too much TV. Mostly comedies."

"No mysteries? I thought someone working in Security would enjoy those."

Connor shook his head. "Too high a concentration level, and I hate falling asleep halfway and waking up wondering what the heck happened."

"I barely watch TV, but I know what you mean."

"I do read them, though." Connor added, "Mysteries, I mean."

"I prefer science fiction. All those alien gadgets they come up with. I think it would be cool owning some of those."

*Too close to work.* Connor understood the interest from Jason's point of view. Many of the alien artefacts he worked with could be easily mistaken for antiques, at first glance at least. He could imagine some old lady admiring the glowing globes they had in Archive, thinking they would go so well with her wallpaper. He hoped Jason didn't notice his flinch as he carefully steered the conversation back to more innocent subjects, like sports.

"Triathlon," Jason said. "You know, a bit of running, bit of swimming, and some cycling. Sometimes I feel I spend more time out in the country hunting down the perfect Tudor dining chair, but I often plan my antique hunting around some tournament or other. I like to keep fit."

"I played cricket for years, until the job became too demanding. I still bowl at charity events, if I can take the time off." Connor didn't think it was wise to mention the large gym at work or the field assignments.

"I have to admit, I've never watched cricket. It's too slow for me."

Connor chuckled. "Not a patient bloke, then?"

"Oh, I can be patient." Jason threw him a lazy smile. "When it's worth my while."

WHEN JASON OFFERED TO DRIVE HIM HOME, CONNOR HAD ONLY been too happy to accept. He gazed at the veins on the back of Jason's hand clutching the gear stick. He'd grab any excuse to avoid taking the train, these days.

Jason lifted his hand and ran it through his hair. He'd been doing it so much, that, in the end, he'd given up on keeping them neatly tucked behind his ears. Connor approved of the messy array of curls. Messy suited Jason.

The night had been brilliant, and Jason had been perfect. He knew exactly what to say to keep the conversation going and had a wicked sense of humour. Yet, no matter how entertaining their conversation, all Connor could think about after Jason's "worthwhile" comment was what Jason would look like out of his suit. Distracting, to say the least. To think, Connor hadn't even wanted to meet the bloke.

He couldn't remember ever being so tempted to invite someone home after only one date—well, two, technically, but the first one really didn't count. He wasn't going to do it, but he'd never wanted to so much.

It took Connor a while to realise Jason had stopped the car and was watching him.

"So…" they both said at the same time.

Connor closed his mouth.

Jason smiled and reached out to cup Connor's face. The moonlight brought out the gold in his hazel eyes. "I had a great time tonight."

"So did I," Connor answered, leaning into Jason's hand.

Their lips met in a hard and needy kiss. Jason was a demanding kisser, claiming control from the start. Connor let him, enjoying the way Jason held his head close while he skimmed Connor's chest with his free hand. Connor tried to reciprocate, but with Jason's grip on his neck, he needed both his hands to keep from losing his balance. It wasn't the best position to be in, but he didn't care. Jason's mouth was warm and wet, and he tasted of beer and the crisps he'd grabbed on their way out of Clyde's.

When the kiss ended, Connor only wanted more, and his resolve not to invite Jason up was almost gone.

But Connor wasn't the only one not ready to go further, it seemed. Jason excused himself by mumbling something about having an early start. Connor was torn between relief and disappointment as he stood on the pavement, staring at Jason's car until it disappeared around the corner.

He turned to open his door and froze. Was someone watching him? He tried not to be obvious about scanning the street, but the moment he turned around, that odd tingle at the base of his spine reappeared. Yet, there was no one to be seen.

Connor wanted to scream, wanted to ask what the bleeding hell they wanted from him. Would it make a difference if he told whoever was out there that they had the wrong guy, that being Tallis' PA didn't mean he knew her passwords?

Of course, he did none of that. He kept his mouth shut, hating how his hands trembled as he fished his keys out of his trouser pocket and opened his front door.

A loud bang made him jump and turn his head, a move he regretted when his eyes locked onto something grey, and wave after wave of intense emotions assaulted him. *Not again.*

**5**

CONNER KISSING ANOTHER MAN HURT NOAH TO HIS CORE. He'd finally found what he never expected to have again, only to have it snatched away. Noah didn't think he could go through that a second time. He watched, fascinated, when Connor scanned the street after his boyfriend drove off. Connor shouldn't be able to sense him from that distance. Not from across the street, and certainly not with Noah hiding in the shadow of a garden wall.

Of course, then Noah *had* to bump into a stray bin. The resulting racket could probably be heard two streets over. No wonder Connor homed in on him. He'd never meant for Connor to see him. He'd never even meant for Connor to sense his presence, yet he obviously had, and Noah didn't know whether to be proud or annoyed at that.

It was too late for Noah to run now. Instead, he took a deep breath, opened his mind, and waited for Connor's eyes to meet his.

Fear and fury. Wave after wave of sensations as dark as night. Noah recoiled, shaking, and clamped down on the connection. He stared, heaving with effort as Connor backed away. The door slamming shut hurt Noah as much as Connor closing the connection would have.

Out of breath, Noah backed into the nearest wall and slid to the ground. What had he done? What had turned Connor's mind so dark?

His throat closed and his stomach turned. How could he have been so arrogant? *He* was the cause of Connor's fury, and his fear. *His* eagerness, *his* lack of preparation had ignited it. His lack of restraint was unforgivable. He *had* to find a way of making it up to Connor. He shouldn't have retreated so quickly; he should have used the connection to try and soothe Connor, at least calm his fear.

He sighed. Over two hundred and sixty years had he longed for this, to find another human who was compatible. He'd blown it. All he could do now was distance himself from Connor and let the connection dissolve on its own.

"I'm sorry," Noah whispered into the empty street, hoping Connor would understand. "I'm so sorry."

BACK TO THE WALL, KNEES PULLED UP TO HIS CHEST, CONNOR SAT IN the darkness until Isa arrived. He hadn't even noticed he was still holding his mobile when she put a hand on his shoulder and took it away from him, despite the busy tone now echoing through the dark hall.

Then Isa turned the light on.

"Hey," he said, annoyed that he couldn't muster more than a whisper.

"You're scary when you're out of it, you know that?"

"Sorry."

"I've never seen you like this. You want to stay here, or can we sit somewhere more comfortable?"

Connor shrugged. His arse was numb from sitting on the dappled-grey tiles of his hall floor, but he didn't really want to move.

Isa sighed and sat next to him, wrapping an arm around his shoulder. "Tell me."

"I think I'm being stalked." Connor let out a breath and told her what had happened. "After Clyde's last week, it seemed this tingling sensation was never far away. Sometimes, I felt it on my way to work, or on my way back, while running errands, and even on lunch breaks once or twice."

Isa squeezed his hand, and Connor rested his head on her shoulder.

"Sometimes I catch glimpses of a purple blob, a boy, a house. Victorian, I think. They never last long, barely more than a second." These glimpses were nothing like getting caught by those stormy grey eyes. He shuddered as he remembered how he'd frozen, forgetting everything around him as he lost himself in a cloudy grey world permeated with a cacophony of jumbled emotions, unable to focus on anything tangible. The emotions kept slipping past him, through him…

"The worst is the almost constant sense of being followed. It drives me bonkers, wondering who's behind me, what they want from me." He turned his head. Isa seemed deep in thought.

Minutes passed, but she stayed silent. It only made him more nervous.

"Maybe I *am* just seeing things."

"Why would you say that?"

Connor cringed at the disbelief in her voice. "I don't know," he said with a shrug. "Because there's never anyone there. Absolutely nothing."

"Mmm…"

"What?"

Isa shook her head.

"Tell me."

"Could it have been a Projector?"

"What? No! It... What gave you that idea?"

"Mmm, let me see. It enters your mind. Not enough for you?"

A Projector? A creature that used some sort of mind power to override your brain to compel you to do their bidding? Connor shook his head. He knew a group of Projectors was still on the loose somewhere, but he'd experienced a projection once, and this was nothing like that. These were only emotions, jumbled emotions. "It can't be projection."

"Are you sure?"

"Yes. No." He ignored Isa's cynical expression. "I don't know. It wasn't subtle or implicative, and I haven't felt compelled to do something I normally wouldn't. Besides, Doctor Quiggins would have found a trace if it had been a Projector "

Isa's expression turned thoughtful. "You have to report it."

"Like the police are going to—"

Isa slapped his knee. "To Lieutenant Tallis, you idiot."

Right, of course. He had typed up all those reports, after all. Why hadn't *he* handed them in?

"Because you're an idiot. And you're too emotionally involved."

Connor frowned. Had he said that out loud?

"Yes, and you're still talking." Isa got to her feet and held out her hand.

Connor let himself be pulled up, even though he didn't really want to move. "What are you doing?" he asked when she led him up the stairs.

"I'm putting you to bed. You need to rest. I'll help you with finishing those reports in the morning."

Connor doubted he could sleep, but he indulged her

anyway, and even let her tuck him in.

Connor's office, normally a pleasant and roomy space to work in with its wide windows overlooking Kinnon's business area, seemed too silent and oppressive. He glanced at the picture of his parents smiling at him from their sunny spot in front of a Parisian bistro. Meanwhile, the teal wall loomed over him as he watched the clock ticking his hours away. He couldn't put it off any longer. Reports in his hands, he rose stiffly and approached the door to Tallis' office, contemplating whether or not to knock.

He'd spent most of the night sleeping and talking things through with Isa, not finishing and reviewing his reports until the very last moment. At Isa's insistence, he'd added his breakdown. It was out of character for him, and therefore worth mentioning. No matter how much he wanted to disagree with her, he couldn't. No point in dragging it out. He took a deep breath and knocked.

"Come in."

Tallis smiled at him as he entered. "Good morning, Connor," she said, checking the clock on her desk. "You're rather early this morning."

Connor tilted his head in confirmation and handed her his reports.

She frowned. "A new case? I wasn't aware of any activity last night."

"It's...er...personal. I've experienced some startling and unusual incidents these past weeks. I didn't think they were worth reporting until last night." He might still not have reported them if Isa hadn't insisted. She was right. He lacked objectivity because it hit too close to home. Not to mention feeling embarrassed. He worked for Primrose, for fuck's sake, he was trained to deal with weird incidents. Not get freaked out by them.

Tallis browsed the reports, frowning as she pointed at the first page. "This one is time-stamped ten days ago."

"I wrote the report on the day of the incident. I...just didn't turn it in."

"Impeccable as ever, Connor," she said, though he detected disappointment in her voice. "Very well, I'll read these over."

"Thank you, Lieutenant." He turned to leave but hesitated at the door. "Coffee?"

"Please. And, Connor? Anything happens again, you report it immediately."

"Yes, Lieutenant."

THE TERRACOTTA-WASHED WALLS MADE THE CANTEEN LOOK inviting in the hint of sunlight coming through the tinted windows. The scattering of tables, all in different earthy colours, buzzed with people having lunch. Isa and Connor sat smack in the middle of all the lunch room noises.

"So? How did it go? What did she say?" She chewed on her sandwich and stared at him.

Connor swallowed. "Nothing. Well, she said I did the right thing, but I haven't heard anything from her since."

"Nothing?"

"Every time she buzzed me, I nearly jumped, thinking she'd want to rip me a new one about not coming to her sooner. Instead, she only wanted me to call someone or other or schedule an impromptu meeting." Connor took a sip of his coffee. He'd have preferred screaming to this endless waiting.

"It's been driving me bonkers."

Isa squeezed his hand. "If she didn't think it worth investigating, she would have told you already. Now, stop fretting and eat your lunch."

"Yes, Mum," Connor took a bite from his sandwich.

"What's that bleeping?"

"What bleeping?"

Isa glared at him. "Seriously? You're not hearing that?"

She leaned over and patted down his suit jacket, shaking her head as she fished his mobile from the inside pocket and handed it to him.

He stared at it, finally recognising the low beeping as the ringtone he'd set for his messages. "Oh, that bleeping." Why had he put his mobile in his pocket? He hadn't even used it after rescheduling his date with Jason.

"Yes, that bleeping. It's been doing that since we left your office. Are you going deaf or something?"

"Too preoccupied, I guess." He checked his missed messages. Three of them. All from Jason.

"Anything interesting?" Isa asked, shoving her empty plate aside to get a better look.

Connor blushed as he read the first one, sent late last night, and tilted his phone so Isa could read it, too. It pleased him to see her turn red, and he barely kept himself from mentioning what curiosity did to cats.

"Er...wow...you're really working fast, aren't you?"

"We hit it off, yes." Connor read the second message. Though it was just Jason telling him he was thinking of him, it made Connor smile.

"Hit it off?" Isa said. "Hit it off? It's a wonder you two didn't end up in bed together right away."

"That's called *restraint*," Connor said dryly, not looking up from his phone, and unwilling to admit he'd been but a hair's breadth away from doing just that. "Oh."

"What?"

"He wants to know if I'm free for lunch some time."

Isa stacked their trays. "Today's a no, obviously, but no reason you can't go out to lunch tomorrow or the day after, is there?"

"No reason? Are you sure you work here?"

"Oh, come one, just text him you'll try to make it tomorrow. You can always call him if something comes up."

"I know that, but…"

"Not buts, just text him."

Connor rolled his eyes at her, but still texted Jason that he'd meet him tomorrow, with a question mark.

"So, your date," Isa started. "I didn't really want to ask, after…"

Connor smiled and sighed.

"Oh, that good?"

"Oh, yeah! He's gorgeous and witty and—"

"Kinky, if his text message is anything to go by."

"There's that." Connor blushed at the thought of finding out more about *that*.

"Agent Smith?"

Connor looked up to find a young agent standing next to their table. "Yes?"

"Lieutenant Tallis needs you to report to lab H-Fourteen."

"Thank you," Connor said, but as soon as the agent left, he cursed. "Bugger!"

"Well, you knew she'd call you in sooner or later."

With a sigh, Connor shoved his chair back, but didn't get up. "Yeah." He worried about what would be waiting for him in lab H-Fourteen.

"Go on, don't keep her waiting. I'll clear this lot away."

"Ah, Connor." Tallis handed him a loupe and pointed at what looked to be a piece of melted plastic. "What do you see?"

This was not about his reports, then. He wasn't certain whether to be relieved or disappointed. He studied the plastic. What was this? Then it dawned on him. "Is this the test CD they found in Langham's computer?"

Tallis nodded. "What do you see?"

Connor looked again. There were some faint markings on the surface. "Handwriting?"

"Yes. Now compare it to the other one," she said as she pointed to another CD.

When she'd previously done this—letting him work out what she no doubt already knew—right after his promotion, Connor had wondered why she'd wanted him to figure out what Research had solved already. Now he knew it was just the way she worked.

The other CD hadn't melted. There was more handwriting, but different this time, with sharper edges. Darker ink as well, though that might be because the writing on the melted CD was so faint. "They weren't written by the same person."

"Very good. Even if it doesn't prove much." She sighed. "The police ruled out arson because there was no sign of breaking and entering, nothing was missing, and Langham had told them it wasn't the first time he'd left the gas on after making tea."

Connor followed Tallis to a computer at the far end of the lab.

"They either didn't check the CCTV, or didn't pay much attention to it." She played a video clip and told him to watch closely.

The building went up in flames. The clip replayed three times, and each time Tallis asked him what he saw. She seemed disappointed by his answers.

"I'm sorry, Lieutenant. I have no idea what you're expecting me to see," he said when she played it a fourth time. "All I see is a burning building."

"The fire started in the kitchen, right?"

"Right." The reports said so.

"Where was the computer?"

He closed his eyes, trying to remember the layout of the house. It wasn't hard, he'd been staring at the blueprint often enough in the past week. "Right above the kitchen. The explosion took out part of the flooring."

"Yet the computer was only partly burnt." Tallis showed Connor a photo of what was left of the computer.

The office was completely burnt out—even the screen had melted to the desk—but the computer tower looked mostly intact.

"Research discovered traces of a fire-retardant material coating the tower," Tallis said, "It seems whoever did this wanted us to find that CD."

# 6

J ASON AND CONNOR WALKED IN SILENCE, BIRDS TWITTERING around them as they crossed the park and ate ice cream. Jason's hand rested lightly on Connor's hip, and all Connor could think about was how nice it was to do this with someone not Isa. He loved Isa, but it wasn't quite the same, and Zack... Zack had never been interested in anything as mundane as walking in the park, let alone during lunch on a Monday. Clubbing in Pole Street was the only thing Zack had enjoyed. Not that Connor hadn't, but, well, not Zack's kind of clubbing. Not flirting with all and sundry, rubbing up against them, and always looking for something new, not caring he was already dating Connor. Or that Connor didn't share. Zack had said that wasn't a problem. Like hell it hadn't been.

"You're not thinking about work again, are you?" Jason's voice close to his ear interrupted Connor's thoughts.

"No, not about work," Connor said in-between licks, trying to keep his ice cream from melting all over his hand. Though he doubted thinking of his ex was any better than thinking about work. When they'd had lunch together on Friday—Thursday something had come up, of course—Connor had felt miles away, and Jason had to keep dragging him back into the conversation. Jason had never lost his patience, though. He'd only reminded Connor of their agreement, and that was that.

"Good, good." Jason stopped and turned Connor towards him, wiggling his eyebrows. "So, tell me, Mr. Smith. Where to now?"

Connor looked at his watch. Only about half an hour left before he needed to head back. "We could sit down for a while? Enjoy the sun, chat a bit."

Jason smiled and dragged him over to an empty bench. Connor was tempted to lean his head on Jason's shoulder, but didn't want to seem needy. Jason, apparently, had no such qualms, and pulled Connor against him. After an awkward minute of playing will I, won't I in his mind, Connor gave up and leaned his head on Jason's shoulder, anyway. "I know you don't want to talk about work, but I have to ask. Why antiques?"

"Oh, I don't mind. My father's dragged me along to auctions since I was twelve, I think. He taught me when to bid and when to let it go. It stuck. Though it's more about the chase for me. I like taking the time to sift through all that rubbish to pick out the one thing that's worth more than a month's salary."

"Ah, family business then?"

"Yes, though my folks have their own business up north. What about your father?"

Connor shrugged. "I think he was an accountant, but I'm not certain. He was already retired before I hit my teens. To me and my friends, he was a stay-at-home dad, and I never bothered to ask."

"Why do you think he was an accountant?"

"He had a real gift with numbers. Mum always said I got that from him. She had more of a knack for languages; she was a French teacher."

"Are they..."

Connor closed his eyes and swallowed. "They died in a car accident, shortly after my twentieth birthday. It had been freezing, the road was slippery, and Mum must have lost control..."

Jason kissed the top of his head. Connor had made peace with it, especially after receiving the picture of the two of them on sort of a second honeymoon in Paris that his mother had sent the week before the accident. They'd seemed so happy in that photo, and that had made it easier, though he still missed them.

"No siblings?"

"None. They never even expected me. They had given up on having children years before I was born. You?"

"One older sister, happily married, or so they say, three children. They emigrated four years ago, so I don't see them much. Weekly emails, phone calls, and text messages, though. We were quite close."

Connor smiled. "I used to nag my parents to give me a little brother every single birthday for years. They thought it was hilarious, even if it drove them nuts. Apparently, I cleared part of my room and put in a self-made cot."

"You're kidding."

"If Mum were alive, she'd be quite happy to show you the photos, though I barely remember any of it."

"You must have been one cute kid."

"My parents thought so." The base of his spine tingled. Connor shot up, scanning the crowd, but it vanished within seconds. No greyish clouds, no freezing, nothing. Just a tiny tingle that barely lasted a couple of seconds.

"Everything all right?" Jason asked, frowning at him.

"Yeah. Sorry, I thought I heard someone calling my name." He hadn't felt it in almost a week; he'd even considered telling Tallis to drop the case. Now he was glad he hadn't, though he wasn't looking forward to writing another report.

Jason raised an eyebrow but said nothing as he took Connor's hand and rose from the bench. "So, same time tomorrow?"

Connor shrugged. "I can't promise anything. As I said—"

"It's busy, I know. You know what? Call me if you can't make it, otherwise I'll see you here around noon tomorrow."

How could he say no to that? Connor followed Jason, but not until after he'd scanned their surroundings one last time. He sighed, not looking forward to reporting this to Tallis.

NOAH BRUSHED HIS FINGERS ALONG THE SPINE OF THE BOOK. BOUND in full leather. A red spine with raised bands and green boards. Gilt border lines and marbled endpapers. A bit roughed up, but no nicks, no scratches, nothing that a bit of tender love and care couldn't fix. It would be a fine addition to the shop.

He cut through the park, not wanting to leave Lily alone in the shop for too long. He didn't think it would be busy, but when Lily got restless, she reorganised the shelves, and it would take him hours, days even, to find some of the books again. He rewrapped the book and put it into his bag. Still, he couldn't wish himself a better assistant. Lily understood the computer better than he did, knew her numbers, was always on time, didn't bring strange boys into the shop to make out in the back room, and never had to be reminded about food and drink in the shop. Not to mention that for some reason, she seemed to like him.

Noah's spine tingled, and for a moment, he stood stock still, revelling in the sensations. He spotted Connor across the park, sitting on a bench with his head on another man's shoulder. When Connor suddenly jumped up and scanned the park, Noah took a last look at both men and turned, taking the first exit out of the park. He kept walking until he was at a safe distance and wouldn't be tempted any longer.

Out of reach, Noah's body reacted to the broken contact as if in withdrawal. It craved more, and while the fear and anger he had felt from Connor might be enough for him to stay away, it didn't stop his body from wanting more. It took all his willpower to stay put instead of walking back and *taking* more.

He'd made a promise to leave Connor alone, and he would keep it. Of course, he hadn't expected to run into him like that. This was going to prove harder than he'd thought it would be, in more ways than one.

Then there was the man Connor was with. Noah sighed. He could never compete with someone that young. Maybe it was better he had promised to stay away. The last thing he wanted was to break up a relationship, and if he and Connor connected, that would surely happen.

"It wasn't his computer?" Connor looked up from the document and turned to Tallis. "So, they not only have the CD, they have Lieutenant Langham's computer as well, including some very rare, made-to-spec hardware. That must have taken weeks, if not months, to plan."

She nodded. "We need to find out who they are, how they knew about the programme, and what else was on that computer."

"Lieutenant Langham made a list of the most important data he kept on it. It's at Research, but I can get you a copy," Connor said. He frowned. "I remember something about a list of archived artefacts."

"Yes, thank you. Check into that with Archive, will you? Make sure those artefacts are still in our possession."

"Of course, Lieutenant."

Dousing a computer in flame-retardant material in a house that was about to burn to hide the theft of a test CD was over the top, but stealing both the CD *and* the computer at least sounded more logical. Especially if you knew whose computer it was.

Someone had gone to great lengths to cover their tracks and mislead Primrose. Two years. He shook his head.

"Find out if there are more CCTV cameras in that area and have them examined, provided they still have recordings that far back."

"Anything else?" Connor asked as he wrote it down.

Tallis shook her head. "Not right now. Not until I hear more from the lab, at least."

"Right, I'll get on it as soon as I've arranged for a copy of that list."

"Good," she said with a sigh. "This is a mess, Connor, and one we need to clean up as soon as possible. Who knows what the thieves are doing with those artefacts?"

Even the tiniest of alien artefacts could be dangerous. A shudder ran through him. Numerous reports of accidents had passed his desk over the years, and those were regular people finding artefacts in their back gardens.

He put his pen away and grabbed his report of the lunchtime incident. He had hesitated typing it up, but she'd wanted to know everything.

Tallis grabbed it and skimmed it. "You didn't experience anything peculiar this time?"

Connor shook his head. "Nothing. I felt the tingling, but when I jumped up to see where it was coming from, it disappeared."

"Sit down, Connor."

He sat on the edge of his seat, hands on his knees, watching her take an envelope from a stack of papers, and he couldn't bring himself to relax.

"I received this after you went out to lunch. We might as well go through it now. Your reports have rather stirred things up around here. As expected, the other board members were none too happy that you didn't come forward about this earlier."

He opened his mouth but closed it again when she motioned him to keep quiet.

"I managed to placate them by telling them I trust your judgement and commending the fact that even though you didn't report it immediately, you had kept notes of your experiences meticulously."

"I'm sorry," Connor said, before she could quiet him again.

She waved her hand in a vaguely dismissive motion. "Oh, nonsense. You handled this as well as could be expected. We sometimes forget that with everything we've seen, we're only human at the end of the day. We don't expect to get this involved."

She opened the envelope and took out a file. "Now, Lieutenant Matthews has been appointed to lead the investigation. I would have loved to take this on myself, but that's impossible considering your involvement."

Standard protocol. Connor could even name and quote the article, if asked.

"He has already ordered Research to check CCTV for a trace of whoever or whatever was following you. As long as it's visible, some camera somewhere is bound to have picked something up. Your detailed descriptions should make their job a lot easier."

CCTV. Connor could hit himself for not thinking about checking himself. Though he was uncertain which was more frightening, something showing up or finding nothing at all.

"Doctor Quiggins expects you to drop in as soon as possible. She's out of the office this afternoon, so I advise you to visit her first thing tomorrow. She'll set you up with a tracker and will give you a thorough check-up. We're taking everything into account, even Agent Griffin's suggestion you might be dealing with a Projector."

"I don't think it's a Projector."

"We agree with you. Aside from Doctor Quiggins not picking up a trace, Projectors do not stalk their victims after first contact. They don't need to. First contact is all they need to establish a link to enable full control. No victim ever mentioned anything you described. In fact, no victim of a Projector has any recollection of anything they did while under control. That said, your stalker may well be capable of controlling your mind without actually possessing you twenty-four seven. We're not taking chances."

"Of course, Lieutenant." Something else he hadn't thought of. He really needed to brush up on his knowledge of Projectors and other aliens using mind-control.

"That's all for now." Tallis closed the file and leaned back in her chair. "We *will* find your stalker, Connor, you can count on that."

Sooner rather than later, Connor hoped. He wanted it over with, so he could concentrate on his job again.

**7**

NOAH WAS SEEING A CUSTOMER OUT WHEN A GROUP OF black-clad military-looking types entered the shop. Before he had a chance to step back, two of them seized his arms while another pointed some sort of weapon at him. Noah tried hard not to struggle against the tight hold, not wanting to give them a reason to hurt him. His heart pounded in his throat and his knees wobbled. If the men weren't holding him, he wasn't certain he'd still be standing.

Lily screamed and grabbed a piece of two-by-four she insisted on keeping under the till. Her bright green eyes had gone wide, making her seem much younger than twenty-two. A woman from the group approached her, talking to her in soft, dulcet tones. Noah couldn't hear what she was saying, but Lily put the two-by-four away and crossed her arms in front of her chest. Her stance was the complete opposite from the friendly, cheery openness she normally showed. She looked as worried as Noah felt.

"Are you Noah Jones?" a man standing next to the one pointing the weapon at him asked.

"Yes, I am."

"Mr. Jones. I have orders to take you in."

Noah should have known. The moment he recognised the

building where Connor worked and the ever-changing names of the cover companies Primrose hid behind, he should have known. It was just his luck to find a source who worked for the organisation he'd tried to avoid—successfully—for over one hundred years. Until today.

"What? Who are you? Are you nuts? You can't do this. He's just a book seller!" Lily shouted. "I want to see some identification."

"Lily..." Noah began, but one of the men holding him pushed his hand against Noah's mouth, and all the fight left him.

Noah didn't struggle when they cuffed his hands and took him to an SUV parked haphazardly next to the shop. He didn't struggle when they sat him down in it and fastened a seatbelt that seemed more appropriate for a child, with bands crossing his chest to fix him to the back of the seat.

Lily, on the other hand, kept shouting, despite the woman trying to calm her down, and when they finally left, Lily stood on the pavement with two uniformed men holding her back as she screamed, her floral dress fluttering angrily in the breeze.

As they drove through Kinnon, Noah could only think of the shocked expression on Lily's face. He hated that they hadn't let him talk to her. Still, he knew she was more than capable, not to mention level-headed enough, to keep the shop running in his absence. Although there'd be hell to pay for giving her such a fright when he got back. *If* he got back.

No. He wasn't going to think about that.

He recognised the Eastworth Building immediately. Despite his predicament, he smiled as he read the names on the front of the building. Ironclad Security, Red Weed Catering, Ottershaw Medical, and Ogilvy Research and Development. The names of Primrose's cover companies had changed a bit since it was founded, but they all came from the same book as Primrose itself. A book Noah kept displayed in a prominent place in his shop as a reminder—first edition, of course.

The SUV stopped in a large underground car park, next to a lift Noah was led into. After a short trip down—at least, he thought they were going down—he was brought into a bright, sterile room with a table and two chairs bolted to the floor. The chairs looked like they were made of aluminium, but felt more like plastic as they sat him down. No doubt they were made from some non-conductive alloy.

Both his wrists were cuffed to a chain connected to the arm rests. It seemed over the top, but considering the sort of creatures Primrose dealt with, it was understandable. Annoying, but understandable.

Noah took a deep breath and closed his eyes when the men left, forcing himself to think happier thoughts. Like how he had told Dafydd what he was in a sex-induced sleepy haze one night. Dafydd had treated it the same way he had treated all the stories Noah told that were too outlandish for him. He had smiled that sweet smile of his and shut Noah up with a kiss. The next day, Dafydd didn't seem to remember a single word.

Noah had no doubt a man like Connor would remember every detail, afterglow or no afterglow. Too late now. He'd handled it badly and lost the only source of energy he'd come across in over 270 years.

He concentrated on the tiny hint of residual energy—all that remained of Connor's presence in his mind. With all Earth's words, no explanation ever sufficed to explain the wonderful gift Connor had given him, or would be enough to express what it meant to him. If only he'd had a chance in trying to explain it to Connor, but it was useless even thinking Primrose would permit him contact with anyone.

What sort of information did Primrose have on him,

anyway?

Noah stretched his spine and neck, and leaned back, hoping Lily was coping all right.

Jason's antique shop didn't look half bad. It was spacious, modern, and decorated in neutral colours—a blank canvas for antique furniture like the table Conner caressed as though it were a cute puppy. The old oak table had caught his eye the moment he'd entered the shop. It would look great in his flat, the perfect size and colour, if he was willing to pay this much for a dining set.

It seemed to be a quiet Friday afternoon, and Jason was nowhere to be found, but Connor wasn't bothered. Jason had told him to wait in the shop, and he wasn't expecting Connor this early, anyway. Eager to meet up, Connor had left while Tallis was still in a meeting with Lieutenant Ubanks to avoid being called back in again.

He wondered if Jason's trip abroad had been successful. When Jason had texted earlier to say he was back, he hadn't mentioned anything about it. Connor wondered if the table came from one of Jason's trips. Maybe even *this* trip. Jason had sounded so apologetic when he'd called late Monday evening to cancel their Tuesday lunch date in favour of checking out some remote estate sale.

"Looking for something particular?" a voice, male and definitely not Jason's, asked from behind him.

Connor turned around to face an older bloke with a pinched expression, immaculately dressed in a black pinstriped suit. He looked down at Connor's frazzled jeans with dismay.

"I'm waiting for Jason Powell."

The bloke raised an eyebrow. "Who can I say is asking for him?"

"Smith, Connor Smith."

The bloke narrowed his eyes. "Right. If you'll wait here, Mr. Smith, I'll inform him."

"Thank you," Connor said, turning back to the beautiful table. He sighed. It really would look great in his flat, and he could afford it...

"Connor. You're early." Jason's voice sounded a bit off, almost irritated.

"I didn't want to risk being called back in," Connor said as he looked up. If Jason's voice had sounded off, his expression seemed the complete opposite—smiling and cheerful—and Connor wondered if he'd imagined Jason's bad mood. "I can wait if you're not done yet. No problem."

"There is something I need to wrap up, but it shouldn't be long."

"I'll just stay here and admire this beautiful table."

Jason had already turned around and was walking over to Pinstriped Suit. The bloke looked from Jason to Connor with narrowed eyes, as he spoke to Jason. Jason shook his head and disappeared through the door, while Pinstriped Suit kept his eye on Connor.

The bloke could watch him all he wanted. Connor returned to admiring the table. The wood was smooth under his hand, but not perfect. Connor loved the small signs of wear and tear. It reminded him of the table his father had made from a set of old doors he'd found next to the road. It had been heavy and uneven, but Connor's mother had loved it and white-washed it. He missed that table, but it had been far too big for his place.

An angry whisper made him turn around. Pinstriped Suit seemed to be facing off with Jason now, looking none too happy. Jason's expression was hard to read, and he kept glancing behind him into his office.

What was going on? He couldn't hear what they were talking about, but whatever Pinstriped Suit was whispering didn't seem to faze Jason. He merely shrugged, slapped the grumbling bloke on his shoulder, and made his way back to Connor again.

"So, where are you taking me again?" he asked, all smiles and cheer.

"Are you sure you're all right to leave?"

"Don't be silly. Of course I am. Simon's grumpy because he has to close up."

The way Pinstriped—Simon—glared at Jason, Connor doubted having to close up had anything to do with it. Still, it wasn't his problem. He was here to take Jason out. "I was thinking fish and chips and a film. Unless you feel like going posh."

"Sounds like a plan." Jason looked down at his pressed trousers. "I think I have a pair of jeans tucked away in my car somewhere."

Honestly, Connor didn't care what Jason wore, as long as he got to peel him out of it later.

A LOUD BANG SHOOK NOAH AWAKE. HE CURSED HIMSELF FOR dozing off.

"Mr. Jones." A broad-shouldered man with a hawk-like nose and harsh brown eyes stood in front of him and dropped a thick file on the table in front of him. Behind him were two black-suited men.

"Yes," Noah said without hesitation, looking from the man to the file and wondering how extensive it was.

"I am Agent Oswald Parker, and I will be conducting this

interview."

His words and tone seemed sincere, yet his posture said, "Give me a reason and I *will* use violence".

Noah would give him none. When he'd first found out about Primrose, early 1918, when it was still a four-man operation, Noah had decided to answer all questions truthfully if they ever got wind of him. The aggressive posture of his interrogator would not change that. Lying wouldn't get him anywhere.

One of the black suits uncuffed his hands. Noah rubbed his sore wrists.

"Sorry, 'bout that, Mr. Jones," Agent Parker said. "It's protocol, I'm afraid. I apologise for leaving you waiting for so long. It's been quite busy today. Can I offer you something to drink? Coffee or tea?"

"I'll have a glass of water, please."

Agent Parker raised an eyebrow and turned to one of the black suits. "Bring Mr. Jones a glass of water."

The black suit nodded and left the room.

"Right, now that that's out of the way, let's start this interview. I am required to tell you that this interview will be recorded, both audio and video, and will be monitored by one of my colleagues at all times. Do you understand?"

"Yes."

"Good." Agent Parker looked down at the file for a moment. "According to our information, you are Mr. Noah Jones of Two-Forty-One Church Street, and you are the owner of First Edition, a bookshop at the same address. You are single, born..." Agent Parker frowned, browsing through the file, though Noah doubted he was reading it for the first time. "We have a multitude of birth certificates, all with different dates of birth. The same day and month every time, but different years. The most recent seems to be April 6th, 19—" Agent Parker paused as the black suit returned with a bottle of water and a glass. He leaned back to watch Noah as the black suit opened the bottle, filled the glass, and put both on the table.

Noah wrapped both hands around the glass, enjoying the chill against his fingers, and took a sip.

"Right," Agent Parker continued, a slight smile on his face. "The most recent date of birth is April 6th, 1968. Seems believable enough, you do look forty-ish, but the others? Can you tell me what that's all about?"

Agent Parker's smile didn't reach his eyes. For a moment Noah contemplated giving his standard answer, but he'd made a promise to himself, and he was going to keep it. "I arrived here on April six, 1648."

"Arrived in 1648... Right. Remarkable. The earliest date we have here is late 1700s. Seems pretty old for a man just in his forties, doesn't it? So, tell me, Mr. Jones. What does that mean, you arrived here in 1648?"

Noah took a deep breath. Dafydd had been the only person he had ever told, but that had been in a time where space travel was even further away than it was now. He sighed. Dafydd had been so young, so willing to believe any story Noah told him, though Noah had often thought Dafydd was only humouring him.

Sweet Dafydd, who had died too young. He couldn't have been much older than Connor when an illness had taken him.

Over 270 years later, Noah only had to close his eyes to feel Dafydd's arms around him, hear his sweet laughter, and see his beaming face. Young and innocent Dafydd had been one of the few humans who went through life truly happy.

"Mr. Jones!"

"Yes. My arrival." Noah pushed all memories of Dafydd firmly to the background in an attempt to clear his mind. "I was recording on the planet you call Ix, when two creatures of an unknown... species ...grabbed me and dragged me onto their ship. I think they stole it; they had far too much trouble flying it."

"So, you were abducted?" Agent Parker's voice was flat, but Noah had never expected to be believed immediately.

"Yes. I think they wanted to sell me. The inhabitants of Ix are considered a delicacy on the planet of Olomas. I was only disguised as an inhabitant of Ix, but lacked speech, and I couldn't tell them I wasn't who they thought I was.

"They bound me to a wall when they fled the planet, and one of them kept an eye on me at all times, making it impossible for me to change back to my original form and escape unnoticed.

"Their lack of skill in handling the ship caused us to crash into an asteroid just outside Earth's atmosphere. They were both thrown into the walls by the impact and lost consciousness...or died. I didn't check. I only survived by changing back."

"You freed yourself by turning back into your original form? You can change shape?"

"Yes. My kin—my species—are energy beings." Noah paused, trying to find the right words to explain. "Have you ever seen a film called *Flubber*, Agent Parker?"

Agent Parker raised his eyebrows, but nodded nevertheless.

"My kin resemble *Flubber* in a way, though in a shade of purple and more see-through. We can temporarily copy the form of any other species. It isn't permanent, and we don't become that species. We cannot communicate or interact in any way—we merely take on the appearance of a certain species."

"Seems rather useless to me."

"It is very useful to my kin. I was—am—a recorder. That's the closest word I have found in your language to describe what I am. I visited other planets, recorded my experiences, and then returned home to share them with my kin."

Another raised eyebrow. "Then what? You plan an attack?"

Noah's jaw dropped, though he really shouldn't have been shocked or surprised at such a reaction. Not after all the time he'd spent on this planet. "No. We simply enjoy experiencing new things. It's like a virtual reality, in which we feel, taste, sense everything the way other species do."

"Are you saying your species are peaceful?"

"We do no harm. That is not our nature."

Agent Parker frowned, looking at the file in front of him and back at Noah. He didn't seem inclined to believe Noah's story. "So, how do you travel to other planets, as an energy being? Do you beam yourself there, or do you have some sort of vehicle?"

"We have pods that resemble large eggs. Almost every planet has eggs of some sort, which makes them easy to hide."

"What, not even an invisibility gadget?" Agent Parker asked with a sneer.

Noah simply shook his head, refusing to rise to the bait.

"How long do you usually stay on a planet? Can't be long, considering you can't communicate with them."

"Usually no more than seven of our planet's rotations as a copy. Longer in our original form."

"Seven rotations. A week. And that is because..."

"I think it's more like ten days, in Earth days. Our energy is limited when we travel off-world, especially as a copy, and we have yet to encounter a world that produces a compatible energy for us to live on. Ten rotations, roughly fourteen Earth days, is the maximum any Rei ever achieved, but they could not return on their own accord."

Noah shivered as he recalled the stories of the agony his kin had gone through for several rotations afterwards—and his own pain, once his final transformation had finished.

"Seven rotations is deemed safe and allows us two or three extra rotations for emergencies."

"Emergencies?"

Parker's tone of voice was getting on Noah's nerves, but he had to see this through. "Sometimes getting off a planet is more difficult than anticipated. I once forgot where I left my pod and spent three rotations looking for it." There was so much beauty on the planets he visited. Noah often simply took a path or followed another creature and saw where it would lead him. He never got stuck, but sometimes finding his way to the pod had been challenging.

Noah smiled until he met Agent Parker's disdainful expression. He lowered his gaze and grabbed his glass to take a few gulps. Telling the truth was one thing; rambling on about unimportant things was another altogether. *Stick to the basics. Don't tell him more than you need to.* He took another sip of water. What *should* he tell next?

Agent Parker answered that question for him by asking about the energy his species needed. As if Earth had anything the Rei could use.

"Our energy sustains us, like food and drink do Earth humans. Only our bodies need more energy than humans do, a lot more. Our planet provides us with plenty, but as I said before, we have never encountered another planet with the same conditions. I cannot describe our energy to you. I have no words for it."

Agent Parker narrowed his eyes, looking straight at him as if trying to catch him lying.

Had the answer not satisfied him? Noah suppressed the urge to fidget and forced himself to calmly pick up his glass, only to discover it was empty. He leaned forward and refilled it. Then he sat back again and took a sip, and another, and another, all the while trying to keep calm and wondering what was going through Agent Parker's mind.

Some long, tense minutes later, a knock on the door finally put an end to the uncomfortable staring. Someone handed a large sheet of paper to one of the black suits, who immediately handed it over to Agent Parker. As he studied it, a deep frown formed on his face. It did nothing to make Noah feel less uncomfortable.

Eventually, Agent Parker looked up again, but only to glare at Noah as he got up and left the room. The two black suits stayed behind, but at least Noah's hands were still uncuffed.

What was going on?

Noah had no idea how long ago Agent Parker had stormed out, but he'd had enough of the black suits watching. Even when he rested his head in his hands, elbows leaning on the table, and could only see the black suits' legs, he sensed them watching him. It made his skin crawl.

When Agent Parker finally stormed in and threw another file on the table, cursing as he did so, Noah was almost relieved not to be alone with the staring, watchful eyes of the black suits any longer.

"Nice stories, Mr. Jones, you really had us going for a moment," Agent Parker said, opening the file and turning it around so Noah could see it. The page showed a lot of squiggly lines in three different colours, with something Noah guessed would be DNA markers, or whatever Earth scientists called them.

Noah sighed. It wasn't hard to guess what Agent Parker was so pissed about.

"Human, Mr. Jones! Both scans say you're human."

"I am."

"So, why the stories?"

Noah looked Agent Parker straight in the eyes. "I did not lie, Agent Parker. I can't help it the scan gave you the information before I could."

"Now you're going to tell me this wonderful story about how you turned human. Right?"

"I wouldn't call it *wonderful*, no. Excruciatingly painful, yes. Desperate, certainly, but not wonderful."

"You think I'm going to believe you?"

"I will not lie to you." He wouldn't, but he wasn't going to beg his interrogator to believe him, either.

Agent Parker once again stared at him. Noah held his head high and kept from looking away, even though he desperately wanted to. He didn't like Agent Parker.

Still, Noah knew if they looked closely enough, his story would be supported by the same scan that told them he was human. If they looked closely, they would notice the differences, and they would believe him.

When Agent Parker finally broke eye contact, Noah hoped it was because he had read the truth in Noah's eyes, and not because he'd decided he'd had enough. "Well, don't keep us waiting," Agent Parker said, arms crossed in front of his chest. "Tell us your story."

# 8

*T WAS RUNNING OUT OF TIME.*
*Almost twenty-four rotations on Earth, as the human species called this planet, and it had yet to find a way home. Not even their books held a solution.*

*While not many Rei studied the written languages of the species they visited, it found them fascinating, and easier to decipher than spoken languages. They were often a mix of information and wonderful, entertaining stories. Both added to its understanding of species, and its younger kin certainly appreciated the more adventurous stories.*

*If only it had time for an adventure story now.*

*It spent most of the first ten rotations in its original form, roaming this library in the quiet times, studying the thick books chained to the shelves. The more it absorbed the symbols in the books, the more it understood their meaning.*

*When it needed more time to study, it copied the human form to move more freely among the species. It found shelter, too. A shed near the woods, far outside the city. Half the back wall was gone, and most of the furniture inside broken. No human had approached it since it had found it. It would be safe there.*

*If only its research was going as well. The more he studied,* the more it became clear that human imagination seemed more advanced than their technology.

They could neither travel through space nor help him contact his kin, only write about it.

Which had left it two choices: fade or transform.

It didn't want to fade, or worse, be stuck as a copy of a human, unable to converse with them, until it ran out of energy. It shuddered. It had been bad enough the past fourteen rotations. It could not bear to spend what was left of its time like that.

It didn't want to transform, either, but it had no choice. Not if it didn't want to fade.

It should have transformed four days ago when it had more energy left. But it hadn't been able to take that final step or give up on its kin.

To honour its kin, it was determined to retain its task as a rememorari, another wonderful human word. It wanted to continue storing its experiences, so that its kin, no matter how long it would take them to find it, could experience its life on Earth.

It had been reading as many books about the anatomy of the human species as this library held, but it had been avoiding transformation until the last possible moment to give its kind more time to find it.

For a moment, the world around it turned the deepest black. It flailed its human arms, clutching at the shelf the books were bound to. When its sight returned, the letters swayed across the page, the way it was swaying on its feet. Its energy depleted fast.

If it did not transform now, it would not have energy left, and fade.

Yet it could not force itself into action, could not make its human feet move towards its shelter until the keeper of the library chased it out with a jingle of his keys at closing time.

*Reluctantly, it made its way to the shed through the rain, still no closer to solving the transformation of its storage. Once there, it took its clothes off, hung them to dry, and lay down on the blanket it had found in a corner. It was full of holes, but still warm enough to shelter it from the cold. Human bodies didn't like the cold.*

*Staring at the sky through a hole in the roof, it feared losing itself. Feared losing its...memories, as humans called them.*

*If this was its last night on Earth, it might as well enjoy one more story. Its favourite.*

*Snuggled underneath the blanket, it replayed the story about a human named Noah, who had taken two of every species from Earth and put them on a boat to ensure their survival after an enormous flood.*

*Noah had been brave to set himself aside from others and do what his God, his deity, had told him to do.*

*It. No, he. As he resembled a male of the human species, he should be a he.*

*Like Noah, he stood aside from his kin and had to be brave. He wanted so much to be brave like Noah.*

*In the comfortable calm that followed, he accessed all the recorded books he needed, and set his transformation in motion.*

*The pain began the moment he started, and he almost stopped. Almost. Noah's story reminded him to be brave, that he couldn't go back now. He had to finish.*

*As he built himself up, he couldn't tell where he hurt. The pain was everywhere, in the heart, and the brain. In the bones, the veins, and the muscles. So many parts to remember. So many to put together, to fill his human shell.*

*He writhed on the floor, his new brain tormented by the signals of pain the rest of his body sent it. Piece by piece, his body became whole. Though it was hard to concentrate through the pain, he sensed his parts seeking connections, creating links, and, finally, communication.*

*He was whole; exhausted, but whole. His vision blacked out temporarily, but he didn't need his human eyes to continue. Not yet. He might be human, but with enough Rei left to still function as one.*

*Instead, he focussed on how his new human body worked. Interesting. Much better than any of the books he'd studied.*

*Unfortunately, none of his internal organs had spare room for his storage, least of all the brain. His stomach cavity, which had seemed a possibility on paper, could not be filled entirely without killing his body.*

*The more Rei energy he lost, the more tired he became, and the harder it was to concentrate.*

*At long last, he found one area he had not even considered. The skin. It had the largest surface. Not the cuticle, the outer layer of the skin, which was too close to the surface and too thin. However, the skin beneath the cuticle was protected, had moderate healing capacity, and would absorb human energy easily enough. It would have to do.*

*He only had one shot at this. If this failed...*

*He cleared his consciousness and focused all the Rei energy he had left on transferring his storage to the skin. It would have been better if he could have tested it, but there was no time. Not anymore.*

*There was no resistance, and his storage transferred much faster than expected. He even finished the complete transformation with a small amount of energy left.*

*His last thought as he succumbed to his fatigue, letting darkness surround him in something humans called sleep, was that he had done it.*

*He was human.*

*A human with a Rei storage hidden inside his skin, who had been brave...like Noah.*

CONNOR WAS ABOUT TO FOLLOW JASON INTO THE CINEMA WHEN HIS mobile rang. He fished it out of his pocket and read the text message:

*WER R U?*

Connor rolled his eyes at Isa's text speak and texted his location.

*MEET ME OUTSIDE,* Isa texted back.

*WHAT'S GOING ON?*

*HV SUMTHIN FOR U.*

With a sigh, Connor turned to Jason. "Sorry. It's Isa, she needs to see me for a moment. Why don't you get the tickets?"

Jason's expression became unreadable, just like it had when Connor had picked him up at his antique shop, but it was gone so quickly, Connor wondered if he'd imagined it.

Jason smiled at him. "Don't be too long."

"I won't." At least, he hoped he wouldn't be.

Connor watched Jason go in and cursed. Of all nights, this had to be the one where Isa interrupted a date. He was...

"Psst."

That had to be Isa. Connor entered the alley next to the cinema. "What are you doing?"

"I don't want CCTV picking up me handing this to you," she said as she opened her bag and pulled out some papers, handing them to him. "Research found your stalker. As of six o'clock tonight, he's being held for questioning. I thought you'd like to know, despite protocol."

Connor's mouth fell open, and his heart raced as he

looked down at the papers. "They found him?" he asked, suppressing the urge to read them right here, right now. Instead, he folded them and stashed them in his left back pocket. "It's only been four days since your boss took the case."

"Turned up twice on the CCTV around your house."

"That doesn't seem enough to—"

"His paperwork is suspicious. You'll see when you have the chance to read them."

He put his hand over hers. "Thank you. You didn't have to do this. Thank you."

Isa beamed. "You're welcome. Of course, it means I'll probably be working all weekend. But hey, you can't have everything. Now, go back to your boyfriend and enjoy the film."

Connor knew there was plenty Isa wasn't saying, but he was wise enough not to ask her. Instead, he kissed her and returned to the cinema.

Jason had come back outside and smiled at him. "I was afraid you had to go back to work."

Connor took Jason's hand. "No chance of that tonight."

They wouldn't allow him anywhere *near* Primrose right now. Bloody protocol.

When Noah opened his eyes and met Agent Parker's narrowed ones, he wondered whether the agent had any other expressions.

"That was a heart-breaking story, Mr. Jones, just heart-breaking."

The sneer in his voice told Noah that he wasn't in any way willing to give him the benefit of the doubt.

"A storage unit in your skin. Very imaginative. I have to give you points for that," Agent Parker said, his voice even more derisive. "But, Mr. Jones, you were taken in because you were stalking someone, attacked him using some sort of mind probe, and none of what you told me convinces me of your innocence."

The door behind him opened and a young woman with auburn hair entered. She seemed vaguely familiar to Noah.

Agent Parker turned around and bellowed, "What?"

"I'm sorry, sir, but considering the late hour, Lieutenant Matthews is calling a halt to this interview and instructed me to put Mr. Jones up for the night."

For the first time, Agent Parker's expression changed. This one far less stoic and more unbridled anger. Noah was glad it wasn't directed at him. Still, the young woman didn't bat an eyelid, but waited patiently for a reply.

Agent Parker pushed his chair back with force and turned around, towering over the young woman, who remained calm. "You can tell Lieutenant Matthews that I want him back in this interview room at eight tomorrow morning."

"I'm sorry, sir. Lieutenant Matthews has scheduled a thorough medical examination for Mr. Jones first thing tomorrow. You will, of course, be notified when he is ready," the young woman said, voice unwavering even as she stood almost nose to neck with Agent Parker.

Noah admired her strength. He studied her profile, trying to remember where he had seen her before, when it suddenly came to him. She'd hung around with Connor a couple of times. Maybe she could talk to Connor for him.

"Cuff him," Agent Parker barked to the black suits as he stormed out and slammed the door shut.

Instantly, one of the black suits moved towards him. The young woman opened her mouth, then shook her head and shut it again.

Noah held his arms out and suppressed a shiver as the cold handcuffs pinched his flesh. The black suit pulled him upright and grabbed him by the shoulder to lead him out, but the young woman waved him away.

"No need to manhandle him, Mott," she told the black suit as she opened the door.

Noah followed her through a maze of corridors until they reached an open door. If anything, the room seemed barer than the interview room had been, despite the pillow and blankets on an uncomfortable-looking bed. Noah tried not to sigh.

The young woman threw him an apologetic look and motioned him inside. The two black suits moved out of sight, probably taking up position on either side of the door.

"I'll have some food and water delivered, and something more comfortable to sleep in. You'll be woken at eight for your examination."

Before Noah could ask her about Connor, she was gone, leaving Noah alone in his cell.

AFTER GAZING AT EACH OTHER THROUGH MOST OF THE FILM, AND Jason drawing circles on his thigh as he was driving, Connor had no doubt where the evening was headed. He didn't bother asking Jason for directions to his place, but drove straight home, stomach in knots. It had been a while.

By the time they arrived at his flat, Jason's fingers were lazily travelling up and down Connor's cock through his jeans. Connor let out a breath of relief when he managed to park his car without hitting the ones on either side. Of course, when he turned to Jason to tell him off, Jason merely smirked and winked as he got out of the car in a supple and elegant move. Connor leaned his head back and tried to get his breathing under control, eventually following Jason in a far less elegant manner. He hoped none of the neighbours were looking out of their windows. Though not skin-tight, his jeans did a poor job of hiding his erection.

The minute Connor closed the front door behind him, Jason was all over him, driving his tongue into his mouth in a rough and demanding kiss while he rid Connor of his clothes at the same time. Not even the jeans gave him pause. Connor tried to reciprocate, but Jason was firmly in the director's seat for this one, though he did let Connor undo the buttons of his shirt.

"Up," Connor suggested when Jason pulled back to undo his own trousers.

Jason raised an eyebrow.

"We need to go upstairs, we are not doing this in my hall."

Jason apparently agreed and pulled Connor towards the stairs. He wanted to complain about the clothes lying about, but Jason kept pulling, and Connor gave in and let him.

"Which way?" Jason asked in a low, husky voice as they reached the top.

Connor pushed past Jason, still holding his hand, led him through the first door on their left, and stumbled over the hoover he had left there that morning.

"Oops," he mumbled, as he hopped on one foot and then landed face first on his queen-sized bed, dragging Jason half on top of him. "Sorry."

Jason planted a loud kiss on the top of his spine, then turned him over and wormed one hand underneath the waistband of his pants.

Connor's breath hitched. He spread his legs to provide easier access and encourage more touching.

"You look so hot right now," Jason whispered, lips trailing the shell of his ear, his curly hair tickling Connor's cheek.

Connor shivered and groaned as Jason found his target. If he kept this up, Connor would come in his pants. He tried to push Jason's trousers down, but Jason grabbed Connor's wrists in his free hand and held them down.

"I..." Connor started, unable to finish what he wanted to say when Jason claimed his lips for another demanding kiss. Connor tasted beer and popcorn. He stopped struggling, stopped thinking about regaining control, and lay back to enjoy what Jason was doing to him.

With every stroke of Jason's tongue across his and Jason's hand on his cock, Connor soared higher, moaning and writhing until he finally flew apart.

Breathing hard, Connor let Jason pull him to his side, his back plastered against Jason's chest. Connor reached back, intent on showing Jason a good time in return, but Jason grabbed his wrist and held it as he whispered, "Catch your breath. I can wait."

# 9

CONNOR WOKE UP WITH HIS MOUTH DRY, HIS MUSCLES protesting any movement, and something warm plastered against his right side. Eyes still closed, he turned towards the source of that warmth and draped his free arm over Jason's waist as images of last night replayed in his mind.

"Morning," he mumbled when Jason's breath hitched.

"Mo'ing." Jason's voice sounded as hoarse as his own, making Connor smile even more.

He opened his eyes, but all he saw were Jason's curls. "That was one heck of a night."

Jason uttered a noncommittal sound.

Connor snuggled closer, kissed the top of Jason's head, and closed his eyes again. "Don't you have a shop to open?"

Jason shook his head and mumbled something again. The only word Connor could decipher was 'Simon'. With Jason making no effort to get up, Connor saw no reason to, either, and let himself drift off again.

The next time he woke up, the space beside him was empty and cool to his touch. He shot up, only to let himself fall back again.

Jason sat cross-legged at the foot of the bed, watching

him, backlit by the sunlight coming through his window.

"Good morning, again," Connor said, his voice still a little hoarse.

"Morning. I've brought up your clothes." Jason pointed at the chair in the corner, next to his oak dresser. "And I've been rummaging through your kitchen, trying to make breakfast, but I have no idea whether you prefer tea or coffee in the morning."

Now that Jason mentioned it, something smelled awfully good, and he didn't mean Jason, though he smelled pretty good, too. "Tea, I drink enough coffee at the office as it is."

"Why not drink tea at the office, then?"

Connor raised an eyebrow. "Are you kidding? They have no idea how to brew a proper cup there."

Jason frowned at him. "I guess you'd better make the tea, lest I ruin it for you."

Connor moved to get up.

"No, no," Jason protested, holding his hands up, "stay here. I'll boil the water and bring the tea things here."

Jason definitely didn't have the first clue about brewing a proper tea. Connor shook his head, got off the bed, and made his way into the kitchen, trying hard not to notice that Jason was wearing his trousers and couldn't even be bothered to grab his pants.

Connor froze in the doorway. His normally spotless counter was doused in flour, a number of cooking implements were piled in his sink, and open canisters filled his kitchen table. It was a mess.

"Bloody tea," Jason mumbled behind him.

Connor blinked. "You know what? Forget the tea, just bring me some orange juice." He slowly backed away from his kitchen and shuffled straight back to his bed.

"Great. Just relax and I'll have breakfast ready in about ten minutes," Jason called out after him.

Connor groaned, itching to start cleaning. Instead, he hid his face under his pillow and let Jason have it his way.

Nine minutes and forty-three seconds later—not that Connor was counting—Jason came in with breakfast. He put the tray on the bed and climbed in next to Connor. The tray was filled with wonderful-smelling scones and buttered slices of toast, orange juice, and Connor's small selection of jams.

Connor moaned as he tasted the scones. Jason might be pants at brewing tea, but he wasn't half bad at baking. "These are good," he admitted, licking the jam and clotted cream off his fingers. "So, good conversationalist, great in bed, and a wonderful cook. I might just keep you."

Jason threw him a satisfied smile. "I aim to please."

They ate in silence, but as soon as they cleared the tray, Connor put it down on the floor and leaned forward to kiss Jason, who tasted of bread and butter and jam and clotted cream.

"Time for dessert, I gather?" Jason said, licking his lips as he pushed Connor onto his back.

Connor grinned as Jason crawled on top of him, still clad in jeans. All thoughts of his messed-up kitchen disappeared as Jason claimed his mouth in a hard kiss.

It was definitely a good morning.

OF COURSE, NOAH DIDN'T SEE THE YOUNG WOMAN AGAIN, NOT during his medical or any time afterwards. Instead, he'd been sitting in the interview room for who knew how long, alone. Though he imagined black suits stood guard outside the door.

The medical examination hadn't been as bad as he'd thought it would be. The doctor was friendly, taking the time to explain every procedure and test as he hooked Noah up to this or that machine. Noah tried to remember all the tests and whether he knew of them, but there had been too many to keep track of.

No matter what the results of all those tests were, he wasn't looking forward to facing Agent Parker again, though he hoped the tests supported his story. If they didn't... Noah shuddered as he imagined the worst.

The door swung open, and in strode Agent Parker. Talk of the devil. "Well, well, well, who figured that, an alien telling the truth."

Noah folded his hands and tried not to look smug.

"At least, you seem to have the doctor convinced."

It was obvious Agent Parker didn't like that much.

"Doesn't mean we're ready to let you go just yet," Agent Parker continued, a familiar sneer on his face as he slammed the files in his hands on the table. "There are still too many questions left unanswered." He sat down. "The doctor confirmed that, according to your physiology, you are approximately forty years old, yet you claim to have arrived in 1648, which would make you at least three hundred and sixty years old."

Though it was a statement, Agent Parker made it sound like a question.

"I studied what was known about the human body in 1648," Noah began, "but two weeks were not long enough to understand it all, let alone something like mortality." He wasn't completely certain how to explain the flaws in his transformation.

"Go on."

"My kin multiply when two mates connect—when their essences, their cores, connect—but we do not die, not in the way humans do. Lack of energy is our biggest threat, but our planet provides plenty. Time and age have no meaning to us, though we do grow in size and are able to absorb more as time progresses. We may start small, but we have no real childhood or adulthood."

"Your species cannot die?"

"Not as such, no." Noah wasn't so foolish as to tell Agent Parker how his kin could be killed. He had promised himself to tell the truth, but this was an exception.

Agent Parker opened the file to one of the last pages. "Yet you age."

"As a human, yes. Part of the transformation consisted of embedding my original form into the human one. But, as I mentioned, aging has no meaning to us. I only understood it from a Rei point of view. As a result, I age very slowly, at the growth rate of my original form."

"At what rate?"

"I seem to age a year about every twenty-four years."

There was that eyebrow again. Noah tried to keep from squirming under Agent Parker's scrutinising look, but the man gave him the creeps. Which was probably why he did it.

"Right," Agent Parker said about five minutes later. "Let's go back to you telling us about your species being peaceful with no desire to conquer other worlds. All you want is to experience what other species experience. Is that correct?"

"Yes."

"How, then, do you explain your victim's nosebleed and disorientation after his first encounter with you?"

"Not being prepared."

"Prepared for what?"

"Connecting our essences—our minds, as humans might say—is the only way my kin connect and communicate with each other." It had taken him a long time to accept he would never feel the presence of his kin, or even a mate. "Only twice in my time on Earth have I experienced such a connection with a human. The first time was barely a hundred years after my arrival, when I had not yet lost hope of finding such a connection. This time..." Noah took a breath. It was hard to think about it. "This time, I understood too late what was happening. By the time I did, the damage was already done."

Of course, he wasn't going to mention his unwillingness to let go and his desperate attempt to keep hold of what he'd found, even after he became aware that he was hurting Connor.

"What does this... connection entail?"

"The exchange of information, the asking and answering of questions."

"That's it?"

"Yes. Like I said, it's a form of communication." Noah tried to keep it generic, having learned long ago that humans did not believe in soul mates, no matter how much they loved writing and reading about them. 'Soul mates' was perhaps not the right expression, but it was the only one Noah could think of that came close to describing the connection in the English language.

"Communication, you say. You don't gain control over the other person?"

"No. It's comparable with what humans call friendship. The better we get to know each other, the deeper we can enter into the connection, the more private the exchange of information can be." The more energy could be exchanged. Noah suppressed the urge to close his eyes and search out the last traces of Connor's energy inside him. This was not the time nor the place.

Instead, he focussed on Agent Parker's insinuation that he'd tried to control Connor. "I cannot learn what the other does not want me to know, and I cannot, at any point, force them to do or give up anything. The connection is not about control." Something he should have let Connor know, instead of following him around, trying to create a connection between Connor's essence and his without getting to know him, so desperate for contact that he'd forgotten all about it being a two-way street.

"You're telling me you can't control someone, but you can hurt them?"

"Yes." Noah hung his head. "When I sensed the connection, I dove into it full-force, without taking protective measures to prevent me from pushing too hard, too fast. It has been over two hundred and seventy years since I sensed a connection. I was too eager to care. As soon as I became aware of what I was doing, I pulled back, but it was already too late."

Noah shuddered as he recollected the pain Connor had broadcast through the connection. "I know you don't want to believe me, but it's very rare for me to connect to humans the way I did my kin, and I missed that contact. It should not have happened. I should have proceeded slowly and carefully. He would not have been in pain then."

And Noah wouldn't have ended up here.

Lips still tingling from their last kiss, Connor closed the door and leaned against it for a moment, wrapping his robe tight around him. He could get used to this, though he was hesitant to let Jason into his kitchen again. At least he had cleaned up the mess himself instead of leaving it for Connor to do. Connor had almost expected him not to. Jason seemed used to getting what he wanted.

Isa might have just found him the perfect bloke. He should send her a thank you note.

Oh, bugger. *Isa!*

Connor ran up the stairs, taking two steps at a time, and into his bedroom, almost pulling his chair across the room when he attempted to retrieve his jeans from its back. The documents weren't in his pockets. He was sure he had put them in his back pocket, but both pockets were empty.

How had his jeans ended up here again? Oh, right. Jason had picked them up from the floor in the hall. Maybe the documents were in the hall. No. Connor shook his head. He'd have seen them when he let Jason out. They could have fallen out.

Connor pulled the rest of the clothing off the chair and shook it all out. He let out a breath when the documents fluttered to the floor. Isa would kill him if he'd lost them.

He folded his clothes, picked up the papers, and settled cross-legged in the middle of his bed. Now he would finally know who or what was messing with him.

*Noah Jones, date of birth suspicious.* Connor snorted. Suspicious. What did that mean? How could a date of birth be suspicious? He pressed his lips together. He'd read all that later. He flipped through the papers. There, on the last page, an old photo. A black and white photocopy, and not a particularly good one. Still, it was clear enough to form an idea of what Noah Jones looked like, wavy hair and all.

Though older than the type Connor usually fell for, he couldn't deny the bloke was handsome. It was the eyes that drew him in. Even in this crappy copy they seemed the lightest grey Connor had ever seen. Yet friendly and inviting and...

He threw the papers to the floor. What was he doing? It was bad enough this bloke or creature or whatever he was had been stalking him. Now Connor was what? Ogling him? Ridiculous.

For a long time, he stared at the bunched-up papers on the floor, torn between his curiosity and his disgust at the burst of attraction. In the end, his curiosity won out, and he picked the papers back up again, determined to know all about who had attacked him.

"Wavy lines."

Across from him, the severe-looking Agent Ruddock wrote Noah's answer down and held up another card, facing her.

Noah barely took a second to consider. "Square."

He kept naming cards. Squares, circles, stars, crosses, and wavy lines followed each other in random order until Agent Ruddock announced the end of the test. Of course, Noah had no clue as to what was really on those cards.

Though she refused to tell him anything about the results, Noah knew he had shown no psychic talent at all. It wasn't as if he hadn't tested it himself before. Not tests like these, but in the first couple of centuries, he had contacted various mediums, from fortune tellers to seers, to see if he could connect with them. It had never worked. Noah had tried telling the woman that, but she wouldn't hear of it, saying she trusted no results but her own, and that had been the end of it.

"Send the first one in."

Noah looked up to see an older man walk in and take a seat opposite him.

"Mr. Jones. This is Harry Gerhardt, one of our most talented psychics. We want you to try and form a connection with him."

Noah straightened up in his seat, suppressing the urge to sigh. He closed his eyes, but he didn't even need to focus to realise there would be no connection at all. There was nothing to grab hold of, no spark, nothing. He opened his eyes again and found Harry looking at him.

They stared at each other for a while, until finally, Agent Ruddock coughed and asked whether it succeeded.

"He's like a blank screen," Harry, said, "I can tell he's

trying, but I feel nothing from him. I can't read him."

"Mr. Jones?"

Noah shook his head. "I sense nothing."

"I was going to ask if you are actively shielding yourself against such an intrusion."

"No." It was a ridiculous question.

"You're not trying to keep Mr. Gerhardt from connecting to you?"

Was she serious? "I haven't been able to experience any sort of connection for over two hundred and seventy years. I welcome such a connection more than you could ever begin to understand. I have no reason to shield myself." Noah cursed himself for his inability to hide his irritation from Agent Ruddock, who seemed taken aback by his outburst.

"I am sorry, Mr. Jones. I had to ask." She turned to Mr. Gerhardt "Thank you for your time, Harry. Could you please ask Monica to join us?"

None of the other three psychics she brought in managed to connect either, not even when she had two of them try a second time, just to be sure. Noah only shook his head at this, hoping she'd see reason soon enough. He had lost track of time, but he was starting to get hungry.

# 10

CONNOR SAT IN A CHAIR WITH ELECTRODES ATTACHED TO HIS head, leaning on the table in front of him as he stared at the white wall opposite. Called in for a psychic evaluation. On a Saturday. Only catching a glimpse of Noah Jones would keep this from being a wasted trip.

"Good afternoon, Agent Smith. Thank you for coming in on your day off."

Agent Ruddock didn't wait for him to acknowledge her. She moved around a transparent polycarbonate divider to a desk containing several big computer screens. She tapped away on a keyboard, a serious expression in her eyes, then came over to check the electrodes and sat down opposite him. Though her hair was up in a tight bun, she ran her fingers up both sides of her head as if to catch any loose strands. "You know the drill, I assume? I hold a card up and you name the first shape to enter your mind."

Connor nodded and tried to concentrate. The first card was held up, but nothing sprang to mind, nor did it on the second, third or fourth cards, reminding him of the very first time he'd had to take the same test. They'd told him then that it was nerves, trying too hard to get a result and ending up drawing a blank. Connor knew better now.

He just couldn't read the bloody cards, and when she held the next one up, he randomly picked a shape. "Square, circle, square, wavy lines, cross, circle..." It went on and on until all the cards had been used.

Connor understood the reason for this psychic re-evaluation, but he doubted he'd scored any better than he had last time. They might think what had happened awakened something in him, but he couldn't see it.

He leaned back and waited patiently for Ruddock to write her report, so she could start the next part of the test. A sudden spark shot up his spine, and Connor only barely bit back a gasp. He closed his eyes.

Images shot through his mind—too fast to see, but they startled him into opening his eyes again.

He tried to get his breathing under control and leaned forward, resting his head on the cool table.

Noah Jones had to be close. That had to be it.

"Agent Smith, are you all right?"

Connor shook his head. Couldn't she see he wasn't?

"Are you in pain?"

He shook his head again.

"Do..."

He held a hand up and pointed to the computer behind the divider. He couldn't believe she was focussing on him instead of her computer. The electrodes stuck to him were bound to have picked up something, weren't they?

The scraping of Ruddock's chair echoed through the room, followed by the clacking of her heels as she made for her computer.

"Nothing," she said, sounding surprised. "I see nothing. Whatever..."

Connor raised his head.

Ruddock moved her face close to the screen. "Oh, now that's interesting." She grabbed the phone and pressed a button, no doubt calling her superior. She turned her back to Connor as she spoke. When she put the phone down, she turned back to him and frowned. "Are you sure you're not in pain, Agent Smith?"

He nodded. He still sensed that odd tingle, but no pain this time. He was sure he'd be all right as long as he kept his eyes open and didn't get drawn into a fast-spinning slide show again.

Sooner than Connor thought possible, three research agents burst into the room. They joined Ruddock at her desk, the divider keeping Connor from hearing them. Their gestures were funny to watch. Their hands never stopped moving, not for a second, as they talked.

Ruddock grabbed the phone again. How many more people would be needed to solve this?

He received his answer about fifteen minutes later, when Lieutenant Matthews entered the room. His boyish smile made him seem charming and friendly, but Connor knew he had one hell of a bite.

"I hear you've been giving the staff a hard time, Agent Smith," Matthews said with a wink, running a hand through his thick, stylish hair.

Connor raised his eyebrows. "I guess they ran out of guinea pigs."

Matthews's smile widened. "I'd better order some new ones, then."

"Lieutenant Matthews?" Ruddock called out from behind the divider.

"I probably should go and see what all the fuss is about." Matthews joined the rest in looking at the screen.

The researchers immediately started talking over one another until Matthews held up his hand and pointed at Ruddock. He seemed more patient than Connor could ever be. No wonder Isa liked working for him so much. He, probably more than anyone, could rein Isa in when she was off on a tangent and get her focus back where it belonged.

With a shake of his head, Matthews rounded the divider and sat down opposite Connor. "No one bothered to ask you what you were experiencing during these readings?"

"It's partly my fault. I was still trying to catch my breath when Agent Ruddock asked me. I pointed towards her screen instead. I guess the readings were interesting enough that she forgot."

"It's no excuse for their negligence. So, what *did* happen?"

Connor told him about the spark, the connection, and the images he saw when he closed his eyes.

Matthews frowned. "Do you think you'll see those same images again if you close your eyes now?"

"I think so."

Matthews turned towards the researchers. "You heard him, ladies. Get that computer set up for another test. And have someone bring in a better chair." He leaned back in his seat. "When we have you safely strapped into that chair, try to keep your eyes closed for as long as you can stand it. The longer it lasts, the more accurate the reading."

Connor nodded, though he wasn't looking forward to doing it. He was tempted to ask about Noah Jones, but didn't, since he wasn't supposed to know about it officially.

Fifteen minutes later, the table and most of the chairs had been shoved into a corner, and in their place stood a sturdy, padded chair with more straps attached than Connor cared to count. The material of the chair was soft and comfortable, though his comfort level plummeted when Ruddock strapped him into it.

Eager expressions faced him through the divider. The researchers seemed raring to go. Connor less so, yet he still closed his eyes when he was given the go ahead.

Images flooded his mind like a whirlwind, sliding by too fast to recognise individual objects. The speed made him want to hurl, but he stubbornly kept his eyes closed. The longer the images whirled past, the more similarities he picked up. They were the same pictures, shown over and over again.

Once Connor managed to focus on individual images, he was able to pick out some sort of snowy landscape and a house—Victorian, maybe, though it looked as if it had been built recently, and not centuries ago.

A hand on his shoulder startled him out of his concentration, and he opened his eyes.

"You can stop now, Connor," Matthews said, his voice sharp, but shaky. "We have enough information."

"But..."

"No. It took me fifteen minutes to snap you out of it. I can't let you do it again."

"Fifteen minutes? Felt more like seconds."

Matthews leaned in and squeezed Connor's shoulder gently. Then he sat back and straightened himself. "The reading showed additional brain activity compared to the spike we registered the first time. What changed?"

"I recognised a pattern in the images. As long as I focussed on one at a time, I saw them much clearer."

"That's all? You were watching images?" Now Matthews sounded even more concerned, and his meaning slowly sunk in.

"You think I'm being brainwashed. You think there's some sort of hidden message in these images?"

"You tell me."

"A newly built Victorian house and a snowy landscape." Connor shook his head. "I can't imagine either having some sort of hidden meaning that I'd react to."

"Those were the only images?"

"No, there were more, many more, but you interrupted me."

Matthews narrowed his eyes. "Connor, it was dangerous enough to leave you in that state for this long. You seemed almost catatonic."

"I thought your objective was to find out if my stalker is dangerous?"

"It is."

"Well." Connor cocked his head. "This is the way to find out. Hook me up to whatever machine you want to. I'm doing this."

When nothing but pressed lips and a grimace answered him, Connor thought he'd gone too far.

Matthews looked away and minutes passed. Finally, he turned his gaze back on Connor. "Would it help if we moved Mr. Jones closer?"

Connor started. He didn't want to give Isa away.

"I knew Isa had copied the file as soon as she handed it to me," Matthews said. Connor opened his mouth, but Matthews stopped him with a single gesture. "Can we focus on the task at hand, please? Would it help?"

"Haven't you moved him closer to test my reactions?"

"The spike? You thought it happened because we moved him closer?"

"Yes."

Matthews shook his head. "We didn't, but it's something we've been discussing."

"It might intensify the connection, but I don't know if it'll make it easier or harder for me to focus. If you've read my reports, you know that I had almost no control during the incidents."

"You froze."

Connor nodded.

"I suggest we keep him at a distance, for now."

Noah listened to the machine next to him softly bleeping. He'd been hooked up to it from the start of this interrogation, but no one had bothered to tell him what they were monitoring.

"No, I have no way of reaching my kin. Nor do I have any means of getting back to the planet," he informed Agent Parker yet again.

Sensing Connor entering the building threw Noah off balance. Part of him wanted to connect to Connor, while the other part didn't want Agent Parker to notice. He had more and more trouble concentrating on the questions.

"You had a pod."

Noah huffed. "Yes, over three hundred and sixty years ago. On the planet Ix, which is light years away from here, and I—"

"Have no means of getting off of Earth. Yes, yes. You're stranded here. I get it."

Finally, he understood. Noah tried to keep the connection under control, tried not to give in, but it was becoming harder and harder.

"You mentioned a signal. Any idea why your...kin never picked it up?

Noah shrugged. "Earth is outside our range."

"Yet you kept trying."

Noah suppressed the urge to roll his eyes. "Plenty of species travel the galaxy, Agent Parker. One would have been enough." Enough to get off the planet, assuming they were a friendly species. Maybe enough to go home.

The door opened, and someone in a lab coat came in to mutter something to Agent Parker. Agent Parker rose with a grunt and followed the lab coat out of the room.

Home. For a long time, Noah had longed to convey the true essence of books, of these humans, to his kin, yet these days, going home was the furthest thing from his mind.

As Noah lost himself in thoughts, the connection between him and Connor flared to life. He cursed and gasped, knuckles white from grasping the armrests. What little control he still had was gone as all his senses overloaded. Connor seemed to be consciously searching him out. He couldn't be. An advancement like that needed touch, as well as proximity.

So long ago, with Dafydd, he had gone through the same thing. Noah sighed. Lovely, innocent Dafydd, who had made him feel more alive than he had been in the hundred years before. Noah hadn't had any control over the connection then, either.

As soon as a Rei connected to another, their essences shared their life stories. Only it hadn't worked that way with Dafydd. Dafydd couldn't process the flood of images the way a Rei did, like the simple stream of data it was. He hadn't known what he was doing.

They had been holding hands when Noah's essence had sensed a kindred one and a connection between them had flared to life, and Dafydd had been so overwhelmed. He had tried, the poor boy; he had tried so hard.

Noah had received a continuously repeating data stream as his essence detected an incompatibility. Yet, instead of breaking contact, his essence kept trying to connect to Dafydd, repeating the flood of images over and over until Dafydd blacked out and ended up with an excruciatingly painful headache that had lasted days.

In the end, their connection had been one-sided, instead. Noah had been able to sense Dafydd, but Dafydd had never been able to sense him.

A sharp tug on the connection made Noah grasp the arm rests even tighter. This time, the headache was his.

Connor had not been born in the 1700s. He was a twenty-first century man working for an organisation that monitored alien activity on Earth. Maybe it was his knowledge or this technological age, or maybe it was because Connor had none of the innocence Dafydd had. Whatever Connor was doing, Noah's essence was reacting to it, and Noah could only let it happen.

The data stream flowed out of Noah, repeating itself. Noah sensed certain images being picked out, as if Connor was consciously browsing through them. It put an extraordinary amount of strain on Noah's system—too much strain. It was draining his energy much too fast.

Noah tried to get a grip, tried to slow it down, but he couldn't regain control.

Then, just like that, the strain was gone, and all that remained was the soft pull of a cementing connection between his essence and Connor's. Noah sagged into the chair, torn between worry and relief. His head lolled forward, and he was too done in to even try and lift it up.

He hoped Connor was all right.

Connor let go of the image of a young bloke with thick, long brown hair held together with a black ribbon, dressed in early-1700s clothing, and took a deep breath. Four images done, but none seemed to indicate anything out of the ordinary, even though early-1700s clothing wasn't exactly common. Still, Matthews hadn't stopped him yet, so Connor focussed on a new image.

The process seemed easier with every image. This one, an unusual swirl of purple, barely took effort at all. What did it mean? It wasn't dense enough to be candy floss. It didn't make any sense.

Was this how Noah Jones gained access to Connor's brain? With an innocent picture of purple swirls? No, that didn't ring true. Yet, unlike the other images, this one called up something from deep within him, calm, and a sense of longing.

The image broke in little pieces. Little snippets flew away, changed into a whirl of barely tangible emotions clearer than anything Connor had ever sensed. Bit by bit, they settled inside him.

They came from Noah. They *were* Noah. They seemed so familiar, as if Connor had always known him.

This was no evil plan to take over the world, not a way to influence him, to use his mind. None of that. Just a connection between two...creatures bringing an intense sense of belonging.

Connor relaxed into the chair with a smile and watched the images. Would Noah sense his acceptance?

All of a sudden, the flood of images and connected sensations stopped cold, as if the power had run out.

Noah?

The connection was still there, but...

A sharp sting broke Connor's focus. He opened his eyes to glare at whoever stung him, only to meet three sets of concerned expressions. "What is it?"

"Jones collapsed. Agent Parker is going apeshit," Agent Zabrowski, a slightly pudgy woman with a faintly eastern European accent said as she pushed her glasses back onto her nose.

Spots swam in front of Connor's eyes as he glanced at Matthews. "Did I do that?"

Matthews nodded. "I wouldn't have thought it possible, but the read-outs confirm it."

Full circle. Connor's stomach turned. All this time he'd been worried about being attacked, being stalked, and now he'd hurt another without meaning to.

*Without meaning to.* "He never *meant* to hurt me."

"Yes, Agent Smith. I think you may just have proven Mr. Jones's claim of innocence."

Somehow, that didn't make Connor feel better at all. Not until he knew Noah would be all right.

## 11

OAH SENSED CONNOR PULLING ON THE CONNECTION again. *Oh, please, not now.* He was too weak, too tired to stop him, and now Agent Parker watched him like a hawk.

*Stop.* Connor didn't seem to hear him—shouldn't be able to, since the connection hadn't advanced that far yet—but Noah had to try. He had no desire to black out in front of Agent Parker, even if it might convince him of his innocence.

What was Connor doing? Was this what he'd felt when Noah had drawn energy from him? Had Connor figured out how to do it, and was he now getting revenge? Noah couldn't stop the questions from flooding his mind, even though he sensed no ill will from Connor.

Noah breathed deeply in and out and braced himself against the impact of Connor's onslaught. Exhausted as he was, he tried pushing him out. Nothing happened. All Noah could do was hold on as his core, his essence—triggered by Connor actively searching him out—attempted to share his life story through the connection.

He bit his lip to keep from crying when Connor manipulated the images. This shouldn't be possible. Humans were incompatible. Dafydd had come close, but even then it hadn't worked.

Connor had far more control over the connection than Noah thought possible. He flipped through the images, one by one. Soon, he would reach the one image that would unlock every aspect of Noah's existence, before and after turning human.

Torn between elation, despair, and pain, Noah welcomed Connor into his core, hoping the fast depletion of energy wouldn't destroy him. Connor wasn't aware he was tapping into Noah's energy, not his own, and with Connor not hearing him through the connection, there was no way to stop him.

Noah slipped away from his body and saw, more than felt, his head fall back against the chair in slow motion, his lower jaw relaxing. Agent Parker's voice came from somewhere far, far away, but Noah couldn't make his mouth work. He had no strength left, but still felt like smiling when Connor's acceptance seeped through the connection.

Then everything stopped.

Connor paced up and down the waiting room of the Medical Department, waiting for someone, anyone, to tell him what was going on. It had been at least half an hour since the staff involved in the testing had rushed upstairs, and the not knowing was driving Connor bonkers. The light green walls, the white chairs and dark green pillows, the magazines stashed on top of a small table—browsed without seeing a word—he'd had enough of it all. He'd even counted the chair legs.

He bristled at being dismissed like this, to not be allowed to join them. Still, aside from grabbing a quick cup of coffee,

Connor didn't want to stray too far. He needed to know how Noah was, needed the connection he had wanted so much to get rid of, now that he knew Noah.

He needed it to satisfy his curiosity about what he'd discovered through it, needed it to fill the sense of emptiness its lack left, but mostly he needed it so he could show Noah how sorry he was for hurting him.

"What did you think you were playing at, Connor Smith?"

Connor jumped at the shrillness in Isa's voice. "What?" he asked as he turned to her.

Isa glared at him with narrowed eyes and crossed arms. "I can't believe he let you do this. What if you got stuck? What if you had gone catatonic again? What if you had ended up like... like him!"

"Noah? Have you seen him? Is he all right?"

"What? Jones? Yeah, he's fine. Still unconscious, but his vitals are fine. He seems severely exhausted, though. It might be a while before he wakes up."

Connor sighed in relief and sank down in one of the chairs set against the wall. Noah was fine. He was going to be all right.

"What's going on with you?" she asked, her voice softer and almost concerned as she sat down next to him.

"I did that to him. I hurt him."

"He hurt you too, Connor."

"He didn't mean to hurt me." Connor knew that now, and all he wanted was for Noah to be released to continue his life as a shopkeeper and be with his precious books. He didn't want Noah to end up on one of the alien islands.

Isa opened her mouth, closed it again, and gaped at him. "You really believe that."

He deflated. "Yes. I do. He's harmless, Isa."

"Based on what?"

How could he explain what he had sensed, had seen, what

he knew? "Gut instinct?"

Isa snorted. "My, my, Agent Smith reduced from logic to gut instinct. Maybe I should ask Lieutenant Matthews to run some more tests."

"Ha–bloody–ha."

She put a hand on Connor's arm, her eyes filled with concern. "I can't say I'm thrilled about this connection you seem to share with him, but the strange thing is, I think you're right. I've seen him, talked to him, very briefly. Nothing about him seems fake or dishonest. He was driving Parker mad."

That, Connor could easily imagine. Parker, despite being extremely insensitive, was the best at sussing out a lie or misdirection. He could rattle anyone he interrogated into telling him the truth. "Wasn't too happy, then?"

"Not at all. Parker's never liked interviewing those who aren't trying to hide anything." Isa shook her head. "Parker said Noah answered every question he threw at him truthfully. Parker played his bit, letting Noah think he barely believed half of it, but he couldn't catch Noah at lying. Parker absolutely hates that. Called it a waste of his time."

A door opened, and a young agent entered the waiting room. "Agent Griffin? Lieutenant Matthews wants you."

Isa sighed. She squeezed Connor's hand. "Go home, Connor. Get some sleep. Be a good boy, and I'll see if I can get you permission to see him tomorrow."

"Yes, Mum," Connor answered half-heartedly, but didn't move as Isa followed the young agent through the door.

He'd go home soon. Just not right now.

He closed his eyes. He knew Noah. How strange did that sound? Though he could barely decipher half of what he'd experienced, he clearly imagined the purple, see-through, floating blobs. One in particular grabbed his attention. Connor tried to caress it. It was Noah, from before he became human, and he was beautiful.

It should have freaked him out, but it didn't. How could it? He knew Noah.

*THE HAND IN CONNOR'S WAS WARM AS THEY STOOD ON THE SANDY* plains. *A soft breeze blew past, rustling the leaves of the large, reddish trees alongside them. A peculiar clucking sound came from behind, but when Connor turned his head, there was nothing to see.*

*He had no idea where they were, but it was nowhere near home. It was warm here. Connor raised his hand to wipe his brow, only to find his arm wrapped in the most multi-coloured, shimmering fabric he had ever seen. He looked down and was glad he was wearing sunglasses. The fabric appeared to be on fire, so brightly did it shine. Why were they dressed like this?*

*If disco music started playing, someone was going to die.*

*The hand holding his squeezed him, and Connor looked to his left, catching the most amazing grey eyes watching him. They seemed familiar somehow. He knew them, but his brain didn't seem capable of reaching beyond grey eyes and sandy plains, no matter how hard he tried.*

*"Connor. Stop thinking. Just be."*

*Just be. That seemed so easily said. He could never just be. He needed to know everything, every detail, cataloguing, memorising. He...*

*"Connor... stop!" The voice came from within.*

*"I can't. It's too much."*

*"Focus on me."*

*Wasn't that what he was doing?*

*"Open your eyes, Connor."*

*Connor did. When had he closed them? He gazed into the grey eyes. They were like clouds, grey clouds on a stormy day. Always a stormy day.*

*Everything stopped. The soft wind that had ruffled his hair nary a minute ago died down. Neither the leaves nor the sand showed even the tiniest ripple. Everything had stopped.*

*Noah blinked.*

*All but them.*

*Before Connor could ask what was happening, Noah leaned closer and kissed him—a soft touch of lips on lips, barely more than a brush.*

*Connor stopped caring about the strangeness of it all.*

*"This is where I left my pod," Noah told him. "The last planet I visited, before Earth. They have the most beautiful sunset. It lights up the sand. Will you watch it with me?"*

*Connor nodded and watched the world around him come alive once more, like an enormous IMAX 3D film with surround sound. It was odd to feel the world move around you, yet not move yourself.*

*The clucking noise sounded again, this time from next to him. Connor turned to see a pale yellow, chicken-like creature hopping up and down, trying to pick berries from orange shrubs.*

*"No, I don't know its name."*

*More questions popped into Connor's head, like what sort of trees the reddish ones were, why the fabric shone so brightly, why*

*—*

*"Stop thinking and just experience. See, hear, smell, feel." Noah twirled Connor around, pulling Connor's back against his chest.*

*Connor did. He stared at the odd creatures passing them and smelled flowers that seemed almost familiar, but not quite. He watched the sun sink into the sand, turning it into a giant bowl of pale light. For the first time in his life, he just was.*

*Until his phone rang. He patted the shimmery fabric to find it, but it wasn't in his trousers.*

*"You need to wake up now, Connor."*

*Connor looked at Noah beside him.*

*Noah smiled. "Thank you for being here with me," he said as the world around them disappeared.*

Connor found himself staring up at his bed from the floor next to it. How? When had he come home?

His phone rang again. He dragged himself over to the chair in the corner to fish it out of his trouser pocket. "Mo—"

"Where were you? I've been trying to call you for almost an hour."

Isa.

"Connor?"

"I'm here." Though he wasn't quite sure of that.

"You sound like you just woke up. It's two p.m., Connor. What are you still doing in bed?"

"Sleeping." Dreaming. At least, he thought he'd been dreaming.

"Lieutenant Matthews released Noah Jones about an hour ago. Parker deemed him adapted to life on Earth enough to allow him to go home. Though he did get a thorough search out of it. You know how Parker is."

"Other than an arse? At least Noah is free."

"Yeah. Sorry you didn't get to visit him."

Connor remembered the stormy eyes in his dreams and smiled.

"Connor? Are you all right?"

"Yes." He was. Noah was free. He could visit Noah at home now, and work would be just work again. "Yes, I am."

Sunk into his favourite chair, Noah watched tiredly as black suits checked his flat out, millimetre by millimetre. They took all the pillows out of his sofa and opened all his walnut bookcases, even taking out most of the books. That they carefully put everything back into place came as a surprise. Noah had half expected them to plough through like bulls in a china shop. The agent in charge never said a word to him. He divided his team into groups, assigned them rooms, and stood in the middle of Noah's living room overseeing them. Or overseeing him.

Why now? They'd had ample time to search his flat and bookshop when he was locked up. The warrant they'd handed him had Agent Parker's name on it. He had seemed none too happy about Noah being released. Was this his way of venting his frustrations?

Noah closed his eyes, close to nodding off even with an agent standing in his living room. If only they would hurry up and leave, so he could finally get some decent sleep.

When they finally did leave, as quietly as they had conducted their search, all Noah felt up to was sinking deeper into his chair and letting himself doze off.

Scenes flitted by as if Noah were sitting in a cinema. All that was missing was the popcorn. Scenes without sound, but filled with a myriad of emotions that echoed through his body.

None of the impressions lasted longer than thirty seconds, which seemed too short to understand what he was looking at. Still, the emotions were clear enough, so Noah hung on and enjoyed the ride.

It could have been any small boy holding his mother's hand, but there was something in the way he smiled, something about the way he walked that was so Connor.

In the next one, Connor sat on his father's lap as he learned his times tables, which shifted into a scene where he was helping his mother cook.

More and more scenes of Connor's childhood passed by, memories of a happy boy, treasured by his parents. He had his mother's hair, the same hint of a curl in the muggy weather, and her smile. He had his father's nose and hands, not to mention his head for numbers.

Connor's teens seemed to go by much faster, showing him Connor crying as his first girlfriend walked by with someone new, his first kiss from a boy, and scenes from his cricket days and summer jobs mixed with more interaction with his parents.

Noah's chest ached from the despair and loneliness Connor exuded, standing at his parents' graves barely a week after their deaths. He reached out, longing to be with Connor in his darkest moment, when the image changed into another cricket scene.

He missed the next few as he calmed himself, and picked up again at Connor's first day at Primrose, a bundle of nervousness and enthusiasm. From there, Connor's life as an adult shifted from work to meeting Isa, a number of boyfriends, and more work. Most of it intrigued Noah, but some of it was too dangerous for Noah's taste.

When Noah woke up, the one scene he couldn't get out of his head was of Connor wrapped in his boyfriend's arms. A blond man with damp curls who pressed soft kisses between Connor's shoulder blades as they made love. They looked good together.

With heavy heart and a stomach tied in knots, Noah sat up. Would Connor forgive him once he grasped the true nature of their connection?

# 12

CONNOR JERKED AWAKE WHEN THE DOORBELL RANG. HE checked his alarm clock. Seven p.m. Had he really been sleeping all day?

With a yawn, he pushed himself up and planted his feet on the chilly floor as he tried to decide whether to put on yesterday's clothes or the robe hanging next to the door.

The doorbell rang again.

"I'm coming!" He grabbed his robe, coughing away the scratchiness that always seemed to gather in his throat when he'd slept so long. He shuffled down the stairs, yawning and trying to tie his belt. If he had slept all day, why was he still so tired?

There had been a presence in his head. Or had it been a dream? It was all so hazy. He remembered Noah, though. He had been right there with him, wherever "there" had been. Now, if he could only remember what Noah had told him.

The doorbell rang a third time when Connor opened his front door. Jason was wearing jeans again, and Connor looked him up and down, want flaring up inside, all thoughts of Noah forgotten. "Hey," he said.

"Hello, Gorgeous." Jason had a big grin on his face that turned into confusion as he took in Connor's appearance.

"Did I wake you?"

"Yes," Connor frowned, barely able to stop himself from yawning again. "Did I forget something?"

Jason shook his head. "Just felt like visiting you. Man, you look tired. I didn't drain you that much, did I?"

"No more than reasonable." Very reasonable, indeed. He wouldn't mind a do-over right now.

"So, what have you been doing all weekend to look this ragged?"

"Work. Had to go in yesterday and didn't get home until two or so this morning." That much, he *did* remember. "Feel exhausted. Been in and out of sleep all day."

"Until the doorbell woke you. Sounds like what you need is a massage." Jason closed the door and dragged Connor up the stairs to his bedroom. "You do have some oil I could use, don't you?"

Pushed onto his bed, Connor couldn't do much more than nod, hoping Jason found it on his own.

"Take off your robe."

That would mean he had to move, which he wasn't inclined to do, but somehow, he still managed.

Connor closed his eyes and was half asleep by the time Jason's slightly cold hands dug into his shoulders.

"Man, you're tense."

Yes, he had noticed.

"Don't worry, by the time I'm done, you'll be as pliant as a cat."

Jason's hands worked like magic, travelling up and down his spine, loosening kinks in Connor's back he hadn't even realised he'd had. It was bliss. Connor felt warm and a little sleepy, and if he'd been a cat, he'd probably be purring right now.

After Jason massaged his feet, up to and including his little toes, Connor was more relaxed than he'd been in ages. Jason could massage him as often as he wanted.

Jason's hands drifted down to his arse, rubbing his cheeks and circling closer and closer to his crack. "Pull your knees underneath you."

Connor hesitated, not sure he was up for what Jason was planning. The moment slick fingers pried his cheeks apart and rubbed up and down his crack, Connor forgot all about being tired and moaned in appreciation.

"Like that, do you?" Jason asked when Connor squirmed.

"Uhuh," was all Connor could utter.

Slick fingers brushed his balls, skimmed his cock, and scratched the backs of his thighs, turning Connor on more with every touch.

Jason seemed to enjoy teasing, his touches light and slow, leaving Connor high and wanting. He definitely wanted, wanted it now. Silent begging obviously wasn't enough to get the point across. Jason never changed pace.

"Please."

Jason trailed a finger up his crack and pushed it into him. Connor nearly lost it. He barely held on.

Jason still wouldn't be hurried along, though, and he was driving Connor bonkers with his slow movements. In and out, in and out.

Finally, Connor had enough and pushed back, impaling himself on Jason's finger. He groaned as Jason gave up all pretence of wanting to go slow and pressed another finger alongside, and another, going a little deeper with each push, each sound and shudder he dragged out of Connor.

When Jason at last grabbed hold of his cock and jerked him off, Connor nearly screamed. He clenched and unclenched his hands in his duvet with every brush across his gland, every squeeze around his cock, until he couldn't hold off anymore and came hard.

CONNOR PUT HIS COFFEE ON HIS DESK, DROPPED HIS BAG, AND TOOK the mail into Tallis' office. Since she'd be in a meeting elsewhere for most of the morning, he took his time sorting and filing into the correct trays.

Back in his own office, he turned his computer on and took Jason's note out of his trouser pocket. It was silly, dragging it along, but none of his exes had ever written him a note like this. He couldn't stop reading it.

If only Jason had woken him up when he'd left, waking up alone wouldn't have been so disorienting. Between dreaming about Noah and Jason's massage, Connor had had difficulty grasping what had been real and what not. In fact, if not for the note, Jason's visit might well have been a dream, too.

Connor ran his fingers along the edge of Jason's note. He was glad it hadn't been.

Jason leaving breakfast out for him had been a nice touch, from his table set with bread, butter and orange juice, to all the spreads he owned arranged around his plate. Jason had even left him a fresh pot of coffee. It was the second time in a couple of days that Connor had decided to forgo his precious tea in the morning.

Jason's note had leaned against his mug.

*Good morning, Gorgeous*

*I know you probably prefer to have breakfast with me, but I have an early flight to catch. There's this triathlon in Germany in three days, and I really need to get some training time in before that, so I booked myself a flight for today. I don't know when I'll be back. Germany is a good country to go antique hunting in, so I might be a while.*

*Pity you were so exhausted last night, but I hope my massage helped you get some rest.*

*Don't get into trouble while I'm gone.*

*Love,*

*Jason*

Connor's body still thrummed from Jason's heavenly massage and the terrific sex that had followed it. Was there anything that bloke wasn't good at? Connor sighed. Why did he have to go abroad again so soon? He had just returned.

A knock on the door dragged Connor out of his thoughts. He slipped the note under his desk pad and said, "Come in."

The door opened to reveal a courier with a large envelope in his hand. Connor thanked him and took the envelope, even though he didn't remember requesting something from any of the departments recently. Then again, with all that had been going on in the past week, he'd been more than a little distracted.

He'd definitely been waiting for this, though. The report on the CCTV recordings from Langham's house that Research had gone over with a fine-tooth comb, per his request.

Tired as he was, Connor browsed through the photographs Research provided. The one with the partial shoe-print in the back garden's flower bed seemed usable, as did the photo with the shadow of someone standing next to the house, even if it only gave them an estimated height of the suspect.

The report revealed several curious glitches in the recordings, enough to prove that the CCTV had been tampered with. There were at least three, respectively two days, three hours, and fifteen minutes before the fire. That, plus the discovery that the computer had been stolen as well, might just prove the fire had not been an accident.

After Connor finished the complete report, he sent Research an email to have them run that calculation for the suspect's height.

He made copies of the file, put the original in an envelope, dropped it into his outbox, and rang for a courier to pick it up. The faster he had the results, the faster he could get on with it. The copies he'd give to Tallis later.

Waiting for the courier to arrive, Connor picked up the file he had been working on before the weekend. All but one of the artefacts on Langham's list had been recovered. Connor had been trying to find that one all week. No luck yet. It was time to let Research have a go at it.

NOAH COULDN'T MOVE, NO MATTER HOW HARD HE TRIED. THERE was something stuffed in his mouth, too. He tried to spit it out, but it was stuck, and it felt awfully like a ball gag. He wasn't averse to bondage, but he didn't appreciate someone binding him without his consent—and not to a bed, either.

No, the surface he lay on was hard and cold and anything but comfortable. The bands around his wrists were definitely metallic, but not heavy enough to be iron. Personally, he preferred soft and supple leather.

He could barely see any walls from where he lay. A large room with a grubby two-floor high ceiling and old fluorescent lamps.

This wasn't his week, was it? First Primrose had invaded his life, and now... Noah frowned. At least, he didn't think this had anything to do with Primrose. They wouldn't do this to him, would they?

*Don't be so stupid.* Not even Agent Parker would bind and gag him, no matter how much he wanted to. It wasn't the Primrose way.

A door opened and closed, hinges squeaking loudly. "Mr. Jones. How nice of you to join me."

Noah craned his neck, but he couldn't turn his head far enough to see who was talking. He didn't recognise the voice, either; even Agent Parker sounded warm in comparison.

"Imagine my surprise when I swung by Primrose to pick you up, only to find you had skipped the joint. Nothing pisses me off more than having to change my plans. It messes up my schedule."

Right, no Primrose then, but he knew of them. What was picking him up at Primrose about?

"The moment I read your file, I knew *they'd* want to have you. Primrose has information on you going back to the late 1700s. That's over two hundred years ago."

It sounded like the information he possessed was the same Agent Parker had when he'd first interrogated Noah. His captor didn't appear to have Primrose's latest information. And who were *they*?

"How does a man live so long?" the man asked.

Footsteps echoed behind him, if only he could turn his head and see who had abducted him from his home, not even a day after being released. Lily would be ever so annoyed to find out he had gone again. He frowned. Lily might not even know he'd been released yet.

"Of course, you're not really a man, are you? You may look like one, but you're not human at all. What are you?"

Definitely no knowledge of what he'd told Agent Parker. Did he expect Noah to answer while gagged?

"What's your secret? Regeneration? Immortality? What are you?"

Regeneration—now, that was an interesting term. Noah

mostly referred to it as healing. It was a slow and exhausting process. It had only happened once, of course, and it had been self-inflicted, as well. A foolish accident in the mid-1800s when he'd attempted to repair a broken window. The wound had been too serious to wait for it to heal at a normal rate. The healing had nearly drained his energy.

"You're disappointingly quiet. If that rubbish about a mind link was true, you would have answered me already or tried whatever voodoo tricks Primrose seems to think you know."

That's why he was gagged? To test his psychic abilities? Suddenly, the testing at Primrose seemed so much more benign.

"Psychic abilities rate very high with my clients. Of course, your age alone should be interesting enough for them. I have no doubt you'll fetch me a nice sum."

Fetch him a nice sum? This man thought he could sell Noah? To whom?

"First, our doctors are going to perform some tests."

All the man had to do was access his files at Primrose, and he'd have all the results he needed. Noah couldn't imagine there were any tests left to do. That was, until two men suddenly entered his vision. Two men who looked nothing like doctors. No lab coats, no stethoscopes, but black leather outfits. They wouldn't look out of place as bouncers in a club he used to frequent. The knives they carried seemed more appropriate for an autopsy than a doctor's consult.

One of them lifted his knife. Noah froze and followed its descent, but the bouncer did nothing more than cut his paisley shirt open. Noah took a shuddering breath. It was one of his favourites, too.

The sharp pain of the blade slicing across his stomach took his breath away.

Noah blinked at the bouncers, who merely grinned at

him. Tests? This was no test, this was torture. What were they looking for? Noah tensed as the other bouncer lowered a knife to his chest.

"One is enough, boys. All we need to know is how long it takes him to regenerate...for now."

The bouncers turned and walked off.

They cut his stomach and wanted to do more? Sick is what these people were, sick.

"We'll be back later to see how you're doing. I might even bring you some lunch, if you can stomach it," the man said, chuckling at his own joke.

Footsteps retreated, and a door behind Noah closed, and he was alone. Alone, strapped down on a cold table with a bleeding wound that hurt like hell, and his favourite shirt cut to pieces. Fuck, did it hurt. This was just a nick, he tried to convince himself, a large one, but still, just a nick. It wasn't as bad as the accident with the broken window, when he'd had several deep gashes on his chest and arms. Six hours, maybe seven, considering he hadn't even had breakfast yet.

The pain made it much harder to concentrate on the wound itself. Noah closed his eyes and concentrated on his breathing, slow and steady. He needed the pain to fade to focus.

Breathe in, breathe out. Forget about the pain.

WHEN CONNOR NEARLY DOUBLED OVER FROM A SUDDEN, SHARP cramp in his stomach, he was glad he was alone in the lift. He grabbed hold of the bar next to him and breathed through the pain. It was gone as quickly as it had started, leaving a dull throbbing and a severe bout of nausea. He watched the lift's progression as if looking at it would speed it up. The last thing he wanted was to puke his guts out here.

The moment the lift doors opened, he made a run for the toilet and knelt in front of the nearest bowl, dry heaving. With any luck, he was coming down with a stomach bug.

When his stomach settled, Connor hoisted himself up. He looked like crap. He washed his hands, splashed some water into his face, fixed his hair, and dragged himself into his office, sinking into his chair and leaning his head on his desk. Tired didn't even begin to describe it.

Someone walked up behind him, but Connor couldn't be bothered to lift his head up.

"Are you all right?" Tallis asked.

"I'll be fine," he whispered. His desk was nice and cool against his forehead.

"If you're feeling ill..."

"I'm not. Wasn't." Connor lifted his head and glanced at her. "I had a sudden stomach pain in the lift, right after the meeting ended."

"You should take the afternoon off."

"I'll be all right." A good cup of coffee might revive him.

"Are you sure?"

Connor nodded carefully, crossing his fingers that his stomach would keep quiet for the rest of the day. The last thing he needed right now was the flu.

She put an envelope on his desk. "A courier handed me this in the corridor."

Back within a day. Research must have stepped it up a notch. "Thank you, Lieutenant. I'll start on that right away."

"Take it easy. If you start feeling worse, go home."

"Yes, Lieutenant."

He wouldn't, and she knew that. Too much to do. She gave him a stern look as she disappeared into her office.

He pushed himself upright and opened the envelope, hoping Research had turned up something useful. Not so much, it seemed. It wasn't even about the Langham CCTV recordings, but a follow-up on the traces found near Presly Green. The first page was familiar, and Connor was convinced there had been a mix-up—they'd received the same report two weeks ago. The attachments were new, though. A quick read later, he got up and entered Tallis' office.

"Sorry to disturb you, Lieutenant. I received an interesting police report," Connor said, handing her the Presly Green file.

Tallis opened it, and Connor stood in front of her desk, waiting for her to finish reading. "I guess the reprimand worked," she said as she put the file down. "Agent Hughes came through for us, albeit still too slow. We should have had this ages ago."

"Still, a truck stolen two villages down the road from a suspicious sighting doesn't normally raise any flags. Not for us."

"You'd be right, if the police hadn't found traces of a suspicious substance on the truck." She pointed to the last page of the report. "Agent Hughes saved us some work by matching those traces with the substance we found at Presly Green."

"So, whatever was picked up at Presly Green has something to do with the Noren. Their space ship, perhaps?"

"Perhaps. But who has it? What are they going to do with it? Sell it? It's not exactly a small item."

*Sell.* That word sparked Connor's memory. "Collectors."

"Collectors?"

"Didn't Primrose shut down a group of collectors years ago?"

"The eBay group." Tallis nodded. "Yes, I see where you're coming from, but we're monitoring all auctions, both online and offline. Have been since early 2002."

That was the case Connor meant. Primrose had arrested a brother and sister who had stumbled onto some Kraugat rings and tried to sell them through eBay. They had inadvertently alerted Primrose to the existence of a group of collectors interested in alien goods, mostly active on eBay.

"No movement at all?"

"Nothing worth mentioning. Nothing from known collectors."

"What if they found a different way of getting what they wanted?"

"What are you thinking of, Connor?"

"I think our artefact thief might be working for the collectors directly. No auction houses, no eBay, but private contracts, all handled by the same person."

"A private artefact hunter, possibly using the stolen A-Watch program. Sound thinking. Well done. I'll talk to Rupert about taking a closer look at our eBay files. He can dig up a list of known collectors and see what they're up to these days."

"I'll see if I can scrounge up some more CCTV recordings. One of them might have picked up that truck."

Tallis shook her head. "I'll have Rupert look into that as well. You're looking far too pale. Go home. Your work will still be here in the morning."

Connor was about to protest, but her expression brooked no argument, and who was he to say no to wrapping up early?

# 13

TALLIS WAS OUT OF THE OFFICE WEDNESDAY MORNING WHEN Connor received the list of known artefact collectors from Research. The list was more extensive than he'd expected. He'd had no idea there were so many collectors of alien artefacts. It must have been a very profitable market, before Primrose monitored all auctions.

According to Holloway's notes, only a few of them turned up in suspicious sales over the past ten years. Most of them seemed to have focussed their attention to antiques, charity and…golfing.

Quite a number of names on the list belonged to the same Golf Club. The Westland Golf Club. Connor tilted his head and Googled the club as he read the rest of the report. It was a weak connection, but a connection all the same.

The Westland Golf Club was owned by the Westland Group, an elite fundraising organisation based in Milridge that raised sizeable amounts for different charities every year, through legit, alien-artefact-free auctions. The Golf Club itself was located on the west side of Presly Green, close to where they'd found the Noren wandering around.

Now, *that* would be worth looking into.

He was about to call Research when someone knocked on

his door and came in without waiting for permission.

Connor turned his chair around, facing Agents Kovach and Viera from Internal Security, and frowned. "Can I help you?"

"Agent Smith?"

"Yes."

"If you would be so kind as to follow us, please."

Connor rose and reached for his backpack. "What's going on?"

"You can leave that here," Kovach said.

They said nothing further as they led him down to one of the lower levels, and into one of the interview rooms.

"Hand over your possessions, please, Agent Smith," Viera told him, his lips thin stripes beneath his moustache.

Questions were futile. He emptied his pockets, watching Kovach, a surly bloke who wasn't known for his conversational talent, collect everything into a small box. He sat down when Viera asked him to and rested his head in his hands as they left, locking the door behind them.

Connor racked his brain, but couldn't come up with anything that might have earned him an interrogation. Unless it was about visiting *First Edition*, Noah's bookshop, Monday evening. They hadn't issued a warning about staying away from Noah, but it was all he could think of.

Besides, Noah hadn't been in, and his assistant hadn't seemed aware Noah had been released.

A little over an hour later, the door finally opened, and Tallis entered, a grave expression on her face. "Good morning, Connor." She sat down and put a folder down in front of her. "You know the protocol. I think it's best if we proceed immediately, so we can clear this mess up."

Connor nodded.

"Yesterday, Agent Lassiter, Lieutenant Nunnink's personal assistant, visited Archive to retrieve the Ling artefacts he had requested, only to discover you had checked them out on Monday at a quarter past five in the afternoon. Both Archive and Research have been trying to retrieve them from your office, but they're not there. There is no trace of the Ling artefacts anywhere in the building."

"There has to be a mistake. I was nowhere near Archive on Monday. You sent me home early that day, so I wasn't even in the building at five."

The Ling artefacts got their name because of the similarities between Mandarin and the symbols found on the artefacts. As far as Connor knew, they had five of them, all made of the same unknown material, gathered throughout the years. One of them held a silvery, non-poisonous fluid that cleaned metals, as far as Connor remembered. He hadn't really studied them.

"I know. We believe they were stolen by someone using your ID." She grabbed a photo out of the folder and pushed it towards him.

*Jason.* No. No. He couldn't have. Connor's hands trembled as he dropped them in his lap. "That's my boyfriend, Jason—"

"Powell. Owner of Powell Antique Acquisitions, Fifty-One Carlton Close, Kinnon. According to the CCTV recordings, he arrived at your house Sunday night around eleven and left Monday morning just before six."

"Yes," Connor said. Of course, they'd checked him out. "He had an early flight to Germany. He's participating in the triathlon over there." Which at least meant he had nothing to do with this.

"Do you have any reason to think he might have been snooping around your flat?"

Connor shook his head. "No. He thinks I'm a PA at Ironclad Security. Besides, I don't keep work related documents at home..." That wasn't true, though, was it? He didn't want to create trouble for Isa...

"What is it, Connor?"

She sounded more concerned than stern. Connor sighed. If Matthews knew, it was reasonable to assume she did, too. "There is that file on Noah, but I had that in my back pocket, and brought it back into work the next morning. It's in the bottom drawer of my desk."

Tallis glared at him for a moment, then glanced at the mirrored wall to the side. "Check that."

I'm sorry, Isa.

"We also checked your tracker logs. You visited Noah Jones in his bookshop on Monday, around the time of the theft."

How silly did it seem now to think that might been the reason for this interrogation. "He wasn't in. When I asked after him, his assistant, didn't seem aware he had been released yet."

"No, she wasn't. Not until we informed her this morning."

There was more. Connor saw it in her eyes.

"Jones seems to have disappeared. Miss Davies hasn't seen or heard from Jones since we released him. She waters the plants in his flat every day around lunchtime, and he hasn't been there. She even checked with some fellow book lovers he meets up with now and then, but no one has seen or heard from him."

"You're not suspecting him of the theft, are you?" Connor couldn't believe Noah would do that.

"No." Tallis pinched the bridge of her nose. "Team Echo found the chip Doctor Quiggins embedded in the bin in his kitchen. And his flat was clean—too clean."

"Did he know about the chip?"

She shook her head. "No, he didn't. Which makes us believe that someone else removed it."

Her tone alarmed Connor. "You think someone's taken him."

"That's my theory. Which brings me to why you're here. I know what the tests showed, Connor, and I know it's not Jones' intention to harm, but he has access to you, and we need to assume that whoever took him knows that."

Connor sighed. He wanted to kick and scream, but it wouldn't help. She was right. The connection made him a liability, even if Noah would never wilfully harm him. "You're suspending me, then?"

"Yes. Until we retrieve Jones."

There really wasn't anything left to say. At least they were searching for Noah.

He was well on his way home when it dawned on him that Primrose might be able to find Noah through their connection.

THIRTY-FOUR HOURS. NOAH HAD SERIOUSLY OVERESTIMATED HIS condition and the influence of being drugged and hungry on his ability to heal himself. It had taken thirty-four hours.

Thirty-four hours of lying on a cold table, bound and gagged, willing his body to heal itself and trying not to let his frustration at how little energy he had and how much it took get the upper hand. The wound had barely closed when he blacked out

How long had he been out of it?

His body might have healed, but he was still cold, exhausted, hungry, and thirsty. Even a single drop of water would be bliss.

He turned his head as the door opened and couldn't believe his eyes when a creepy butler walked in with a large plate of sandwiches and a glass of water. He blinked a couple of times, clearing his vision to confirm he wasn't dreaming and what the butler carried wasn't stale bread and water.

No, they truly were sandwiches.

The bouncers released his bindings and took him down from that wretched table. Every muscle in Noah's body screamed in agony with each step he took, though the bouncers were carrying him more than he was walking himself. They sat him in a high-backed chair in front of a rickety wooden card table and tied his legs and torso to it, with rope this time.

He sagged against the chair's back. It still wasn't comfortable, and he could use a new shirt, but at least he was sitting up and his arms were free for now. They took his gag out, too.

Noah took the opportunity to look around him. It seemed the only furniture in the huge, empty room were the two tables and the chair he sat on. There were no windows at all.

The bouncers disappeared, leaving the creepy-looking butler.

"Eat!" he snarled at Noah, pointing at the plate filled with sandwiches.

Noah hesitated. It might be a trap. He expected the man in charge to appear the moment he took a bite to tell him he had been poisoned to see if he healed himself from that.

"Eat!" the creepy butler snarled again.

The sandwiches did look delicious, and trap or no trap, Noah was hungry. Besides, he couldn't risk the food being taken away again because he'd waited too long.

He grabbed one of the sandwiches and wolfed it down, same with a second one. They were good. *Food, glorious food.* He downed half his glass of surprisingly cool water. He finished all four sandwiches within minutes. Had there been more, Noah would have probably eaten those as well.

He had barely finished the last of his water when the creepy butler took everything away and the door squeaked again. Great. They couldn't have let him savour lunch a little longer?

"I figured it out, Mr. Jones. Clever me, huh?" the man said.

That a man needs food? Very clever.

One of the bouncers grabbed one of Noah's hands and tied it behind the back of the chair. His meal was officially over.

"You're not going to ask me how I figured it out?"

"I have no doubt you're going to tell me whether I ask or not," Noah said without thinking. He hoped the man wasn't in a vindictive mood. He sounded way too cheerful.

The man continued as if he hadn't heard him. "You're quite talkative when you're delirious. Too weak, you said. You were too weak to heal quickly, but you're fed now. Quite a show you gave there, gobbling up those sandwiches in record time."

One of the bouncers appeared in front of Noah, across the table, holding a sharp-looking knife and a bottle of water.

*Oh, no. Not again. Please, not again.* Noah tensed. This wasn't happening again.

The man chuckled. "Oh, don't worry. I have no patience to wait another two days, so you have a few hours yet. You might even get more sandwiches first."

That wasn't what Noah was worrying about. Though he didn't doubt the man knew that. The bouncer filled his glass and set the bottle beside it. He pointed at Noah's right hand and stood back, the knife dangling carelessly between his fingers. Noah eyed the knife as he picked up the glass, vaguely aware of the creaking door closing. Nothing happened. The bouncer stood there as a reminder of what was to come.

RELENTLESS KNOCKING ON HIS DOOR DRAGGED CONNOR OUT OF bed. He cursed and grumbled all the way down the stairs. It had been silly to think Isa would give up.

He didn't bother to hide his irritation as he yanked his front door open.

"About time." Isa looked worried, a little annoyed as well, no doubt because he'd left her waiting for so long.

"You could have used your key, you know."

"That's not how this works," she said, tapping her foot. "Aren't you going to let me in?"

He shrugged and let her pass, closing the door behind her. "Not really in the mood for a visitor," he told her. Or anything, really. He'd left several messages for Tallis with his idea to use his connection to Noah to find him, but she had yet to contact him. He'd thought about contacting Isa about it, too, but…she'd have to go through Tallis anyway, and maybe they just didn't need him.

"I can imagine, but I don't count as a visitor, do I?" Isa hung up her coat and ran up the stairs.

Another shrug. "I guess not," he mumbled into the empty hall. He followed her up the stairs to his living room and sank down on the sofa, staring past her at the aubergine wall behind her.

She glared at him, but he had no intention of getting up again. "I'd love a drink, Connor, thank you," Isa said, crossing her arms. "Mind getting it yourself? I'm a little out of sorts… Of course not, love. My pleasure."

Connor just stared at the floor as she strode into the kitchen. It was good of her to come, but that didn't mean he could pretend all was well. They'd suspended him. Wasn't he allowed to wallow in misery for even a little while?

He studied the grain in the dark wooden floor and didn't look up as she sat next to him, but he did take the glass she offered him. It felt cool against his cheek.

"Connor. You know she had no choice."

"Of course, I do. Doesn't mean I have to like it." He ran a hand through his hair. "How would you feel if they fetched you from your desk to lock you up with no idea what's going on?"

"I get your point."

"Do you?" He sat up and glared at her. "*My* ID was used to steal artefacts, and even though they know I didn't do it, I'm suspended because of a connection with an abducted ex-alien."

"Ex-alien?"

"Are you telling me you didn't read *all* the reports?"

"Of course, I did, but how do *you* know?"

"The documents you gave me."

"There was no mention of Jones being alien in there."

Bugger. All he was supposed to know was that Noah possessed some sort of mind-reading power.

Isa narrowed her eyes. "Spill."

*She's your best friend.* He took a deep breath. "Through the connection."

She gaped at him. "What? How? The reports said humans weren't com—."

Connor blinked. "Com what?"

"I shouldn't have said that." Isa plucked at the hem of her cardigan.

"Come on."

"Nosy pillock. All right. Compatible. The reports said humans weren't compatible."

Interesting. Connor wanted to ask more, but doubted Isa would tell him. Instead, he told her how his focus on the images had triggered something through the connection to Noah. "It was like unlocking a door. All it took was one specific image, and I got this stream of information."

"From one image?"

"Yes. Though, I discover a little more every time I dream."

Isa's eyes narrowed again. "Dream? You're connected when you dream?"

"No. Yes. Maybe. I don't know." It was hard to tell her about this. She might take it the wrong way, might think Noah had been invading his mind. He had no problem telling his best friend, but she wasn't just his best friend. She was a colleague, and one with a healthy dose of suspicion for the abnormal.

Connor crossed his fingers and hoped she'd give Noah the benefit of the doubt. "What I did triggered a deeper connection, I think. I don't know. I don't even know why it happens when I dream—might have something to do with being in a REM state or something like that." There wasn't a lot of information to work with here. "Anything in those reports?"

"About dreaming? No."

Pity. Last night's dream had been much clearer than the others. "It's like I've got this database of information dumped on me. The knowledge is there, I just need to know how to access it."

"So, you're having these dreams even though he's disappeared?"

"Yes." It kept him from thinking Noah was dead. "I feel the connection as well—a sort of humming in the back of my mind. It's there all the time now."

"You haven't done anything foolish, have you? Like initiating contact through your connection?"

Connor didn't know whether to hit or kiss her for suggesting that. "Why didn't I think of that myself?" He rolled his eyes. "Oh, wait. I know? Because last time I did something like that, I knocked Noah unconscious." And he didn't want to put Noah at risk. Still...

"Oh, no you don't," Isa said. "I'll see what Lieutenant Matthews thinks, but don't try anything on your own."

Connor didn't want to lie, but he couldn't promise not to try. It might just be worth the risk, especially when finding Noah was taking this long. Isa looked at him with narrowed eyes, and he sighed. "All right. I promise." He hoped he wouldn't regret it.

"Good. Now, tell me something about him. About Noah."

Connor shook his head.

"Oh, come on. I don't need to know if he wears boxers or briefs, just something that's not in the report."

"He loves books."

"He owns a bookshop, it goes without saying. Come on. Tell me something no one else knows."

"I—" His glass slipped out of his hand, splattering juice everywhere as pain lanced through his stomach. "Shit!" He pushed his heels into the floor and tried to breathe through the pain.

"Connor?"

He slid to the ground and pushed himself up on hands and knees, gagging and dry heaving.

Isa rubbed his back. "What's going on?"

"I don't know. A stomach bug or something. Hurts like hell."

"Can I get you anything?"

He shook his head, regretting it when even the tiniest movement made the room spin.

Isa's hand was warm against his forehead.

"No fever. Something you ate?"

"Twice in the same week?"

"Wait. What? This happened before?"

"Monday, at the office." Connor dropped his head to the floor in relief as the pain and nausea faded. He breathed slowly in and out until his stomach settled. "It was the reason why Tallis sent me home early."

He hoisted himself back onto the sofa, ignoring the wet, juice-stained rug. Might be time for a new one.

"Are you sure—?" Isa shifted away from him and touched her earpiece. "Griffin... Of course, Lieutenant. I'll be right there." She looked at Connor, her hand resting on his knee. "Are you sure you're all right?"

"I will be." He'd better be. "Work?"

Isa nodded and got up. "They have a lead on Jones."

Connor sagged into the sofa and pressed his palms to his eyes. "Go on. I hope you find him safe."

"I'll let you know as soon as I have news."

If only he could go with her.

# 14

CONNOR ITCHED TO DO SOMETHING. HE WAS SICK OF SITTING at home, mulling and waiting for news on Noah—news on all his cases. He'd promised himself, promised Isa, he wouldn't do anything foolish, but if Isa or Primrose didn't contact him soon, he was going to try connecting to Noah. Consequences be damned.

He hadn't heard anything from Jason, either. The race was over, he knew that much. He had no idea when Jason would be flying back.

When the doorbell rang, he practically threw himself down the stairs. "You've found Noah, and I can go back to work."

"Ah. Not exactly." Isa gave Connor a quick hug, grabbed his hand and led him back up the stairs to his living room.

She sat on his sofa, tucking her feet under her, and smiled apologetically as he sat next to her. "That lead we had? Got us nowhere. The man looked nothing like Noah. Though the strip club was fun. It took Roderick and me about half an hour to get all the men to leave. Got a free beer out of it and all."

"On duty?" he asked. Strip club. An image of a half-naked girl dancing for Noah sprang to mind; it made Connor smile.

Isa winked at him, and Connor was glad she didn't know

what he was thinking of. "Nah, we clocked out as soon as we found out the lead was a dud."

"So, if not that, what *have* you got?" As funny as it was, Connor was anxious for real news.

"Do you know Agent Vaine?"

"Francis, yes. He's a video engineer. Has only been with Primrose a couple of months, I think. He's been put on the CCTV recordings." Connor wondered who was handling his investigations now that he was suspended. Whoever it was, he hoped they didn't mess up.

"Video engineer? More like an all-round computer whiz. Anyway. Agent Vaine—Francis—scoured the internal cameras for the theft. Nothing showed up around five p.m. on Monday, when the theft supposedly happened, but he did find glitches around three a.m. that morning."

"Glitches?"

"Yes. Glitches. Same glitches he found on the recordings of the Langham theft."

"Same glitches, same thief?"

"That's what the boy wonder says. Apparently, it's got something to do with the way the videos are cut and pasted onto each other. According to Francis, they're misaligned by a frame. Only the thief used some sort of filter first, which means that only part of that frame is visible. The filter isn't a standard one, either. Bottom line, for two different videos to have the exact same non-standard filter is too much of a coincidence."

Connor frowned. "Did those frames bring us something?"

Isa held her hand up. "Be patient. I'm not done yet. Turns out, the CCTV recordings at Noah Jones' place early Monday morning show the exact same glitches."

"The thief went from Primrose to Noah's?"

"That's what we think. Especially after Francis discovered someone's been hacking into the computers. He isolated the point of access and closed it, but the hacker had already downloaded all the information we have on Noah Jones and the Ling artefacts."

Why those? Well, the Ling artefacts, Connor could understand. But what did they want with an ex-alien who... He shook his head at his own stupidity. An ex-alien who was over 360 years old. Of course they'd be interested.

"Francis is still tracking them, but he kept muttering about being routed all over the world and other complicated technobabble that I can barely follow, I had to get out for a while. Suffice to say, he's determined to get them."

Primrose agents were like dogs with a bone when they were on a case. "What about those frames?"

"From the internal cameras? One of them shows a shoe. A black shoe."

Now, that sounded familiar. "Don't tell me. Same make and model as the shoe print from the Langham theft."

"Exactly the same."

That was something, at least. Might still not be enough, but a photo of the shoe meant they at least had the colour. "Good work."

He took a deep breath. She hadn't said anything about the connection, but Connor needed to know. Needed to feel useful, suspended or not. "So, what did Lieutenant Matthews say about trying the connection?"

Isa fidgeted with the hem of her blouse. "He said he'd think about it."

Think about it. Right. Meanwhile, they still hadn't found Noah.

Isa squeezed his hand. "We'll find him, Connor. With or without that connection of yours, we *will* find him." She leaned back, still holding his hand. "Now, is there any chance of getting a decent cup of tea before I have to get back to the office?"

"So, what about that triathlon? How did it go?" Connor put his fork down and took a sip of water.

"Didn't even place," Jason said after finishing the last of his salmon. He'd landed earlier today and had driven straight to Connor's from the airport. "Had a good race though. Did I tell you about the German writing desk I found? In near-mint condition."

Connor smiled and put his hand over Jason's. "You texted me about it."

"It's being shipped as we speak. It's gorgeous."

"You'll have to show me when it arrives. So..." Connor trailed off when his mobile vibrated in his pocket. He fished it out. "Sorry. It's work." He rose and walked into the hall before answering.

"Be outside your front door in ten. You're coming with us," Isa blurted out.

The call he'd been waiting for since Isa's visit the day before. He glanced at Jason leaning back in his chair with his eyes closed, and hesitated. "Jason and I just finished dinner," he said. "He's taking me to see a band later."

"Well, you'll have to get him out of there, because we're picking you up. We had another lead on Jones, and Lieutenant Matthews wants you on the team."

Connor sagged against the wall and ran a shaky hand through his hair. "I'll be outside in ten."

"Good. Sorry to ruin your evening," Isa said before ringing off.

He closed his eyes. How the hell was he going to send Jason home when he'd just returned?

"Work?"

Connor nearly dropped his phone. He opened his eyes

and threw Jason an apologetic smile. "Yes. Sorry." He hadn't even told Jason about the suspension.

He expected Jason to be irritated he had to cut their date short, but Jason just shrugged.

He took a flyer out of his back pocket. "Here. If you make it back in time, this is where you'll find me."

Connor read the flyer. He'd looked forward to seeing the band, but it wasn't to be. "I don't think I'll be able to make it."

Jason pulled Connor to him. "Call me when you're done," he said and kissed him.

Connor leaned into the kiss. He'd missed this, so much that he was tempted to call Isa back and tell her he'd changed his mind.

No. Noah was still missing, and Primrose needed Connor to find him. *Connor* needed to find Noah.

"I think your mind's already on the job," Jason said as he pulled away.

*Great going, Smith, thinking about another bloke when you're kissing your boyfriend. Just lovely.* He opened his mouth to apologise, but Jason put a finger on his lips.

"I'll see you later."

When the front door slammed closed, Connor shook himself out of it and inspected his outfit. They'd have his gear in the car. His boots and jeans would have to do. He wasn't going to get dressed in that bloody SUV again.

The SUV pulled up as he was closing the front door.

The drive took a little over half an hour. Half an hour of donning his field gear, being briefed by Isa, hooked up to a portable brain function monitor, and instructed to focus on his connection with Noah.

The closer they got to Greater Ickly, their supposed destination, the more disappointed Connor became. He sensed the hum of the connection, but no tingle, no sign that they were getting closer to Noah. He shook his head when Isa caught his eye.

Zabrowski from Research didn't stop fiddling with her glasses and equipment.

"First assignment?" Connor asked.

Her eyes stayed glued to the screen that monitored Connor and the connection as she nodded.

He was about to say something soothing when a slight tingle joined the hum. Zabrowski raised her hand and glanced at Connor. He raised his in confirmation. Were they getting closer to Noah after all?

Two miles on, the tingle disappeared, and Connor exchanged glances with Zabrowski.

"Didn't we pass another road back there?" she asked without looking up.

Connor blinked at her. Apparently, she'd been paying attention to more than just the screen.

"Turn around, Evans!" Isa instructed team Charlie's driver. "We need to go back."

Evans, a young agent who tended to treat the SUV as if it were a sports car, turned around and drove back until they reached a T-junction. It was more a dirt track than an actual road, but faint as it was, the tingling returned.

"You sure?" Isa asked when Connor told Evans to turn onto it.

"No, but it's our best bet."

"Do it, Evans."

The tingle intensified as they progressed down the track. Connor kept his eyes on the road in front of them—in as much as he could see, sitting in the back—but the tingle levelled out and stayed that way for the next five minutes.

He frowned.

"Connor? What is it?"

"I think he's moving. Might be in a car driving the same direction."

All eyes were suddenly focussed on him.

"Zabrowski? Can you confirm this?"

"There was a slight spike when we turned off the main road, but now I see no change. It's level. Agent Smith might be right."

They drove twenty minutes, twenty-five, thirty, when abruptly, the tingling disappeared again. Connor felt Zabrowski's eyes on him when he shook his head. "Lost it again. They seem to have turned off somewhere."

Isa had already pulled up the map of the area. It showed barely any side roads at all. There was a road running parallel to theirs, but no connecting road for at least forty miles. Still, Isa told Evans to stick with it and turn off at the first chance he had.

Yet, three miles later, Connor sensed the tingling again. He ignored Zabrowski's enthusiastic reaction and closed his eyes. The tingling became more intense, as if... "They're turning back towards us."

"Are you sure?" Isa asked.

Connor nodded.

"But there's no road here."

Connor leaned back as several agents discussed route possibilities with Isa. None of them came up with a logical explanation.

"We've been looking at the wrong road," Evans chimed in, pointing at the navigation screen on the dashboard. "I think they're on Broad Street, close to Little Ickly. You must have picked up Jones as they turned onto it. It runs parallel with this one for a while, but loops around some old quarry to get to the other side of the ridge."

"Shepherd's Ridge?" Isa asked, eyes on her map.

"Yes."

"We can't get there from here. Not in time to catch up."

"Yes, we can," Evans said. "But we'll have to cross a field

or two, so it'll be bumpy."

"Do it," Isa said.

Connor leaned forward to check out the map himself. There didn't seem to be any junctions on Broad Street, but they'd need to be fast, because if the vehicle Noah was in made the next turn before they managed to get across those fields, they'd never be able to catch up.

Evans wasn't exaggerating. It was more than bumpy. There was no part of Connor left that wasn't bruised, it seemed, but they made excellent time. He lost contact once or twice, and his sense of direction, but small spikes here and there confirmed Noah was still within range. Any minute now, they should see a vehicle coming up on them.

Two minutes later, no vehicle, and then the tingling faded to nothing.

Connor cursed. "Could they have turned off the road before this turn?" he asked.

"No. Not unless they drove across the fields like we did. No one lives around here. Why?"

Zabrowski answered before Connor. "He's lost contact again."

Evans hit the brakes and cursed.

"Can't we—" Isa asked, only to be interrupted by Evans.

"I can't drive out into those fields blind. It's near impossible to guess where they turned off. We've lost them."

As much as Connor wanted to protest and keep at it until they found Noah, Evans was right. He hung his head. Judging from the sounds around him, they were all as frustrated as he was.

"At least we know roughly where to search," Isa commented without conviction.

It didn't make any of them feel better. Losing was not in their vocabulary.

NOAH HAD COME TO IN THE BOOT OF A CAR, BOUND HAND AND FOOT, body jolting with every bump in the road, and dressed in a tight-fitting t-shirt that was definitely not his. All he remembered was a bouncer sticking a needle in his arm. The car had stopped now, but the drive had been rough, and Noah's body protested even the tiniest movement. The one reprieve had been when he'd sensed Connor through the connection.

It couldn't have been Connor, could it? Connor was back in Kinnon, and Noah was who knew where.

Despite his less than stellar situation, Noah only felt relief when the bouncers finally hauled him out of the boot.

"Take him inside, third cell. Bring him something to eat and drink, for cryin' out loud. The members won't want their pet to go hungry, will they?"

Noah frowned at the unfamiliar voice. Who was that woman? Where was the man in charge? Did he know about this?

Noah was hoisted onto a shoulder. They didn't go far before they lowered him to the floor and prodded him until he sat. They took the cuffs off, removed his blindfold, and left him in a tiny cell that looked like a stall and smelled musty. He rubbed his wrists. At least they were going to feed him properly.

One of the bouncers returned with soup and sausages. A dying man's meal. Noah grabbed the bowl of soup. It had been a while since he'd had warm food, and the warmth was welcome.

He had barely finished when his cell door opened.

"Good afternoon, Noah."

Noah saw no point in answering her greeting. Slim, tall,

curly red hair, skin-tight red leather outfit—she and the bouncers were quite a group. He'd dated a woman like her once. Did the man who'd abducted him dress in leather as well?

"Come along. They're ready for us."

She turned around and clicked her fingers, not even waiting to see if Noah followed her. The bouncers entered the cell, and he realised she didn't *need* to wait. She had the bouncers to make sure he followed. He slumped and shuffled out of the cell.

They didn't carry him this time. Noah shuffled between them—barefoot, slow, with stiff limbs—following the redheaded mistress outside. They seemed to be on a farm with a large barn and a paddock. Further ahead stood a large, modern building with plenty of windows that looked nothing like a farmhouse. High, solid fences surrounded the place, far too high to climb.

"Keep up, Noah, we don't want to keep the members waiting."

He did, actually. He had no desire to meet these members she was talking about. He kept up his slow pace. Anything to delay the inevitable.

The elevated podium in the middle of the building was not what Noah had expected to see. Not in a barn. It looked a lot like a boxing ring, with seats surrounding it on all four sides. He couldn't see any empty seats, and he shivered as it dawned on him that these people might organise fights.

Fights between aliens? Though Noah was fit and exercised regularly—when he wasn't tortured or interrogated, that was—he doubted he would last long in any sort of fight where non-humans were involved.

As the redhead preceded him up the podium, Noah breathed deeply in and out, trying to keep from panicking as the bouncers led him towards sturdy-looking stocks. His shaky breathing and their heavy footsteps were all Noah heard—the room was eerily quiet. He'd expected the crowd to go wild at the prospect of another fight. That was what they did, wasn't it? Cheer and yell until the game began?

One of the bouncers put a collar on him and leashed it to the stocks while the other cuffed his hands in front of him. The chain wasn't long enough to leave him a lot of leeway, which seemed impractical if they expected him to fight.

"Good afternoon, ladies and gentlemen," the redhead said into a microphone. "As you can see, poor Noah here doesn't look extraordinary at all, but as we all know, looks can be deceiving."

A murmur ran through the audience, the loudest sound so far.

"You have all received his file—with some delay due to a connection failure, to our regret. In it you'll find all sorts of interesting information, like the location of his planet, his telepathic gift, and..." The redhead looked at Noah with a smirk. "It *is* true, ladies and gentlemen. Noah cannot die."

The audience gasped, and the muttering increased.

"We will have a demonstration later, of course."

He froze. Demonstration? What demonstration? He hoped they weren't going to stab or slice him again.

"His telepathic gift is of no real use to us, unfortunately. As you can read in the report, he apparently caused a young man to suffer a nosebleed, but nothing more exciting than that."

Noah fought to keep his expression blank. What if those reports mentioned Connor?

"Of course, there is nothing to keep the lucky winner from finding out what else he's capable of for themselves."

The muttering became more excited.

Who were these people? Did they truly see him as some sort of novelty or commodity to display and abuse? Noah shuddered at an intensely leering expression from a member in the audience. These were no ordinary people.

"You know the procedure, ladies and gentlemen," the redhead said. "For the next half hour, you can take a closer look at Noah and ask us any questions you might have. No bids allowed during the viewing."

Bids? Noah swallowed. He wasn't expected to fight. They were auctioning off aliens—were auctioning *him* off. He needed to get out of here. If only he could contact Connor through the connection.

Whoever bid on him, whoever bought him, he was never going to be free. Humans could be impossibly possessive. It would be just his luck to end up with someone who put him in a custom-made glass box for the next hundred years or so, to be passed on to his children and grandchildren as part of their inheritance.

Where was Primrose when you needed them?

The only positive thing about the next half hour was that the viewers could look, but not touch. Not to mention that he couldn't hear any of the probably embarrassing questions they were asking the redhead. He couldn't, however, avoid the leering expressions.

A loud alarm echoed through the room, and everyone returned to their seats.

"Time for a little demonstration, don't you think, ladies and gentlemen?"

Noah tensed up. Not again. Though it at least explained the meal earlier. They wanted him to be able to heal fast enough for a demonstration.

The redhead showed a large knife, demonstrating its sharpness by cutting a piece of cloth with it.

Noah swallowed and closed his eyes as he leaned against the stocks and breathed deeply: in and out, in and out, in and out. He doubted it would dull the pain, but it might just keep him from squealing like a pig.

A loud scream echoed through the large hall. Noah belatedly realised it had come from him. The redhead cutting his arm instead of his stomach had taken him by surprise. Embarrassing squeal aside, he was thankful it wasn't his stomach this time.

Blood trickled down his arm as he tried to get his breathing back under control again. His stomach might have hurt more, but this was a sneaky, high-pitched pain that, no matter how hard he tried, he couldn't seem to breathe through. All he could do was stare at the blood steadily dripping onto the floor and wait for the pain to fade.

# 15

THE PUB WAS SMOKY, SMELLY, AND LOUD. THE SMALL STAGE added to the atmosphere, and the band was good, very good. Still, Connor couldn't stop thinking about Noah. His head was filled with what ifs and if onlys.

Connor found the distraction he needed in the band's next song. The darker tones of the band's progressive metal style reached deep into him, and when the singer chimed in, Connor instantly fell in love with his voice. Dark, rugged, hoarse, and simply drool-worthy. Jason hadn't lied about him, neither his voice nor his looks. He was handsome, gorgeous even, in a rugged kind of way, but Connor didn't mind a bit of rough. He would definitely be going to more of their gigs.

He smiled at Jason and was about to grab his beer, when a slicing pain shot through his left forearm. He bit his lip to keep from crying out.

Jason turned towards him as he jerked and asked if something was wrong, concern written all over his face.

Connor looked at his arm but there was nothing, nothing at all. It was like that sudden stomach bug all over again. Only this wasn't his stomach. This was his arm. "I don't know," he said. "It's like a knife sliced through my arm, but, look." He showed Jason his arm. "Nothing."

Jason's expression was weirdly blank as he looked at Connor's arm and shrugged. "A phantom pain?"

Phantom pains? Why would he be having phantom pains? He didn't have a twin or... *Oh.* Connor could slap himself. *Of course.* He'd been so busy trying to understand his connection to Noah, yet that this could be Noah-related had never even dawned on him. This wasn't *his* pain, it was Noah's. Noah was in pain. "I need to go home."

Jason offered to drive him, but Connor declined, fumbling for excuses as he told Jason to stay and enjoy the music. He couldn't exactly tell Jason he wasn't going home, could he? Jason mumbled something about him being stubborn, but Connor ignored it in favour of kissing him. Part of him really wanted to stay, but someone was hurting Noah, and Connor couldn't waste more time. He needed to do something before Noah got hurt again.

Connor sighed against Jason's mouth, then straightened up and walked out of the pub. He was already on the phone with Primrose before the door closed behind him.

THE REDHEAD DIDN'T EVEN BOTHER WIPING THE BLOOD OFF HIS ARM as he healed the cut. It annoyed Noah so much he wanted to scream at her, but he couldn't spare the energy.

Ironically, had she wiped off the blood, the audience would have had a better view, but she didn't wipe his arm until it had almost healed. Not that anyone in the audience could see the difference now. From a distance, his arm looked as unblemished as it had been before she'd cut him.

"Thirty-five minutes," she said into the microphone.

Had it really been that long?

"Thirty-five minutes for the cut of a knife to heal. Isn't it wonderful?"

*Oh, yes. Wonderful. Let's do it again, and again, and again.* Noah could almost see the Teletubbies dancing around, begging for a repeat.

"I think we should start the bidding at five. Such a fine specimen. Don't forget the storage filled with endless information on other alien species embedded into his skin. Very clever, don't you think, ladies and gentlemen?"

The applause that followed made Noah roll his eyes. They were applauding as if they'd developed that idea. Ridiculous. Humans weren't capable of manufacturing something so advanced and wouldn't be for many, many years.

"I have five-two in the left corner of section B. Five-four from the lady in section C. Five-eight from... Six. We've reached six. Who bids more?"

Her voice had a harsh bite to it. Noah almost imagined a ruler in her hand, though it was clear she didn't need one to keep this crowd under control.

"Seven!" someone in the audience behind Noah shouted.

"We have seven in section D, ladies and gentlemen. Let's hear more."

"Seven-two," a young man said. He was younger than Connor, but with rough looks and cruel eyes. Noah didn't want to end up with him and almost cheered when someone else raised his hand and the redhead called out, "Seven-six."

"Seven-six, ladies and gentlemen. I think he's worth more. Do I hear more? ... Yes, seven-eight, eight-two, eight-seven, nine." The redhead turned to him. "You seem to be quite popular, Noah."

"Nine-five," someone shouted from the audience.

"A fine bid, Mr. Allen."

All at once the room descended into silence.

"No one to counter this bid?" The redhead browsed the room. "Right. Going once."

Noah trembled. It hadn't felt real. This was real, was it? They were selling him to the highest bidder for... How much was nine-five supposed to be?

"Going twice."

*Someone, please stop this.* This couldn't be happening to him. He wanted to wake up from this nightmare.

A loud bang made him jump. "Sold to Mr. Edward Allen for nine hundred and fifty thousand pounds."

Noah's knees gave way, and he sank to the floor. Nine hundred and fifty thousand pounds. Someone had bought him for fifty thousand pounds shy of a million. All this time he'd been keeping an eye on Primrose, making sure they wouldn't catch wind of him, while he should have been on the lookout for someone else entirely. Did Primrose even know these people existed?

Noah knew he'd read too many mysteries when he seriously considered that a Primrose agent might have infiltrated this meeting. That didn't keep him from taking a good look at the man who'd bought him. He immediately dismissed the idea. This Mr. Allen being a Primrose agent would be too good to be true. Who was he kidding? Primrose probably hadn't even noticed he was missing, even *if* he hadn't imagined sensing Connor close during that awful drive.

Someone helped him to his feet and freed him from the handcuffs, but didn't remove the collar from around his neck. "Well, Noah. I think it's time we got to know each other better. Don't you?"

Edward Allen. His...owner. The word stuck in Noah's throat.

Allen was short and thick-set with greying, thin hair. Strong, though, and with large, piercing eyes that seemed to brook no disobedience.

Noah didn't dignify Allen's question with an answer. All he wanted was to be left alone, to be back in his shop with his beloved books. He tried hard not to blame Primrose or his chance meeting with Connor for his abduction or the auction. It certainly wasn't Connor's fault he was in this situation, since he'd been the one pursuing Connor.

With Allen holding the leash, Noah had no choice but to follow him into a small room, a large cubicle made of wood, more luxurious than the cell he'd been put in at his arrival. It had a bed, at least. He sat down on the bed when Allen told him to, but refused to answer any of his questions, tuning him out by reciting the story of Noah in his head.

A stinging slap to his face brought Noah out of his thoughts. Allen had an intensely cold expression on his face that brought Noah up short. Perhaps he should have answered the man's questions.

"I hope you'll soon understand that it's better to obey, Noah." Allen turned to a guard standing in the corridor. "We're leaving at four. Stay here and keep an eye on him. You know what to do."

For a moment, Noah feared the guard would harm him, but after he let Mr. Allen pass, he closed the door, and left Noah sitting on the bed with the collar around his neck, alone.

"Get me out of here!" Noah yelled.

All he got in return were fading footsteps.

WITHIN MINUTES AFTER HE ARRIVED AT PRIMROSE, CONNOR LAY ON a bed in a lab, hooked up to a bunch of machines monitoring who knew what. Matthews and Isa joined the researchers. It irked Connor that they decided how far he could go, but since he was still officially suspended, he had no choice but to agree.

"You can start any time you want, Agent Smith," Matthews said.

"Be careful." Isa had wanted to sit next to Connor to hold his hand and support him, but Connor was afraid her closeness might be too distracting.

He wasn't sure this would be safe for Noah, but he had to do this, had to try and save him, before they killed him. He closed his eyes and breathed deeply.

Once he shut himself off from the noisy lab, he focussed on the pain he'd experienced during the gig. At first, he concentrated on his arm, but minutes passed without even the barest tingle.

"Connor?"

"Give me a moment, Isa."

He was going about this the wrong way. It wasn't his pain, so focussing on his own arm was useless. He needed to focus on Noah.

A couple of deep breaths later, Connor was ready to try. He closed his eyes and pictured the image of Noah in his original form. Out of all the ones he'd seen, it was the picture that had touched him most deeply.

At first, there was only darkness surrounding Noah. As Connor's focus grew, Noah morphed into his human form. His arm was bleeding. Connor zoomed in on the wound, the pain, and slowly a thin grey line of mist loomed up in front of him.

Connor grabbed onto the mist, holding on, following it through the darkness until he suddenly broke through the dark and found himself standing in the middle of a large building. He stood on some sort of podium in front of a large crowd who were all looking at him.

His arm was bleeding. No, not his arm, Noah's arm. He couldn't look away, couldn't stop staring at the blood that dripped off it, right onto the floor. There was something odd about the wound—it was closing as he watched it, healing itself. What the...?

The room faded, changing into a different one. Connor stared out into the darkness with a head that seemed too heavy to lift. Where was he? Why was he so tired?

At least the surface he lay on was soft, comfortable. The room smelled clean, too. Was this where Noah was now? Could he contact Noah if he was asleep? He had to try. "Noah?"

His body jerked. Connor shuddered. He felt so out of control. "Noah?" he tried again.

"Connor?" Noah's voice was barely audible. He sounded exhausted, but hopeful, too.

Connor willed his heart to slow down. "Yes," he whispered.

"How?"

"I traced your pain. Well, sort of."

Noah stayed quiet for a while. Connor wondered if he should speak up again.

"Can you get me out of here?" Noah finally asked. "I tried to free myself, but the door won't give, and I can't even get this wretched collar off."

"We hope so. They collared you?"

Noah twitched, and Connor tried to soothe him. "Sorry. We'll get that thing off you. Can tell me where you are?"

"A farm, I think, or it used to be."

Noah sent him images, vague and see through, but recognisable. A barn, a paddock, and high fences, but no livestock. Unfortunately, Noah's memories of the trip consisted of nothing more than a lot of shaking and bumping in the dark boot of a car.

Noah trembled when the images dissipated.

"I'm sorry," Connor said.

"You have to get me out of here before my...owner moves me to his estate."

Connor sensed Noah's repulsion. "Owner?"

"I was auctioned off like some sort of commodity." Noah sounded angry, and Connor couldn't blame him.

"Do you know when?"

"Four."

Connor reached out only to find himself grasping empty air. "We'll get you out. I promise."

"Thank you. You need to go now, Connor, cut the connection."

"Why?"

"You're draining us both. It costs too much energy to keep this up."

Energy. That was why he was so tired all of a sudden. "Are you all right?"

"I'll try to sleep. Make sure to eat."

Connor didn't even remember cutting the connection. Or Noah pushed him out. When he opened his eyes, both Isa and Matthews were leaning over him.

Isa squeezed his shoulder, hard. "Fuck, Connor, you scared us half to death. If the computers didn't insist you were perfectly fine, we'd have pulled you out already."

"How long?" Connor forced himself to keep his eyes open. He'd fall asleep if he closed them.

"Twenty-five minutes, but you were in deep."

Despite being exhausted, Connor smiled. "I did it. I made contact."

"You did?" Zabrowski asked from behind Isa and Matthews.

Connor nodded, though she didn't stop studying her screen. He was sure she was trying to find evidence, but he didn't care whether she did or not. He had work to do. He pushed himself up the moment he was released from the chair, and grabbed the armrests tightly to keep from sliding off it.

Noah had told him to eat, but he ignored the dizzy spell.

He'd eat after he brought them up to speed. "He's on some sort of farm with a high fence surrounding it. We don't have much time. He'll be taken off the premises at four."

While Connor sagged into the chair, Matthews and Isa grabbed their phones and bellowed orders to all and sundry. Connor closed his eyes and didn't even try to decipher their commands.

A CATNAP, A PLATE FULL OF SANDWICHES, AND TWO HOURS OF searching later, Connor and Isa weren't even close to locating the farm.

"I'm telling you," Isa repeated for the umpteenth time, "there are no farms anywhere near that quarry."

They stared at Connor's screen, studying the aerial photos from Little Ickly all the way to Dungrove. He shook his head. "It has to be there somewhere. Why are we not seeing it?"

"Because it's invisible."

Connor and Isa turned their heads as one when Francis entered and laid some enlarged photos on Connor's desk. Francis looked as tired as they were. His eyes were bloodshot; his clothes rumpled, and his sandy hair stuck together in odd places.

Connor looked at the photos, but all he saw was the quarry. "What is this?"

Francis pointed at a vague, small black mark that appeared on all three photos.

"For those in the back of the class, Francis. What is it?" Connor prompted.

"On screen, which is how you've been studying these same images, this looks like a dead pixel. Only it isn't."

"Dead pixels don't show up on prints," Isa said.

"The other thing about dead pixels is that they don't move. They're always in the same spot on your screen. These are not."

Connor turned back to the screen. There was indeed a small black spot on the screen. He moved the image to the right and the spot moved right along. He could hit himself for not noticing it earlier, and judging from her expression, so could Isa.

"Right. So, what *are* we seeing?" Isa asked, turning back to the photos Francis had brought.

"Someone's been tampering with the satellite reception."

It barely took a moment for Connor to catch on. "A cloak. You're talking about a cloaking device."

Francis seemed flustered. "Er, I don't really know. I can detect the tampering, but not what caused it."

Connor knew. "A few years back, we found this nice old lady whose house wasn't visible in aerial photographs. Turned out she had a device that hid her house from cameras. Not that she knew she had it. It had been a gift from a friend who'd thought it was a pretty lamp."

"Oh. Wow!" Francis said, his eyes sparkling in an "I want one of those" way.

Connor couldn't blame him. With all the cool artefacts that passed his desk, he found himself tempted to take some of them home, too.

"So... D'you think they have one of these cloaking devices?" Isa asked.

"Or something similar."

Isa looked from the screen to the images, shuffling them to match them up with the screen. "There's no road leading towards it, but I think it's about ten kilometres, fifteen tops, north of the quarry."

Close to where Evans had driven them last time. Connor grabbed his phone. "I guess we'd better get Lieutenant Matthews."

# 16

CLATTERING WINDOWS, SLAPPING BRANCHES, HOOTS, BARKS, and howls—even the softest sounds kept Noah awake, because any sound could mean the arrival of his rescuers or the dreaded Mr. Allen. So, he lay awake with a pounding heart, watching the moonlight ripple on his ceiling, and Connor on his mind.

And Home. Wherever home was. He had been away from his kin for 363 years now. Sometimes, watching the stars in bed at night as he waited to fall asleep, he wondered how his kin were and if they missed him, searched for him. He missed them.

Yet, despite all their flaws, he had fallen in love with the human race. He abhorred their wars and their hunger for control, but he admired their diversity, appreciated their humour, adored their ability to love no matter what, and enjoyed their ability to romanticise. He savoured their stories, devoured their books, and relished their written languages.

He had come to like being human, got used it, to them, and had found a place amongst them.

He often wondered what he would do if his kin *were* to find him. *If* he could go home. *If* they were able to reverse the transformation. *If wishes were horses.* With a shake of his head, he forced himself to let go. It was useless to think of it. Though he couldn't help but think he'd miss his books. His books and Connor. He'd miss Connor.

Connor, who'd come looking for him using the connection between them. Connor, who was trying to find him, was coming to get him any time now. Connor, who probably didn't even know he ran the risk of depleting himself. It scared Noah as much as it thrilled him that Connor cared enough to do this.

Noah still sensed Connor's presence, stronger than it had been before. Part of him yearned to sleep so his dreams would open the connection and he could learn more about Connor. He longed for the moment when the mere thought of Connor would reveal his location.

How much would Connor hate him when he understood the connection was irreversible?

Another window clattered somewhere in the building. Or was it a door? No footsteps, at least. He shot up. Was that a door? No, probably a branch slapping against the wall.

*Stop winding yourself up.* No one was coming for him yet. Noah leaned against the wall. His rescuers were on their way. They'd be here soon.

It became his mantra, repeating it over and over in his head as the hours passed, trying to ignore the eerie sounds that surrounded him.

Finally, a door slammed. He opened his eyes and straightened up as footsteps approached and the door opened.

"Time to go, Noah," Allen said, that same cold expression in his face. "Get him in the car, boys."

THREE TEAMS, THREE SUVS, PARKED IN THE MIDDLE OF NOWHERE, facing an enormous fence. Isa with Team Delta waited on the west side of the gate, while Connor with team Alpha and Matthews with team Charlie were parked next to each other on the east side of the gate, ready to move in.

"Elliot, see if you can scan the area for body heat," Matthews said through the commlink. Connor ordered Kelp to do the same.

"Nothing outside the fence, and there's something about that fence that keeps the scanner from penetrating it," Elliott said.

"No results here, either," Kelp echoed. "Hold on. There's something going on."

"What?" Matthews asked.

"It's blurry, but it seems there's a car coming out of the cloaked area straight ahead. Five passengers. No, wait... there's one more. Looks like one's been stuffed into the boot."

Noah. It had to be. Rescuing him out here seemed better than having to fight their way onto the premises.

Connor tried the connection, but received no reaction from Noah, although he sensed Noah close. The humming got louder. It had to be Noah in that boot. If it was, they'd probably knocked him out for transport.

"No others? Just the six?" Matthews asked.

Kelp nodded, obviously forgetting that Matthews couldn't see that through the commlink. Connor waved his hands to grab Kelp's attention and pointed to his ears. Kelp sighed. "Just the six, Lieutenant. They're coming our way."

"Agent Griffin, close in, but stay out of sight."

"Yes, Lieutenant."

"Kill the lights," Simpson hissed at Flanigan, their driver. Apparently, Evans heard it as well, because Charlie turned theirs off at the same time.

"Evans, Flanigan," Matthews called out. "You two are the

net, keep track of the car. Flank it as soon as it's in sight."

"Yes, Lieutenant."

"Right, Alpha and Charlie, out of the SUVs. Keep behind them and on the outside. Agent Griffin, your team stays in the car until my say so."

"Yes, Lieutenant," echoed through the commlinks.

One by one, they came piling out of the cars as Matthews ordered Iles and Yoshida to run ahead and take up positions in front. "Warn us when the car is close and take up positions behind it if Delta is too far off."

Simpson moved to crouch next to Connor as Iles and Yoshida made their way forward. Connor was glad to have him at his back.

Time slowed down as they waited for a sign from Iles and Yoshida, but the car headlights signalled its arrival before either could call it in. The car swerved as the driver found his way through the terrain.

Both SUVs and agents inched closer to the car at a steady pace. Matthews directed agents this way and that. Connor would be responsible for getting Noah out, and Elliott— inching towards him—was to assist him. Though all agents were trained in first aid, Elliott had an actual medical background—a background Isa had been grateful for a number of times already.

By the time the driver of the car spotted them, both SUVs were too close for them to escape. Evans managed to block it on the driver's side, but the car accelerated as Flanigan moved to block it on the other side and hit Flanigan's SUV at an angle. Not a perfect situation, but it would have to do.

The car's gears ground loudly, but before it could back up, Roderick, Delta's driver, blocked it from behind. Connor gasped as it hit the SUV, but his connection to Noah didn't change. He itched to run in and open that damn boot to check if Noah was all right.

The blokes in the car started shooting, sending most of the agents diving for cover. Connor lay low in the grass next to Simpson, tranq pointed at the car.

"Don't fire until I give the command. Let them run out of ammo. Block them if they try to get out of the car," Matthews ordered.

"Whatever you do," Connor added across the commlink, "make sure you don't hit that boot."

Of course, with Flanigan unable to flank the car, the doors on this side were unobstructed. Both opened at the same time, and two blokes came out shooting.

"Smith, Elliott. As soon as you see an opening, get to the boot," Matthews said.

"Yes, Lieutenant," Connor replied as he inched forward.

"Where do they get their ammo from? They should have run out already," Isa complained. Though Matthews hadn't given the command, Isa's team had joined the rest.

"Beneath the seats, most likely," Simpson said. He moved between Connor and the car, shielding him and distracting them.

Connor crawled towards the boot as fast as he could, ignoring the bullets flying around. Elliott, on the other hand, found himself blocked by Delta's SUV.

"Go around. You can't do anything from there," Connor said as he checked out the boot, focussing on the connection. He only vaguely heard Elliott's "I'll be right there."

The boot was dented on the left side, bent out of shape enough that his pocketknife wasn't going to open it. Connor sensed Noah's presence, but still received no reaction when he prodded him through the connection. "Are you all right?" he asked, even though it was silly. If Noah had been drugged, he wouldn't be able to hear him, anyway.

Elliott appeared beside him, on his hands and knees, holding a crowbar. "Got it from the SUV."

Connor took the crowbar, wriggled it between boot and lid underneath the lock, and put all his weight on it. The lid creaked and shifted, but not enough to break the lock.

"We need more weight," he told Elliott.

Elliott nodded and moved closer. Together, they pushed the crowbar down hard. The lock gave and the lid came up.

As they rose to haul Noah out, a bullet whizzed past, and they dove for the ground.

None of the chatter coming through the commlink indicated they were being shot at, specifically.

Elliott crawled to the side of the car. "I'll check if they're paying us any attention." He stared at the car and signalled Connor to keep his head down. "They're not aiming at us, but they're too close," Elliott whispered through the commlink.

They stayed low for a long time, too long. Connor didn't want to wait any longer. "If they're not paying attention to us—"

"Cease fire. All men secured," Matthew's voice came through the commlink. "I repeat. Cease fire."

Silence fell over them as the shooting stopped, and as one Connor and Elliott rose and threw the boot open. Noah lay awkwardly on his side, unconscious, both hands and legs cuffed. No severe wounds as far as Connor could see, though he did have a bruise on his cheek, just non-responsive. His assumption that Noah had been drugged seemed to be right.

But alive. Noah was alive. Connor swayed and had to grab the car to stay on his feet.

He took a couple of deep breaths and nodded at Elliott. Then he pulled Noah closer, grabbing him under his arms while Elliott took Noah's legs. They hefted him out of the car and carried him to Delta's SUV.

They made slow progress. Bodies were annoyingly limp when they were out cold and awkward to carry. The uneven ground wasn't helping, either. By the time the two of them laid Noah on the floor of Delta's SUV, Connor's muscles were sore, and his arms heavy.

Isa appeared behind them as Elliot grabbed his stethoscope. "How is he?"

"Unconscious, but his heartbeat is steady," Elliott said without looking up. "We need to remove these cuffs so I can take a better look, but they're not standard material."

"Do we have Kellan cutters?" Connor asked through the commlink. Kellan cutters cut through most alien materials, but there weren't enough of them to equip *all* the SUVs, and Connor hadn't been the one to oversee the packing of supplies.

Isa shrugged, but Flanigan answered them. "They should be in my toolbox. I'll be right there."

Noah lay on his back, mouth slack, and bruised cheek turned towards Connor. Connor put a hand on Noah's shoulder. He wanted Noah to be able to see him when he woke up.

Matthews instructed Isa to take a team to check out the gate when Flanigan arrived with the Kellan cutters. She gave Connor a quick hug and took off.

He helped Elliott hold Noah's arms up so Flanigan could cut the cuffs. The legs were next.

Matthews appeared next to the SUV, motioning for Connor to join him as he told Evans to take the suspects to Primrose. "Simpson, Iles. You two take the car."

Reluctantly, Connor left Noah in Elliott's care. "We're taking the car?"

"Yes. Unfortunately, the fifth suspect didn't survive. He was determined not to be captured. I didn't want him stored in the SUV with the others."

"The leader?"

"In the SUV with the other four. A posh-sounding fellow who wouldn't stop complaining about police brutality, so we had to gag him. "

"You need extra hands at the fence?"

Matthews shook his head. "Once Mr. Jones is checked out and secured, you can leave. You're still suspended, Smith." He turned towards Flanigan, leaning against the SUV. "You drive this one. Roderick will take yours."

"Of course, Lieutenant."

Connor hung his head. Still suspended. Of course. He'd only been allowed to join to rescue Noah, and he had. He wasn't officially part of the team.

"Chin up, Smith," Elliott said. "You'll be back at work in no time."

Connor wasn't as confident. He helped Elliott move Noah into the backseat, and secured him with the seat belts.

"Lieutenant, it's no use." Isa sounded frustrated. "The fence is too thick for the Kellan cutters to get through, and there's electricity running through it, too. No way we're getting in right now."

They needed to gain entry if they had any hope of finding out what was hidden inside.

Connor tuned out all conversations about a possible solution. It was nothing to do with him. He was suspended. He laid a hand over Noah's chest, reassuring himself Noah was still breathing. Though both the connection and Elliott verified that Noah was all right, he needed the tangible proof. Whatever else might happen, at least Noah was safe.

Noah woke up groggy in another unfamiliar room. No, it seemed familiar, but he wasn't awake enough to figure out why. At least it was clean—sparsely decorated, but clean.

The door opened, and Noah quickly closed his eyes,

hoping Allen wouldn't notice he was awake yet. He stiffened when he counted more than one pair of footsteps entering the room.

"Do you have any idea when the drugs will be out of his system?"

Connor. That was Connor. Noah wanted to see him, but didn't want to miss the answer. The conversation would surely stop when they realised he was awake. Noah kept his eyes closed and listened.

"Any time now, depending on how fit he was when they drugged him, whether they fed him, that sort of thing. He'll come around when he's ready, Agent Smith."

Noah wasn't thrilled that he was back at Primrose again, but anything beat having to live the rest of his life as Allen's pet alien.

"Can I stay here and wait for him to wake up?"

"Lieutenant Tallis said you have free access to this room, so yes, you can. But I'd appreciate it if you alert us when he wakes up."

"I will, Doctor."

"Good. Don't give him anything but water until we've examined him."

"Shouldn't be a problem. I don't think he drinks anything else."

"It's in his files, but I didn't just mean fluids. No food, either."

The door closed.

"You can open your eyes. I know you're awake."

Connor's eyes were red-rimmed and his skin flushed as if he hadn't slept since he'd contacted Noah. He reached out a hand...and then remembered Connor had a boyfriend. With heavy heart, he withdrew it.

"How did I get here? I remember Allen coming in and one of his men injecting me with something, but nothing else."

"Not surprisingly. That was a pretty heavy drug he dosed you with. Apparently, Allen lives north of Aberdeen. You had a pretty long way to go in that boot."

Boot? They'd put him in the boot of a car? Again? Noah turned onto his side, away from Connor. Connor put a hand on his shoulder and squeezed gently. Noah didn't turn back.

Connor sighed loud enough for Noah to hear, probably full of questions, but those would have to wait. No matter how glad he was to see Connor again, he wanted to sleep and forget.

"I'd better alert the doctor. Please try and stay awake a little longer. I'm sure you can sleep as long as you want to as soon as she's checked you out," Connor said as he got up. "I'll be back later."

Noah nodded, hearing the unspoken "we need to talk" clearly. Connor deserved to know more about the connection between them. He tried to stay awake for the doctor when Connor left the room, but in the end, he couldn't keep his eyes open long enough.

# 17

NOAH GLARED AT THE DOCTOR.

"What do you mean, I can't go home yet?"

"You haven't been cleared to leave." The doctor fussed with the machine next to Noah's bed. "You're still weak and slightly underfed. I'm not letting you go before I'm satisfied you're back to acceptable standards."

*Of course I'm weak and underfed*, he wanted to scream, *I was a prisoner, a commodity to be traded, auctioned off.* Noah turned his back to the doctor and closed his eyes. All he wanted was to go back to his flat, surround himself with his books, and forget any of this happened.

The door closed. He sighed. Too late to ask her for a book, then.

He must have dozed off, because when he opened his eyes again, Connor sat next to the bed, his feet up on another chair and his mouth slightly open, softly snoring. He looked so young, so innocent. Like Dafydd, yet nothing like Dafydd at all. Connor had grown up in a completely different time and was much more world-wise than Dafydd had ever been. Noah smiled. World-wise and clever, using their connection to find him.

Against all odds, the connection between his essence and

Connor's had cemented itself. He was connected to a human. Noah barely believed it.

"Your thoughts are way too loud for a quiet afternoon."

"You can hear my thoughts?" Noah asked.

"I can sense your worry. Worry and exhilaration. Pride, maybe. I don't know. I've been picking up your moods, or whatever they are, since I came in."

Why couldn't he feel Connor's moods? *Because you haven't tried.* He'd expected it all to come naturally. When he was still Rei, it had been effortless, like humans and their breathing. He could be communicating with his kin while playing his recording. Now? Now he could barely remember how it worked.

Noah took a deep breath and focussed on the connection. It was there, stronger than before. He caught a tiny wisp of worry, but he couldn't say if it was his or Connor's. He clenched his jaw.

"Are you all right?"

"It's... I never expected to have this again. I'm a little rusty."

A hand covered his. "You'll get the hang of it again. I mean, if I, a mere human, can make it work, surely you should be able to."

Noah snorted then. "Now you're just placating me."

"Sorry," Connor said, though his expression didn't show it. "I just... it's funny, you know. It seems I know you better than I do me."

Yeah, Noah knew exactly what he was talking about. An image of a very young Connor popped up in his mind. "You had cute curls when you were little."

"Oh, God. This is worse than Mum showing my baby pictures."

"You want to know why the connection happened." Connor was the kind of man who needed to know how everything worked. He needed to be able to take it apart, so he could build it back up.

"I think I know why, but..." Connor bit his lip.

"You have a boyfriend. I know," Noah said, surprised when he sensed no sign of backing off or intention to end their weird relationship. Not that that would be possible.

"I'm sorry."

"Don't be." Connor couldn't help who he loved.

"The report said the connection was about friendship. Why did you lie?"

Noah raised an eyebrow. "I didn't really lie. The connection between our essences is partly how we communicate and get to know one another—form friendships. Mates connect on a much deeper level; much more information is shared between them." *Between us.* Noah tried hard to suppress the urge to reach out to Connor. "Besides, I've been around humans enough to know they only believe in soul mates or love at first sight in fairy tales and fantasies."

"I believe."

Noah raised another eyebrow.

"I do. I blame my parents," Connor said with a smile. An image of them with tiny, curly-haired Connor playing in the snow appeared in Noah's mind. "Mum stepped on the wrong train and bumped into my dad when they both went for the same seat. They'd been together ever since. All right, the story is a lot longer than that, but that's what it boils down to. They met, fell in love, and knew they belonged together."

"They were well into their thirties then, weren't they?"

Connor nodded. "Yes, they were. They thought they couldn't have children. They'd all but given up when I finally announced myself. Mum was reaching forty by then, and Dad was quite a bit older than she was."

Noah wanted to hug Connor. They'd done a good job

raising him.

They sat in companionable silence, until Connor's smile abruptly faded. "You're see-through." His voice shook.

What had brought that on? "I was... once."

Connor squeezed his hand. "You've given up hope."

Noah closed his eyes. "Humans evolve too slowly for me."

"You don't want to go back."

Caught at a lie. Though, he wasn't so much lying to Connor as lying to himself, and Connor had sensed that. "I miss my kin, but I fell in love with Earth, fell in love with your books, your stories. If I return, if they can change me, I will never be able to hold a book again." Not to mention that he wouldn't be able to survive there if they couldn't reverse his transformation.

Connor said nothing, he just held Noah's hand and drew circles with his thumb.

It soothed Noah. He closed his eyes, too tired to stay awake any longer, but even this close to sleep, he couldn't stop himself from admitting, "I couldn't bear to let you go."

As he stared at photos of Edward Allen, Connor had trouble keeping himself from going downstairs and beating the crap out of him. Parker had been questioning him for hours, but Allen refused to talk, except to claim he didn't know why Noah had been in the boot of his car. As if anyone was going to believe that, with four gun-happy crooks in the same car.

Connor rubbed his eyes and yawned. At least he'd been reinstated again. Well, reinstated on probation for mostly desk work, with no clearance for the more delicate cases. It was bloody frustrating. He closed the folder. He needed a break. All that reading wasn't doing him any good today.

"I hear you spent most of yesterday with Noah Jones."

Connor looked up from a desk strewn with pictures and reports at Isa, who leaned against the wall next to the door. "I hear you spent most of yesterday interviewing our newest residents."

"Overseeing, you mean. I spent my Sunday watching four silent men and one hothead."

Connor snorted. "Parker?"

"Got it in one. Parker's taken more breaks during his interrogations than ever. He kept sneaking off to the gym to cool off in between sessions."

That, Connor would well imagine. Two minutes alone with Allen, and *he* would have to be forcibly removed from the bloke. "Yet, they still haven't talked." The images of Noah's cuts popped into his mind. He shuddered. "After what they did to Noah, I'm tempted to petition to reinstate torture."

Isa grimaced. "That's why you're not allowed to be involved." She sat down and rolled her chair close to his. "So, Noah, huh? First name basis already?"

Connor shook his head and looked away. "Don't, Isa, please." It was an unsubtle change of subject, but not a good one.

He felt a hand on his arm. "Oh, man, Connor. This is just eating you up, isn't it?"

How could he tell her how torn he was? Isa was his best friend, but she was also the one who had introduced him to Jason. He sighed. Perfect Jason, even if he was out of the country, again.

Connor had called Jason after he'd finally left Primrose, in need of a distraction, but Jason was short on time. A quick fuck and he was off again, rushing to catch a plane. Serbia this time. As much as Connor had been looking forward to spending time with him, he was almost relieved when Jason had gone.

Connor sighed. How could he tell Isa that he couldn't stop thinking about Noah, despite having the perfect boyfriend?

She didn't say anything. She just studied him, her hand still resting on his arm. There was a spark in her eye that told Connor that despite her abysmal matchmaking abilities, she knew him better than anyone. Except Noah.

Which was what it was all about. Connor's problem was that he wasn't bothered about their connection at all. Everything he needed to know, he could get through the connection. He knew it shouldn't be possible, it shouldn't be easy, yet it felt like it had always been this way. Was *meant* to be this way.

During yesterday's visit, talking to Noah or watching him sleep, the connection had grown stronger and stronger, until Connor barely had to focus to sense what Noah was feeling. He sensed it even now. Noah was tired, and frustrated that he still wasn't allowed to go home. He soon would be, though, and Connor had practically begged Tallis to put him on the protection rotation.

Connor looked from Isa to his desk and sighed. "What do you think?" he asked, pushing the work aside. "Time for lunch?"

Isa beamed. "I thought you'd never ask. I've heard they have chocolate pudding today."

Chocolate. Isa's solution to all problems.

THIS TIME, NO ONE RUMMAGED THROUGH NOAH'S STUFF WHEN THEY brought him home. He had gained a protection detail, however. Not Noah's choice, not a choice at all, not when he could only choose between accepting the detail or staying at

Primrose.

Once the Westland Group, as Primrose called the organisation that Noah had been abducted for, found out what had happened to Edward Allen, they might come after him. Noah reluctantly agreed to the protection detail, considering how easily they'd grabbed him last time. He refused to stay at Primrose any longer.

The protection detail consisted of two agents at his place around the clock. Out of politeness, Noah had offered them the use of one of his guest rooms, which they had only been too happy to accept.

"Can I get you anything before you go to bed, sir?"

Noah looked up into a pair of hazel eyes. He couldn't remember the names of the agents assigned to him, and he wasn't sure he should bother. Apparently, they would be rotating in and out.

"Sir?"

Oh, right. Bed rest. He had hoped the agents had forgotten about the interfering doctor's orders. Bed rest. Noah snorted. All he wanted to do was settle himself into his library with a good book, but no, the doctor had ordered bed rest.

The agent waited patiently, or seemingly patiently, in the doorway. Well, if they wanted to play butler to him, who was he to stop them? "I'd like some books." He wasn't really up to carrying the heavy tomes himself, anyway.

Agent whatever-his-name-was quietly followed Noah into the library—filled with the same walnut bookcases he had in the living room—and grabbed the books Noah pointed at. He carried them up to Noah's bedroom and placed them on the floor next to the nightstand, just as Noah asked.

"Good night, sir."

Noah muttered a quick good night in reply, but the agent had already closed the door. Noah undressed and slipped under the covers. As soon as he'd drawn the duvet up to his shoulders, he let his head sink into his pillow.

He had so missed his bed, missed his home, missed his books, and missed the amber-coloured walls that had the appearance of an eternal sunset when the sun peaked through the window above his bed.

The top one, a seventeenth-century King James Bible, he didn't even plan to read. He just needed to hold it. It had been his first purchase, his most-loved book; the one he had taken his name from. Humans would probably call it his "security blanket".

Whenever Noah felt down, out of sorts, like he didn't belong, he'd take the book out and put it on his night stand. Sometimes he just gazed at it. The soft night light gave the leather a warm hue to which he would fall asleep. Sometimes he would put it next to his pillow, laying his hand on top of it, the way he did now.

The leather warmed to his touch, and it made Noah smile. This book made him feel connected and safe.

"Security blanket" wasn't such a bad name.

"I'm staying a little longer," Jason said through the phone. "The dining set I had my eye on fell through, but someone gave me a tip about a small village across the border."

"I hope you find what you're looking for," Connor answered without enthusiasm. Jason had been gone for four days already.

"So do I, and fast. Serbia is nice, but I'd rather be lounging with you at your flat than sit here in this generic hotel room."

Connor burst out, "So, get the hell back here."

"Miss me?"

"Yes," he whispered. Yet when he hung up, he wasn't so

sure about that.

Jason was funny and attentive, and the sex was great, even if Jason insisted on topping every time. He was perfect. But—there had to be a but—Connor didn't know Jason like he did Noah.

With his protection detail shifts, Connor had spent more and more time with Noah. They didn't even have to talk or be in close proximity. Connor sensed Noah through the connection, sensed his moods, and knew his history. Connor felt cherished, like he belonged.

His feelings for Jason and his feelings for Noah didn't mesh, and it tore at him.

His computer chimed, dragging him out of his thoughts. He stuffed his mobile into his backpack and grabbed his keyboard. His search had finally garnered results. He'd been given the boring task of tracking down Primrose's internal memos to find anything to do with missing aliens. The memos should have been filed to Archive, were it not for the fact that those same dratted memos were also used as betting slips. Not to mention, they got more calls about alien sightings in a year than they could handle, so he had to sift through one fake alien sighting after another to find what he was looking for.

Connor disliked being put on the sidelines even more than being suspended. He was up to date with the investigations, sure, but he wasn't allowed anywhere near them.

Investigations into the farm had hit a dead end. The satellite images showed cars pulling out the minute Matthews and Isa's team had left, but that bloody fence remained impenetrable.

While Allen still wasn't talking, Isa worked her arse off to organise raids on known members of the Westland Group, using the eBay list. The Allen residence had already been searched, of course, as useless as that had been. Someone had made certain there wouldn't be much left to find—nothing alien, at least.

Tallis entered his office, looking ready to go out as he was dutifully sorting all the memos into different categories. "Connor. I'm having lunch with a possible recruit, ex-military. He's been studying one of our larger suspected weapons this past week. I'll be back around two. Can you make sure he can't stray from the tour I'll be giving him?"

Primrose was an odd mix and match of ex-military and civilians. It looked like this one would be an addition to the Development department. "Secure the premises. Will do. Will an hour be enough for the tour?"

"An hour will be fine. Thank you, Connor."

Connor focussed his attention back on his screen. He typed a memo to all departments warning them of the recruit tour and instructing them to lock their doors between two and three and limit mobility as much as possible. With that out of the way, he returned to the internal memos.

Right. Fake alien. Click. Transferred to Island. Click. Fake alien. Click. Reported but not followed up. Bingo. That was what, the fifth out of over a hundred entries? Still many, many memos more to go.

"I have a report for Lieutenant Tallis."

Connor turned in his chair as Francis entered his office carrying a large envelope. "And a good morning to you too, Francis."

"Sorry, sir. Good morning." Francis handed Connor the envelope. He was about to head back out when he caught a glimpse of Connor's screen. "Are those betting slips?"

Connor groaned. Internal memos as betting slips. Whoever had come up with that one had been bonkers. Of course, the 'game' had been created years before he'd worked here, so it was sort of a tradition now. Employees bet on anything from what the next artefact found would be called to the most gruesome way an alien would die.

"Yes. I'm looking for missing aliens."

"That will take you hours."

Days, more like it. That was kind of the point. "Did you find anything more on those frames?"

"Still working my way through it. Nothing on the hacker, either. I have leads pointing to almost every country in and outside of Europe, but none that even comes close to being the origin."

"Right. And the report?"

"Details of the surveillance on the farm."

Oh, that sounded interesting. "Want to join me and Agent Griffin for lunch?"

Francis looked at Connor with a deer-in-the-headlights expression, but muttered a *yes* anyway.

# 18

NOAH SENSED CONNOR'S PRESENCE BEFORE ONE OF THE creaking steps on the stairs betrayed his arrival. Noah inspected his outfit, a blue and purple paisley shirt. He enjoyed the playfulness of paisley. Or should he have changed into something more...? More what? He sighed. Why did he put himself through this? Connor had a boyfriend; he wasn't interested.

But, he was, wasn't he? Even though Connor never let it show—tried not to let it show—Noah sensed his doubt through the connection. Noah tried to keep some distance, but it was futile. Regardless of Connor's feelings now, their connection would only grow deeper.

Noah rose with a sigh, and stood by the window overlooking the grassland behind the shop. Nothing had been built there in over fifty years. He didn't know who owned the land, but the last owner had died in the 1920s. It had been turned into a car park at some point, but when a new one had been built in a more accessible spot a block down, this one had become derelict.

"There's concrete underneath all that grass," he said when Connor stood next to him.

"I know. You were broadcasting, loud and clear."

"Only about the land, I hope." Noah tried to make it sound light. There would come a day when Connor could even pick up on his most private thoughts. Probably sooner rather than later.

Connor turned towards him, a thoughtful look in his eyes. "I'm not prying, Noah. I got the part about the land because you... It was like you were trying to explain it to me. Usually, I only pick up your moods." He turned away from the window, away from Noah. "I sometimes wonder if you can read my thoughts."

Noah put his hand on Connor's arm. "I can't. I promise. You'd have to permit me access, but I can't teach you how to do that."

Connor looked down at Noah's hand and frowned. "I don't get it. Shouldn't it be easier to get in because I have no idea what I'm doing?"

That was an easy one. "No. I know it's hard to understand, but I can't get into your mind when I want to. It's locked, and you're the only one who can unlock it."

"So, why can we sense each other's moods and feelings, then?"

"Those aren't locked or hidden. The connection will broadcast anything that's not hidden."

"All right." Connor said, though Noah wasn't certain Connor understood it. Time would tell.

"Want some tea?" Ever since he'd discovered Connor liked tea, he'd made the effort of brewing it when Connor visited.

"I'll brew it," Connor said, and before Noah could protest, Connor had already disappeared.

Noah shook his head and sat down on his sofa, leaning his head against the back. Connor seemed as obsessed about his tea as Noah was about his books.

Noah blinked and jerked up when something clattered to

the floor, grabbing for his stomach. *Fool.* He was at home and free, not bound and stabbed.

"Sorry. The tray was a bit slippery." Connor's expression told him he had sensed Noah's reaction, but he didn't comment on it. Instead, he put the tray on the table.

"No problem." Noah hadn't meant to fall asleep.

"So." Connor poured himself a cup of tea and handed Noah a glass of water. "Have you ever thought of buying that land, expanding your shop?" The question didn't seem to resonate with Connor's mood. There was something on his mind.

"I don't want a larger bookshop. I like it the way it is. People come here to buy the special editions they've been looking a long time for. I don't need to have a children's section to sell more, or a shop filled with the latest and most popular books."

"So, obsessed with books, but picky," Connor concluded.

"Of course," Noah admitted with a wink. "When people come in, I know they have the same appreciation for books that I do, even though some of them just browse. Most come because I might be able to find them the long out-of-print book they always wanted to have."

"It's strange that I've never been here before. I have some first editions, but I never knew this shop existed."

"It's been here since before you were born."

Connor put his mug onto the tray. "If you love books this much, then why didn't you start your own shop back in the 1700s, or late 1600s, even?"

"Times were different. I was different. I still thought I'd be going home at some point. Besides, I didn't have any money to buy food, let alone a shop. When everyone around me aged, I thought it better to start changing jobs, changing cities, hoping no one would figure out I didn't age."

"What about now? Do people actually believe you when

you pretend to be your own son?"

"They have no reason not to. Humans don't live that long, so I couldn't be the same person, could I?"

"Us humans are too easy to fool, sometimes."

"I am *not—*"

"I...I'm sorry. That was uncalled for," Connor said, turning away too late to hide his flushed cheeks. He poured himself another tea. "I know you don't think we're stupid."

Connor's face flushed even more when Noah caught him smelling his tea. Noah smiled, glad he'd gone for the Earl Grey and not the breakfast tea the shopkeeper had suggested. He let Connor enjoy his tea and forget his embarrassment. Noah should have known Connor hadn't meant to insult him. He'd said it in jest, that was all. Noah... He was still a bit raw, and that wasn't Connor's fault.

"Smells good," Connor said, holding the cup close to his face.

It smelled like some cheap perfume. "I've never liked it much myself."

Connor frowned. "I've never seen you drink anything but water."

Noah shrugged. "I never saw the point. Water quenches my thirst. Everything else is a waste of perfectly good energy, if you ask me."

"Is it the same with food?"

"I'm a little more adventurous where food's concerned. Different food groups, different functions, and all that."

There didn't seem to be anything else to say. Connor stared into his mug. Something still seemed to bother him, judging from the worry and sadness bleeding through the connection. Whatever it was, Connor couldn't seem to bring himself to talk about it.

Understandable. They were only just getting to know each other. Noah rose and went into his library. He grabbed a book at random and sat down to read. He wasn't surprised to sense Connor following him.

"You can't die."

That was what had him bothered? That Noah couldn't die? "I can, and I will, someday when I've grown old. I just don't age the way humans do."

"No, you don't."

It was obvious Connor had more to say, but he didn't come into the library. He stayed in the doorway, looking at the floor with his hands in his pockets, deep in thought. "How do you cope?"

"Cope with living this long?"

"Cope with losing people, cope with being left behind. I know you miss Dafydd."

So, it wasn't that he didn't die, per se, it was that he would be left behind while the people around him died. "Yes. I miss Dafydd. Just like you miss your parents."

"But..." Connor sighed, a sad sound that made Noah wonder what was going on in that head of his.

"I've learned to live with it, Connor. I try to remember the good times and not get stuck on the bad times, because there's nothing I can do to change what I am, nothing I can do to save them."

Connor hung his head and backed out of the library. "I need to go."

Connor ran down the stairs two steps at a time, needing to get away from Noah as fast as possible. He didn't understand why he hadn't figured it out before. Knowing Noah had seemed so natural, but then there was that image of Dafydd, taken before he died. He still sensed Noah's anguish. Now, all he could think of was that when he died, Noah would be the one left alone.

He stopped short of the front door, knowing O'Neill would be keeping watch outside. He didn't want to have to explain why he was running out the door. Then he heard Noah's footsteps on the stairs behind him, followed by coughing, and Connor immediately felt guilty. Though Noah's wounds had healed, the malnourishment had taken its toll, and he wasn't fit enough to walk up and down the stairs.

With Noah already halfway down, Connor leaned back against the wall and waited, rubbing his arms as he stared at the floor. If only Noah would leave it be—leave *him* be.

He didn't. Noah continued until he stood chest to chest with Connor, out of breath, trembling, and raised Connor's chin, forcing him to meet his gaze. Though Noah looked brittle, his voice sounded anything but. "Yes, I lose more people than the average human, and yes, it takes time to let them go. But I never regret having known them."

Connor held his breath to keep from tilting his head and sucking Noah's fingers into his mouth.

As if he knew what Connor was thinking, Noah caressed Connor's bottom lip with his thumb. "I know it's hard to fully grasp what I am, but let me assure you, I will never regret meeting you or connecting with you."

Connor held still. He wanted to grab Noah, wanted to push him against the closest wall and ravage him. Noah cared deeply for him, would welcome him, but the last thing Connor wanted was to lead Noah on. So, even though he craved a kiss, Connor restrained himself.

When Noah stepped back, Connor found himself following the motion, grabbing Noah's arms to keep them both steady as he leaned forward until their foreheads touched. A sudden sense of arousal shot through the connection, and before Connor could back away, he found himself lip-locked with Noah.

He lost himself in the kiss as a multitude of emotions and impressions hit him through the connection. They filled his head, intensifying the experience, and his arousal.

He clung to Noah, unable to think...until an image of Jason entered his mind. With a growl, Connor tore himself away from Noah, moving to the other side of the hall and facing away. "We can't do this," he whispered as he touched his fingers to his lips. "Please, go upstairs. I'll stay outside with O'Neill until my shift is over."

Noah said nothing. He didn't have to. The hint of sadness coming through the connection said enough. Connor swallowed. As much as he wanted to make that sadness disappear, if he didn't go outside now, he'd do something he'd regret. He grabbed the doorknob. "I'm sorry."

"Connor?"

Isa's hair sat flat to the right side of her head, and only one arm stuck out of her favourite robe. Connor shouldn't have come here.

"Did something happen? Do I need to come in?"

"What?" It took Connor a minute to decipher what she was talking about. Work, she thought he was here for work. "No, no. Nothing like that." He shouldn't have come here in the middle of the night. "I'm sorry for waking you. I'll see you tomorrow."

"Oh, come in, you daft git. You don't think I'm letting you go, do you?" She grabbed his hand and pulled him inside, closing the door with her foot. "Get your arse on the sofa, I'll be there in a sec."

Connor did as she said and curled up on her soft and

fluffy indigo sofa, leaning back into the mountain of pillows with a loud sigh.

Isa followed a couple of minutes later with two large mugs of coffee. She handed him one and sank into her favourite chair opposite him, the small tables on either side filled with magazines, books, and crossword puzzles. "So, what did you do? Have an argument with Jason?"

Connor shook his head. "He's still somewhere in Serbia."

Isa narrowed her eyes. "Noah, then."

Her stare was annoyingly intense, accusatory even. It made him want to cringe and turn away.

Suddenly, her eyes widened. "You didn't! Please tell me you didn't."

"Didn't what?" Connor asked, even though he had a pretty good idea what she was talking about.

"You slept with Noah!"

Connor blanched. "No! I didn't sleep with him."

Isa's eyes narrowed again.

"Really. I didn't."

"Then what happened to land you at my doorstep?"

Connor swallowed. "I kissed him."

"Hah!"

"I didn't mean to, but..." He sighed. "I wanted to. The connection..." Connor couldn't explain it.

"The connection made you?"

"No!" He shot up, pacing up and down in front of the sofa. "Nothing like that. I thought we cleared all that rubbish up already."

She held up her hands. "Calm down. Obviously, *something* happened with that connection of yours. Can you blame me for assuming the worst?"

Deflated, Connor sagged into the pillows. He couldn't. Hell, he probably would have jumped to the same conclusion if it was her.

"So, what *did* happen?"

"I was..." He shook his head. He should go further back. "Things were tense. It dawned on me that, living as long as he does, he loses people he loves over and over again." He wasn't explaining it very well. "I wanted to get out, it was too much. He followed me, and I couldn't get the idea of us kissing out of my head. I sensed his emotions through the connection, and I just snapped and kissed him." Even now, he sensed Noah's emotions so vividly.

"You ran, didn't you?" No judging, no placating, only Isa's calming voice.

"As soon as I could. I stayed outside with O'Neill until my shift was over, and then came here." Connor closed his eyes. "It was wrong. I have Jason. I can't...I couldn't...I shouldn't. It's not who I am."

"So, what are you going to do now?"

Connor had half expected her to ask how Noah kissed and was glad she hadn't. "I don't know."

"You can't run away from this."

As if he didn't know that. "It's not fair, Isa. I meet this gorgeous, perfect bloke who seems really into me. Then I meet someone who turns my world upside down with a single thought, and I can't escape it, can't escape *him*."

Isa got out of her chair and knelt in front of him, putting both her hands on his knees and looking him straight in his eyes. "Maybe you shouldn't." He opened his mouth to protest, but she stopped him with a gesture. "Noah can't connect to just anyone, right?"

"No," Connor admitted, "he can't."

"I'm not going to buy that bullshit about friendship, either."

"It's not bullshit, the friendship. But it's not what the connection between us is about, no." Connor swallowed. "It goes much deeper than that." He could admit that now.

"Well, there you go."

"But—"

"Shh. You think too much," Isa said. "Don't think. Feel."

*Don't think. Feel.* Something about that sounded familiar. Could it really be that simple? "How did I get from being dumped to having to choose between two blokes?"

Isa snorted as she got up and brushed the lint off her knees. "Honey. If you ever figure that out, come tell me. I'd love to be in your shoes."

The very first time a human female had tried to kiss Noah, he had recoiled, afraid of what she was going to do to him. It had turned out to be good though—more than good. His body responded to the kissing, violently. Sex, though nothing like the brushing and merging of the Rei, was more than enjoyable, and so diverse. A little clumsy at times, a lot messy, but exploration and experimentation were half the fun of sex.

After all these years on Earth, one would think he'd know it all by now, yet every now and then, he still learned something new. These tactile humans had no idea how precious they were for their inventiveness. To Noah, at least.

On the other side of the equation was love. Humans loved with an intensity that scared him, and yet, their love seemed such a fleeting thing, a curious concept that was so unlike Rei mating. More than a fair share of human lovers had professed their love for Noah, enough for him to figure out he could never love the way they did. There was no instant connection, no brushing, no merging. It made Noah feel disconnected.

He and Dafydd had come close, so close. He'd connected to Dafydd, but Dafydd had been unable to connect to him. Still, it had resembled perfection then, even though their connection was not complete. Pure, innocent Dafydd had been the answer to all his hopes—had been his reason for being for eight wonderful years.

In the 1700s they'd had to be careful, on guard. As much as Noah had wanted to show his love openly, Dafydd had been more important to him. It hadn't been easy to sneak around and steal moments whenever they could. Noah smiled as he remembered how Dafydd had found them combined lodgings, giving them more freedom and a chance to spend each night holding each other without raising suspicions.

With a sigh, Noah opened his beloved Bible and looked at the only drawing of Dafydd that remained. He stood in his best clothes with his hair hanging loose and a hint of a smile on his face. Just a hint, because Dafydd hadn't wanted to sit for the portrait; he hadn't wanted Noah to waste money on him.

Noah was glad he had persisted. "You were worth it, love," he whispered as he closed the Bible again. More than worth it.

With Connor, Noah had received a second chance, there was no doubt about that. The moment Connor had kissed him, Noah had sensed the awakening in him. Connor should have sensed it too, even if he didn't understand what he'd unleashed, yet.

Connor hadn't been back since. It was hard to handle, sensing how torn Connor was. Yet, no matter how desperately Noah wanted to help him, be there for him, there was nothing to do but wait until Connor sorted himself out. Connor would have to come to him.

Noah had no doubt he would. It was only a question of when.

# 19

UNDAY EVENING, CONNOR PARKED HIS CAR ACROSS FROM Jason's antique shop, turned off the engine, and leaned back in his seat. After the busy days at work, still grounded and working on those blasted internal memos, he'd had plenty of time to think about his situation this weekend.

By the time he'd finally made a decision, Jason had called to say he was back in town.

After taking a deep breath, Connor got out of his car and crossed the road. His resolve had faltered for the length of that phone call, but now he was determined to end their relationship. That was what dinner would be all about. Jason had wanted to come straight to Connor's, but Connor preferred more neutral ground.

Jason wasn't in the shop itself when he entered, but the older bloke, Simon, was. Simon took one derisive look at Connor and disappeared into the back, hopefully to tell Jason he had arrived.

If he had, Jason certainly took his time to come out, because Connor spent fifteen minutes gazing at the same dining table he'd had his eye on last time.

He started when Jason appeared beside him, wrapping an arm around his waist. "See anything you like?"

It was the tone of Jason's voice that brought Connor up short. It lacked warmth. Jason seemed tense. Connor shook his head.

Jason smiled and led him outside. "Where are you taking me for dinner?"

Connor frowned. "Don't you have to lock up?"

"Nah, Simon'll do that when he's done. So?"

"I made reservations at Guiseppe's on Harrow Road." Because Jason had told him he liked Italian after Connor had served him his lasagne.

"Italian sounds great."

Connor stumbled over a loose rock on the stone path in front of the shop and dropped his keys. Jason let go as Connor bent to pick them up. As he collected his keys, a pattern in the sand to his right caught his eye. A pattern that looked suspiciously like the shoe print they'd found on the CCTV recordings. It couldn't be, could it? He'd probably been staring at that bloody print for too long and now saw it everywhere. Still, the only way to rule it out was to take a picture. Rather safe than sorry.

As Connor pretended to re-tie his shoe laces, he fished his mobile out of his trouser pocket. All he needed now was a distraction so Jason wouldn't notice what he was doing. It wasn't as if he could tell Jason why he needed a photograph of dirt.

"Jason!"

Connor turned his head, still fumbling with his laces. Simon stood in the doorway of the shop, holding his hand next to his face as if it were a phone and looking none too happy.

Jason sighed. "One minute. I'll be back in one minute."

"That's all right. If you're not here in one, I'll come back to drag you out."

Jason laughed, though it sounded forced, and sprinted

back to the shop.

Connor let out a sigh of relief as he took a couple of photos of the shoe print, including a couple of wide-angle shots.

Jason returned when Connor put the mobile back into his trouser pocket. He slung his arm around Connor's waist and whispered, "Let's get out of here, before Simon calls me back in again."

When Connor glanced behind them, Simon was staring at him.

The drive was unexpectedly silent and their dinner different, less easy going. Jason, for once, didn't seem inclined to keep the conversation going.

Despite his own thoughts distracting him, things seemed to have changed between them, and it wasn't all Conner. Jason telling him about Serbia lacked something. It was as if his heart wasn't in it.

Had something happened to Jason in Serbia? Connor frowned. Or could Jason tell he was having second thoughts? He hadn't been that obvious, had he? Whatever it was, this awkward tension wouldn't resolve itself.

When Connor opened his mouth, Jason put his fork and knife down. "Look, Connor. You're a great guy, but I can't do this anymore."

For a moment, Connor was lost. He was here to break up with Jason, wasn't he? So, why did it seem Jason was breaking up with him?

"I met someone else," Jason continued, studying Connor with dull eyes. "I can't see you anymore."

Connor was at a loss at what to say. He tried, but nothing came out. This was the strangest break up he'd ever had.

"I'm not going to apologise," Jason said.

"I don't expect you to." His voice croaked. Should he tell Jason about Noah after this? Did it matter? Even if it didn't, deep inside, Connor didn't want Jason to think he was heartbroken about it. Still, it wasn't easy to get the words out. His heart pounded in his ears, and in the end, it came out as one long string of syllables. "Imetsomeonetoo."

Jason jerked in his seat, a shuttered expression in his eyes. "You did?"

"We met through work, and we—"

Jason held up his hands and shook his head. "I don't need to know." His tone was short and a little cold.

Connor bit his lip. "Sorry." Too much information. It wasn't like they were friends, was it?

For the longest time, Jason just stared at him, food forgotten, and Connor couldn't help but stare back. For someone who'd just broke up with him, Jason seemed…upset. If upset was the right word for the unreadable expression in his eyes. Suddenly, Jason smiled and wiggled his eyebrows, but the smile didn't reach his eyes. "Guess one last make-out session is out of the question?"

Connor smiled despite himself. "I guess."

Jason nodded. He looked at his watch and got up. "I'd better go, then."

*You haven't even finished your dinner*, Connor wanted to say, but there was no point. Was there?

"It's early. She might still be up."

She? Jason had met a woman? Never once had Connor thought Jason was anything but gay. He felt uncomfortable with the way Jason was watching him. As if waiting for a reaction. It almost seemed as if Jason wanted him to be hurt.

He probably would have been, if the circumstances were different. Or, maybe, Connor had just misread him. He rose and shook Jason's hand. He wanted to kiss him, but decided against it.

"Don't be a stranger," he said.

As he watched Jason walk out of the restaurant, he knew

Jason would never be calling him again.

CONNOR PLUGGED HIS MOBILE INTO THE COMPUTER AND transferred the photos. As he stared restlessly at the screen, his mind drifted back to the break up.

After Jason had left the restaurant, Connor had called Isa, and when she didn't pick up, he'd almost taken the train to see Noah. Almost. It would have been too soon. He kept telling himself that all night to keep from using the connection. If he was going to talk to Noah, he was going to do it face to face.

"Your transfer's finished, you know?"

Connor's screen showed a reflection of Isa's face. "Good morning."

"I'd say the same, but you don't look all that chipper," Isa said, sitting down next to him. "That what the call last night was about?"

It was no use asking her to come back later. The way she looked at him meant she wasn't leaving until she heard the whole story. He still had to try. "I'm working."

"Sure. You've been staring at your screen, but you didn't notice your transfer was done. I wouldn't call that working."

"All right. Jason and I broke up last night."

Isa's eyes widened. "You told him?"

"Not quite."

"Meaning?"

"I was still gathering the courage to tell him when he told me he met someone else and couldn't see me anymore."

Now Isa's jaw dropped. "You're kidding?"

"No. And it's a woman, apparently."

"He dumped you for a girl. That's new. So, how are you?"

"Confused. Relieved. A bit lost, I guess." Mostly because it had been Jason who had pursued him. Had Jason not kept calling him, Connor might have never met up with him again. So, how did a guy go from pursuing a blind date to dumping him a month later?

Not forgetting the unreadable expression in Jason's eyes, as if he'd been waiting for something from Connor. Isa didn't need to know that.

"Does Noah know?"

"I haven't seen him." Though Connor assumed Noah sensed his emotions, even if he might not realise the cause.

Noah felt the same as always. He was tired of having a protection detail around 24/7.

Suddenly Isa shot up, hand reaching for her ear. "Yes, Lieutenant, I'm on my way." She turned to Connor. "Got to go. Lunch later?"

"You're wearing a commlink in the office?"

She rolled her eyes. "Matthews got tired of trying to track me down. Which is funny, since he's the one sending me running all over the place."

It was hard not to be jealous of Isa's work load.

"Don't pout. You'll be back on active service soon enough," she said as she exited the office.

It would be great if she was right. This missing alien goose chase he was on was doing him in. He brought up the photos of the shoe print he'd taken the day before and compared them to the ones on file. Same pattern, just as he'd thought. That didn't mean much, though. It was a popular brand and model, after all. There was no reason for the thief to have been near the antique shop, was there? Still, he needed to rule it out.

The difference in lighting of the pictures made it hard to determine a match in wear pattern, so he sent them off in an email to Research. He also added a request for the CCTV recordings of the antique shop, just in case, cc-ing Tallis. He leaned back and sighed. He might as well get some coffee before diving back into the internal memos again.

When Tallis' office door banged open, he nearly jumped. "Connor, gear up. We're heading out."

Connor automatically stood up and opened his cupboard. Then he froze. "I'm on desk duty, Lieutenant."

"Not anymore, you're not. We're headed for the farm."

"Allen talked?"

"Still not a peep out of him. No. Research broke the shield. They're waiting for us before going in."

That meant he needed to get his arse in gear. Suppressing the urge to jump in the air at being allowed to go, Connor changed into his field gear and followed Tallis out of the office.

Isa and Matthews, surrounded by agents from all the different field teams, waited for them at the gate of the farm. Isa smiled at Connor when he got out of the SUV.

"It's good to see you back out in the field," she whispered.

"I hope it's not a one-time deal," Connor replied.

He stayed with Isa while the lieutenants were laying down the plan, but as soon as they were finished, he joined Simpson at the head of team Alpha.

"They've decided to let you play, then?" Simpson asked.

Connor smiled. "It seems so."

They set the commlinks to team frequency only, to avoid being overloaded with chatter—they'd be hailed if they were needed elsewhere—and led their team through the gate towards the barn. Team Bravo took the east side corner, and Connor took his team to the south-side entrance. He opened the door, and they filed into a narrow corridor with numerous doors on both sides. Team Bravo entered at the other side.

Connor set his commlink to include Bravo's frequency as well, motioning his team to do the same, and greeted Agent Vera Abernathy, Bravo's leader, a sharp-faced woman with short-cropped light brown hair. From both ends of the corridor, they searched the cells on either side until they finally met up in the middle. The silence of both teams said enough. They were all empty.

There was something about the resonance inside the building that didn't sound right, though. Connor stomped his right foot. The floor sounded hollow. "Check the floorboards. Look for something like a hatch," he said.

There was nothing in the corridor, but a quick search through the cells later, Simpson called out that he'd found one.

"It seems to be locked," Simpson said, sounding a bit muffled. "No lock on this side, though."

Connor joined him and frowned. It looked like a hatch, but why would it be locked from the inside? He helped Simpson try to pry it open, but no matter how they heaved, it wouldn't budge at all.

"Got one on this side as well, sir," Agent Ipsen from Bravo reported. "Also locked."

Simpson let go of the hatch. "I think we need to find something to break it."

Connor nodded at Simpson. "Right. I need two agents to go back and bring us some axes. In the meantime, Abernathy, if you can send two of yours to scour for another way down. There has to be another entrance somewhere."

"We'll get the axes," Xiang said, gesturing at Kelp.

Connor nodded and watched them sprint off as he waited for Abernathy to respond.

"I sent O'Donnell and Quadeer to find another way in."

"Good. I don't know what we'll find down there, but caution first." Until they knew what the conditions below were. Though Connor prayed whatever was down there was both alive and docile, he doubted anything was left. Still, the last thing he wanted was for a desperate alien attacking any of them.

"Of course, sir."

Connor hated waiting and was relieved when Xiang came running back with a large axe. "Kelp'll be back with another one for Bravo." He handed the axe to Simpson. Simpson immediately hacked into the hatch, close to where Connor hoped the lock would be.

The wood splintered, but Simpson had some difficulty hitting the lock. By the time he finally broke it, the sound of more hacking echoed in his ear. It seemed Kelp had found an axe for Bravo.

"There's a staircase leading down, I think," Simpson said as he set the axe aside.

Connor helped him open the hatch. He grabbed the torch from his vest pocket and shined it down. There was indeed a staircase, but it was difficult to see anything beyond the dirty floor at the bottom. They had to go in.

"I found a light switch, but it doesn't work," Simpson whispered as they all made their way down the stairs.

Connor shrugged. "Guess we'll stick to our torches, then. Right. I don't know what they kept here, but don't assume this place is empty."

"Yes, sir," the team replied in unison.

Even with the torches, they couldn't see more than a few feet in front of them, but Connor had a feeling they'd landed in a long corridor similar to the one upstairs. Lights flashed at the other end. Bravo had made it down as well.

"Meet you in the middle again, sir?" Abernathy asked.

"Yes."

Connor had checked three cells, all empty, when Briers from Bravo yelled, "Found one," through the commlink, so loud that Connor was tempted to rip the commlink out of his ear.

"Stay cautious," Abernathy said. "There might be more. What's its condition?"

"A female Snychol, it seems. Looks well fed but scared out of her wits. She's not stopped growling since we discovered her."

She had to be growling very quietly, because Connor hadn't heard it, not through the commlink and not through the corridor. He tried to remember what he knew about Snychols. Hadn't he read something about them that drew his attention? What was it? *Think, Smith, think.*

"Music," he suddenly remembered. "They like our music. If anyone has an MP3 player or mobile, turn it on, but not too loud. It'll calm her down."

He barely had time to turn around before Amato found something, too. When he reached her, she was bent over, heaving. "What is it?"

Amato shook her head, face pale. Connor entered the dark cell and nearly stumbled over the bloody mess in the middle. He gagged violently and turned back into the corridor. He was glad they'd got Noah out when they had. This was inhumane and cruel. To torture these poor aliens, regardless of whether they were dangerous or peaceful...

"What do you think it is, sir?" Amato asked, still looking pale.

"I have no idea. There's not enough left to identify, not by sight alone."

"The Snychol has indeed calmed down. I'm having two of my men take her up," Abernathy interrupted through the commlink.

"Anything else?" Connor asked.

"Nothing yet."

Connor hoped they would keep it that way. He turned to Amato. "Get Flanigan to help you bag it and take it up to the SUVs."

"Yes, sir," Amato said, and took off to find Flanigan.

While Amato and Flanigan bagged the dead alien, the rest worked their way along the corridor, checking every cell. He closed his eyes when Simpson called in a dead Noren. Now they knew where the missing one had gone. Connor didn't go in. He didn't want to see another dead alien.

The rest of the cells were blessedly empty.

"I'll be glad to get some air," Abernathy said, voicing Connor's thoughts.

They hadn't even reached the stairs when they were called from the far end. Connor pointed his torch and blinked.

O'Donnell and Quadeer appeared through the wall.

# 20

THE HOLOGRAPH-LIKE PROJECTION OF THE FAKE WALL WAS impressive, to say the least. Connor moved closer and put his hand through. He felt around and tried to locate the projector, but found nothing.

"There's nothing on the other end, either," Indian-born Quadeer said.

Connor nodded and stepped back. He had no doubt they were looking at one of the stolen alien artefacts. He turned to O'Donnell and Quadeer.

"Where does it lead?"

"To the main house. We'd been walking around for a while when Roderick and Young from Delta passed us, mentioning a cellar filled with dark, empty cells," Quadeer said.

"So, on the off chance, we went in and found a similar setup like this on that end," O'Donnell continued, his stocky posture a stark contrast to Quadeer's slight one. "Quadeer was knocking on the walls when he suddenly fell through it. Looked really funny with his feet sticking through it."

A tunnel to move the more dangerous aliens from one building to another without going outside or having to take them up those stairs. Clever. "Right." Connor turned around and faced both team leaders. "We'd best go up and report our findings to the lieutenants."

Abernathy and Simpson nodded and led the teams back to the stairs.

"Would be good to get our hands on that holographic stuff, wouldn't it?" Simpson asked as they made their way to the exit.

"Research will have a field day with it," Connor said. He'd love to study it himself.

They met up with the rest of the teams next to the paddock. He didn't even want to consider what the Westland Group had needed the paddock for. No lieutenants in sight.

"You look horrid. Where have you been mucking about?" Isa asked when she spotted them.

Connor looked down. His clothes were dusty and sooty, and that was going to be one hell of a dry-cleaning bill, even if Primrose paid for it. "The catacombs, a.k.a. the barn cellar, filled with cells."

"Is that where that creature came from?"

"The Snychol? Yes. Has she calmed down yet?"

Isa shrugged. "I only saw her pass, but I think Elliott is in charge of her now. So, she should be fine."

"Good. Where are the lieutenants?"

With a nod towards the main house, Isa said, "Inside with the Research team. We're to wait here for new orders."

"Guess I'll have to report when they get back," Connor said with a sigh. "So, how did your search go?"

"No paper trail, no nothing. One small creature in the whole building, but no aliens."

"Dog or cat?"

"A fox, actually—probably got in through an open window in the back of the building. No idea how it got onto the premises, though."

"So, they cleaned out pretty thoroughly, then?"

"It seems that way. Lieutenants want a more thorough search, though. They hope that the Westland bunch were so focussed on clearing out, they might have been lax with taking precautions and left us some fingerprints."

"Since they left the Snychol, I'd say they were definitely in a hurry to get away and might not have cleaned up properly."

"Good point. Anyway, that's why they're drilling the Research team. They were grumbling about dusting for prints taking up too much of their time, until Matthews told them they're not allowed to go exploring until that's done." Isa rolled her eyes. "They just want to get their hands on the technology."

Who didn't? "You saw the holographic walls, then?"

She frowned. "No. I was talking about the machine room we found in the house."

Machine room. That was where the controls for those holographic walls had to be. "So, what are all us agents doing here when the place needs to be dusted for prints?"

Isa pointed at the main house again. Both lieutenants were coming their way. "I think we're about to receive our new orders."

Now Connor wanted to grumble. He was not looking forward to dusting for fingerprints or going back into the catacombs, unless it was to take another look at those holographic walls again.

IT WAS HIS FIRST DAY BACK IN THE SHOP. HE WAS SORTING BOOKS, and Noah had never felt so uncomfortable in his own shop. The doorbell, at least, was familiar. It was all those other sounds, the less predictable ones, which made him jumpy as hell. People walking into the shelves, the door slamming closed, shuffling feet, rustling pages: they made him want to close up shop and hide in his bed. Not that he would.

He also had his protection detail to contend with—the ones who'd harassed him to let them into his shop to keep a better eye on him. He'd told them they could watch him in the shop with their "friggin' cameras". They were not coming into the shop unless there was an emergency. Noah didn't want them to disrupt his life any more than they already had.

Besides, there was no way he was going to let them come close to his books. It was not acceptable.

"Noah? Didn't we have a Willa Cather first edition somewhere?"

Noah looked up from the books he was sorting. "Yes, we do. We have a copy of *The Professor's House*." He grabbed his written registry. "It came in a month ago," he said as he browsed it. If only he could remember where he'd put it and why. It came back to him when he reached the correct entry. "It's in the vault."

"The vault? Are you sure?"

"Yes. Put it there for preservation. It's not exactly in mint condition."

"Oh. Is it too badly damaged? I think I have a buyer for it," Lily said as she came around the set of shelves blocking Noah's work space off from the front of the shop.

"I'd better go talk to them, then, and see whether they deem it worth the price," Noah said as he rose.

Lily waved her arm in the direction of the customer. "He's all yours."

The man was young, polite, well dressed, educated, and decidedly interested in the first edition, even in its current condition. The way he looked the book over told Noah he knew how to handle them, too. He didn't even blink when Noah named the price, he merely handed him a credit card with the name J.T. Carter on it.

Noah finished the sale and watched the man walk out of the shop. Not until he disappeared around the corner did Noah realise the man had not looked directly at him even once.

He shook his head and returned to his sorting until someone knocked into the shelves close by. He jumped, then jumped again when a hand touched his shoulder. He felt silly when he turned to see it was only Lily.

"You need a break. Go to bed, Noah. I'll lock up later."

He was about to shake his head, but thought the better of it. He did need a break. If he kept on going on like this, he would lose all desire for his books, and he wasn't going to let what had happened get to him like that. With a nod to Lily, he exited the shop through the back door.

His guard was waiting in the hall. "I'm going to bed," Noah told him, not waiting for an answer before climbing the stairs to his bedroom.

He didn't even bother undressing. He let himself slide onto his bed, toed his shoes off, and curled up in the middle. With his eyes closed, Noah focussed on his breathing—in and out—to help himself fall asleep, but his mind kept drifting off to the man who wouldn't look at him. With a sigh, he grabbed a couple of earplugs—a recent experiment in trying to keep all unwanted noise out—and tried the breathing exercise again.

If only it kept the nightmares at bay.

A LOUD PING AND THE SOUND OF THE LIFT DOORS OPENING ALERTED Connor that he had reached the floor where Francis had his office. Despite the maze of desks, giant computer towers, and other electronic equipment, it took him little time to find Francis, who was in the video room watching a music clip with a bunch of girls in bikinis.

Connor coughed to grab his attention.

Francis nearly slid off his chair when he turned to see who was there *and* tried to hit pause at the same time.

"It's just me, Francis."

"Oh, God. You scared me. If anyone had caught me..."

"Caught you doing what?" Connor looked at the screen. "Tsk, tsk, tsk, Francis, watching MTV on the boss's time? Blasphemy!"

"Oh, it's much worse. They don't care if I'm watching TV, but after the first time they caught me using Primrose's computers to make my own video, I got a warning."

"This is *your* work?"

Francis nodded. "My sister has this band, well, something like that, anyway. They asked me to make them a clip."

"Dare I ask which one your sister is?"

"The middle one."

"She's what, sixteen?"

"Eighteen in five months. They think they're the next best thing. Since most of the bands they like barely wear anything at all... they think they need to do the same."

Connor shook his head. The girl seemed pretty, but he wasn't sure they'd sell anything trying to copy other bands. "They should focus on getting into clubs to sing, instead."

Francis closed the window and unplugged his USB stick. "Anyway, enough of the family theatrics. What can I do for you today?"

"You left a note on my desk about the shoe print?"

"Oh, right. I did." Francis rose and led Connor to a room where pictures lay strewn all over a large table.

"So, what's the verdict?" Connor asked as he looked at the pictures.

Francis grabbed two photos and put them next to each other. "These are the photos of the different footprints," he said.

Connor looked at them. They seemed the same to him.

Francis grabbed two new photos, both enlarged with an area marked with a black marker. "Look at these. What do you see?"

Connor grabbed one of them and looked closely at the marked area. "It looks like there's a nick in it." He grabbed the other photo and looked from one to the other. "These are the same."

"Yes. I contacted the manufacturer to check out whether it's a fault in the mould. It's not. They also checked a number of shoes in their inventory, none of those show this nick, either. It's not a fabrication fault."

"So, they match?" Connor barely contained his delight, even if that still didn't answer the question of how the shoe print had ended up at Jason's shop.

"Yes, they match."

"That's good news. That's very good news. Thank you. So, did you have time to check the CCTV recordings out as well?"

"Not until after lunch."

Connor frowned. "You don't have them yet?"

"I do, but I'm checking it for glitches first. Don't want to spend hours watching it, only to find out any useful footage has been deleted." Francis pointed to a screen in the corner of the room. "Still forty minutes to go."

"Guess I'll come back after lunch, then. Or did you want to join us for lunch?"

Francis shook his head. "No, thank you. I'm meeting my sister."

"Ah, the clip."

"Yes," Francis said with a sigh. "My mother will probably kill me if she sees it."

"I bet your sister'll love it."

Francis snorted. "She'll be happy when it gets her

boyfriend drooling."

"WE FOUND THE LING SET," ISA SAID AS SHE DROPPED DOWN INTO the seat opposite Connor in the canteen. "What? No coffee for me?"

"I drank it," he said. "I didn't think you'd make it."

She looked at her watch. "Oh, I *am* rather late, aren't I? Do you have time to spare or do you need to go up?"

"I can stay for a bit." He shoved the tray towards her. He'd saved the sandwiches he had picked out for her.

She unwrapped one and took a bite.

"So, you found the Ling set," he prompted her.

"Yes." Isa's hand froze on the way to her mouth. She put the sandwich down long enough to say, "We found it at the Usherwood residence."

One of the Westland Group members. "Anything else?"

She shook her head, and Connor sighed in relief. No live aliens then—or dead ones. He shuddered as he remembered the poor dead creature they'd found at the farm. Even with the list of missing aliens, they had not been able to determine what species it had been.

"This was the first house where we actually found something. Most of the other houses are cleared out. We had to clear out both cellar and attic, but they were quite the collectors."

"So... Why wasn't the Usherwood residence cleared out?"

"I'd go with arrogance. Aubrey Usherwood is one of those slick-looking car salesmen. He probably didn't think we'd find his stash, but he didn't count on our scanner."

"He must have been furious."

"Close to exploding. We had to gag him to keep him from

screaming. Of course, once we got here, he pulled an Allen and didn't say another word."

Connor looked at his watch. "I'd better go back up. I'm waiting for a call from Francis."

"You should have asked him to join us."

"I did. He already had plans."

"Oh. A date?"

"Lunch with his sister," Connor corrected.

"I should find him a date. What do you think?"

"I think you should eat lunch and go back to the work you're actually good at."

Isa stuck her tongue out, but he ignored it, gave her a little salute, and got up.

"Hold on. I have the list of artefacts we found for you." She pulled some neatly folded papers out of her bag and handed them to him.

"Thanks. Enjoy your lunch."

She waved as she took a bite of her third sandwich.

On his way up, Connor read the list. Usherwood's collection mostly consisted of small pieces, judging from the pictures. The Ling set had to be the most impressive.

He'd never thought about it, but with all the artefacts they'd found through the years, including weaponry and not counting peculiar-looking aliens, they had never found anything even resembling a space ship. He wondered if they would ever stumble across one. If they did, he liked to think he'd be able to take Noah home in it. He knew Noah considered Earth home now, but he deserved to meet his kin at least once more, even if it was only to say goodbye.

A FOREST. IT HAD TO BE A FOREST. CONNOR WAS AT LEAST GRATEFUL it wasn't four-something in the morning this time. He snuggled deeper into his coat to fend off the chill, leaning against a tree as he tried to see through the veil of mist that hung around them. This deep in the forest, he wouldn't have thought it was summer.

He longed to be in Francis' office, getting the latest information. Not that there was any—that was part of the problem. Apparently, Francis' system had crashed during that first scan, and he'd been working most of the afternoon getting it up and running again.

Then this call had come in.

So, here Connor stood in a chilly, misty forest, trying to find a small group of unidentified creatures that were reportedly hanging around a farm to the east.

"What was it we're looking for again?" Xiang asked through the commlink.

"Large, thin, probably four-legged," Simpson replied from behind Connor. "No tail, but what looked like a second head. She couldn't say how many, only that they'd appeared and disappeared all day, and that she'd missed her midday nap because they wouldn't be quiet."

She had also said that they bleated, snorted, and growled, and made far too much noise running around and knocking things over. The description of the possible aliens had been vague, but the woman had been hysterical on the phone.

Connor shook his head as he slowly made his way through the trees, tranq ready and eyes focussed on every hint of movement. A sharp snap behind him made him freeze. That didn't sound like Simpson. He turned around as quietly as he could, finding Simpson turned towards the sound as well. The mist made it nearly impossible to see anything else.

He preferred seeing the creature before he bumped into it.

Another snap, louder, closer. Connor and Simpson

shuffled towards the sound until the mist thinned, and the outline of a large shadow appeared amongst the trees. It seemed four-legged, at least.

With luck, the creature was as hindered by the mist as they were, because if it saw through, they were toast.

"Let's try and box it in," Simpson said. "Don't tranq it until absolutely necessary. Not until we know what we're dealing with."

Connor nodded and kept his eyes on the shadow as he waited for Simpson to go around it. The creature never moved at all. Couldn't it hear or smell them? Or was it observing him, waiting for him to make the first move? It could wait a long time, because Connor was quite happy to let Simpson spook the thing.

Or five minutes. Which was how long it took for Simpson to get behind the creature. Five minutes for the creature to suddenly come alive and run bleating at Connor.

His heart skipped a beat, and his hand clenched around the tranq as it charged at him, but as he caught sight of the creature, all he could do was laugh. A goat, it was just a bloody goat.

Simpson kept asking him what was going on, but Connor couldn't get a word out. There was bleating and growling and snorting all around him, accompanied by startled yelps from the rest of the team.

"A cow? I'm chasing a cow?" Amato asked, while Flanigan yelled something about nearly being run over by a horse.

Simpson, in the meantime, had gone after the goat, still thinking he was chasing an alien creature. When he returned, he too was laughing.

"Seen it, then?" Connor said, in between gasps.

Simpson nodded and burst into another fit of laughter.

"As much fun as this was," Connor said once he had his breathing under control, "I think it's time to catch these animals and find out where they came from."

A cacophony of grumbling protests echoed through the commlink.

"You heard Smith. Catch them and bring them to the meeting point." Simpson's voice sounded giggly at best.

They caught a horse, two cows, two goats, and a sheep. Turned out they belonged to one of the caller's neighbours, whose stable door had been knocked off its hinges a few nights ago.

"I've not had time to repair it, so I put an old trough in front of the door to keep them from getting out," the farmer said in his defence.

There was nothing left but rubble of said trough. Together, the team made quick work of repairing the door while the farmer fed his poor beasts.

Connor had a hard time keeping his face blank, and the moment the team gathered in the SUV, they all burst into laughter again.

# 21

CONNOR FOUND NOAH IN HIS LIVING ROOM, FEET ON THE table and eyes closed. He stopped in the doorway to watch him, even though Noah could sense him. Noah looked better than he did last week. Rested. Handsome in his pink paisley shirt with contrasting red collar and cuffs. A sense of warmth came through the connection as Noah smiled and opened his eyes.

"I knew you were here before you rang the bell."

"Of course you did." It was distracting to feel Noah smile. If he felt that at a distance, he'd never get any work done.

"Sit down. Tea's already brewing."

Connor sat down next to Noah and leaned back. This was the first time he wasn't here as part of the protection detail, and he didn't know what to say. It would be lame to ask Noah about his books again.

Neither of them spoke. They merely sat in silence, leaning back into the dark blue sofa, mostly examining the ceiling. At least, Noah was when Connor glanced his way.

There was a tension between them that Connor didn't like. Noah no doubt sensed something going on with Connor and was waiting for him to speak. Yet Connor couldn't quite make himself say it.

He admired Noah's gait when Noah went to get his tea. There was an elegance to the way he moved. Pity the slacks didn't show off his arse very well. A flash of arousal coursed through Connor, and in the kitchen, Noah chuckled.

*That, he does sense.* Connor shook his head.

Noah set the tea in front of Connor with a wink and settled down next to him again.

Connor looked at the steaming mug. "Jason and I broke up."

Noah's head snapped towards him.

"It was…odd."

"Odd?"

"Yeah. As if something was off. I thought it was me, but then he said he met someone else."

"Oh."

Connor looked at Noah. "Just like I have."

Noah moved his hand on top of Connor's and gazed at the ceiling again. Connor moved closer to Noah and rested his head on Noah's shoulder. A sense of calm came over him, and he relaxed. Noah squeezed his hand, and for a while, Connor let Noah's emotions envelop him, knowing Noah sensed his as well.

The longer they sat there, the stronger the urge to kiss Noah grew. They turned their heads at the same time. Connor used his free hand to pull Noah close and pressed tiny butterfly kisses against Noah's neck. He took in Noah's scent, and it was like he'd come home. He belonged.

He brushed his lips against Noah's and ran his tongue across Noah's lower lip, asking permission. Noah shivered and claimed his mouth in a searing kiss.

Emotions rushed through the connection as they kissed, fast and intense, but good, so good. They slid down the sofa, and as they landed on the floor, Connor paused, aware Stembridge and Torgerson were on guard.

"Forget them," Noah whispered against his lips.

Connor closed his eyes and resumed the kiss. In for a penny...He rolled over Noah, narrowly avoiding the table, and pulled him on top. His cock, trapped between their bodies, came to life. Connor gasped and squirmed, pushing his hips up to increase contact.

Noah explored every inch of Connor's mouth as he pushed back. The hitch if his breath was like music to Connor's ears. He threaded both his hands in Noah's hair as they settled into a rhythm that got them both hot and bothered.

Connor wriggled his hands between them and undid Noah's trouser button and zip. Tugging them over his arse took some effort, and Connor couldn't shove them further than the knees.

Noah shuddered above him, sending a wave of lust through the connection that echoed through Connor's body. He panted against Noah's mouth as he hooked Noah's briefs gently over his cock, and slid them down as well. It was hard and warm and damp in his hand, and he gave it a quick squeeze.

How to get his own trousers out of the way was trickier. For one, Noah refused to stop kissing him—not that he wanted him too—and secondly, he'd *had* to wear tight jeans today. By the time he worked them down his thighs, they were both out of breath and trembling. And incredibly turned on.

Connor moved his hands back to Noah's hair and pushed his hips up as Noah pushed his down. There was no rhythm, no coordination. Yet, they matched. Whether through their connection, sensing each other's emotions, or a stroke of luck, Connor didn't care.

Their rutting became intense and almost too much. Connor gasped and moaned into Noah's mouth and just went with it. They were so fucking close. One more push would be enough to send them both over the edge.

Until Noah stretched his arms, lifting himself up and out of reach, and Connor was left fucking empty air.

"Bugger," Connor said. Out of breath as he was, it came out more as a groan.

Noah grinned, claiming his mouth again, dipping his tongue in and out in a cruel parody. Connor sensed Noah's mirth through the connection and tried to will him into action. Noah, once again, ignored him. He teased Connor with his tongue until Connor was fast on his way to losing his mind. When Noah finally lowered himself and pushed into Connor again, Connor came hard, sensing Noah's release as vividly and overwhelming as his own. Too overwhelming. Connor panted, fighting for breath as his vision blurred, until all he saw was the cloudy grey of Noah's eyes.

Someone pinched his cheek, and Connor jerked, gulping for air as he opened his eyes to find a blurry Noah looking down on him.

"Idiot," Noah whispered, a tremble in his voice betraying his concern. He shook with the effort of not crushing Connor into the floor.

Connor trailed his hands down Noah's chest. "That was..." he began, annoyed he couldn't produce more than a hoarse whisper.

"It was," Noah replied, and silenced him with a kiss.

AFTER A DREARY MORNING FILLED WITH ODDS AND ENDS, INCLUDING yesterday's report on the farm animal hunting, a long lunch with Isa was exactly what Connor needed. He half expected Francis to be there as well.

Though shy and a bit geeky, Francis seemed to fit right in with the two of them. Pity, Francis was still knee-deep in research.

Isa, of course, spent the first fifteen minutes laughing at him for having to chase farm animals, but Connor didn't mind too much. He'd get back at her at some point, that was how it worked. Next time it would be *her* team out on a dodgy call. Besides, as long as she was focussed on their stupid mission, she wouldn't have time to harass him about other things. Like Noah.

They had risen early so Connor could go home and change clothes. Noah had been more than happy to lend him some of his—they'd probably have fit him, too—but wearing Noah's clothes would have been like carrying a banner saying "I got me some".

Connor sensed warmth coursing through the connection. It was like being hugged from a distance. He didn't know if Noah was the whistling type, but he imagined him walking around his shop, whistling as he put books in their proper places.

Isa burst out laughing again, dragging Connor out of his thoughts. He glared at her, but she wasn't looking at him, she was looking at a couple of kids running along the lake. He rolled his eyes as one of the kids mooed. Hadn't she teased him enough, yet?

"Oh, come on. You have to admit it's funny."

He put his sandwich down. "It's always funnier afterwards. Even more so when it doesn't happen to me. Not to mention it was bloody chilly and misty in that forest. The foliage was so dense, it seemed like permanent twilight in there."

"What? Noah didn't warm you up enough, afterward?" she asked with a wink and a smile.

Connor suppressed the urge to groan, and took a bite. As

long as he had food in his mouth, he wouldn't be able to say anything.

Of course, food didn't deter Isa one bit. "Your thoroughly shagged look gave it away the moment you entered my office."

He didn't doubt it one bit. She, of all people, would have recognised that silly grin he hadn't been able to shake off all morning.

"Let's not forget that cute, besotted smile every time you think of him."

When *hadn't* he been thinking of Noah?

"So, spill!"

"A gentleman doesn't tell." Connor knew it was useless pretending she wouldn't drag it out of him, but he tried anyway.

She wiggled her eyebrows. "That good, huh?"

He grinned. "More than good." Even if they'd made out on the living room floor like horny teenagers.

"Anything you can tell me about those four hundred years of experience?"

Nearly choking on his sandwich, Connor thumped his chest as he coughed. He must be red as a lobster, as hot as he felt. "Warn a bloke next time."

"Why? It's so much more fun getting you all flustered." She stuck out her tongue. "At least this way I can tell whether you're hiding something. So, stop stalling and tell me what he's like."

Connor sipped his coffee while Isa stared at him expectantly. Finally, he shook his head and closed his eyes as he told Isa about their night together, from their first kiss—skipping through their horny rutting—to waking up with Noah and the intense feedback through the connection. Connor still shivered as he recalled the way Noah's hands had moved across his back, just shy of touching, wet kisses following in their wake.

With Noah, it had been about being in the moment, about knowing what the other wanted, yet still asking. Connor liked being asked.

Though sex with Jason had been great, Jason hadn't asked. He had called all the shots and assumed Connor would bottom. Connor was as much to blame for that, since he hadn't exactly told Jason what he wanted. Honestly, Connor hadn't even realised how much he'd missed that sense of equality until Noah.

"Ow." Connor rubbed his arm where Isa had slapped him, and glared at her while she looked anything but apologetic. "What was that for?"

"You were miles away." She looked him up and down. "If I didn't do something quickly, I'd have had to dump you into the lake."

It took Connor a bit of effort to figure out what she was saying. Unfortunately, it wasn't just his own arousal he had to fend off. He sensed Noah's as well. "Thanks," he said, willing his cock to go down and making a mental note not to do any remembering in public.

"You're welcome. Any chance of you stopping by mine, tonight? Or is he expecting you?"

"I'm on duty at his tonight."

"Ouch! Till what time?"

"I think O'Neill is taking over around midnight. Claiborne is doing the ten to six sleep over shift." Connor was staying the night, though.

"What about lunch at the Cleo tomorrow?"

The Cleo wasn't as cosy as Isa's place, but the booths would give them a lot more privacy than the park would. "Sounds good to me."

"Right. We'd best get back to the office. Both Charlie and Delta are out on raids, and I'm expecting them to call in..." She glanced at her watch. "In fifteen minutes."

They both rose, and Connor let Isa put her arm through his as they made their way back to the office.

"You look good, you know. You've been far too stressed lately. It's good to see you smile."

He felt good, too. He couldn't wait to get back to Noah's after work. Though he didn't regret signing on to Noah's protection detail, he knew the night would drag on until midnight. Being so close to Noah while working might not have been the best idea he'd had.

As they entered the Eastworth Building, Isa bumped into Francis, literally. Before Connor could ask him about the CCTV recordings, Francis asked Isa if he could talk to her, privately. As they walked away, Francis took something out of an envelope and showed it to Isa while he glanced at Connor, only to turn away again when he caught Connor looking at him.

That was odd.

Noah woke up when a warm, naked body snuggled into him. He had tried to stay up, but after falling asleep on the sofa twice, Connor had sent him to bed with a promise to wake him up after his shift. He moved his arm across Connor's waist. "Time is it?"

"Nearly one. O'Neill was late."

Noah slowly trailed his fingers up and down Connor's chest, smiling as a spark of anticipation coursed through the connection.

Connor yawned and shivered at the same time. "Sorry, it's been a long day," he whispered as he turned to face Noah, but the way he kissed betrayed no trace of tiredness.

Noah moaned into the kiss and moved his hand lower until he touched the soft curls surrounding Connor's cock. Connor pushed his body into Noah's hand.

"I have to get up in less than five hours," Connor said when he ended the kiss.

"We had best go to sleep then." Noah gave Connor's cock a friendly squeeze.

"I'll sleep at the office."

Noah doubted it. He gave Connor a quick kiss, raised himself up, and manoeuvred himself until they lay top to tail and he faced Connor's cock.

"You have great ideas." Connor shifted and moved closer.

Noah gasped when Connor blew air across the tip of his cock. Noah did the same to Connor and snorted as Connor's left leg slipped off his right one and he rolled onto his back. Connor moved back and planted his foot flat on the bed, creating a beautiful tension in his leg. Noah couldn't resist and ran his hand along the taut muscles.

Connor teased Noah's balls as he blew air past his cock again. Noah shivered and mirrored Connor.

They lost themselves in a flurry of tongues, lips, fingers, nails and puffs of air. With the echo of the same sensations coming through the connection, coupled with Connor's emotions, Noah soon forgot who was copying whom. It didn't take long until he sensed Connor getting close, and he sucked Connor in earnest, revelling in the needy sounds he uttered.

Connor didn't stop teasing, never giving him more than a lick or two. When Connor exploded, Noah was so dazed with lust, so close, he barely remembered to swallow. Connor gasped for breath, and Noah sensed an apology through the connection, but all he could think was, *Hurry up!*

The bed dipped, and Connor crawled next to him. He beamed at Noah. "Now that's my kind of goodnight kiss." He kissed his way across Noah's chest and trailed his fingers down to Noah's balls.

A lick here, a pinch there, a caress, a squeeze, and the sudden sensation of Connor's mouth closing around his cock. Noah came hard, hands pushed deep into the mattress and body taut with tension.

Connor rested his head on Noah's thigh, stroking Noah's legs, his stomach, his chest, until his muscles relaxed. He grabbed Connor's hands and pulled at him, or at least tried to. Connor was too heavy, or he was too tired. Not that it mattered, because Connor got the hint anyway and wriggled until he lay flush against Noah's side.

"Shower in the morning?" Connor asked. When Noah nodded tiredly, he brushed his lips against Noah's, and rested his head on Noah's shoulder. "You do know we're on the wrong side of the bed, right?"

Noah smiled as he put his hand on Connor's hip and closed his eyes. "Don't care." With Connor plastered against him, it was warm enough not to need the duvet.

# 22

CONNOR ENTERED ISA'S OFFICE AND FROZE AT THE SIGHT OF A concerned Isa and a downright nervous Francis standing in front of her desk. Instead of sinking down into one of her lounge chairs as he usually did, he leaned against the doorpost. "You had some information for me?"

Isa nodded and looked at Francis.

Francis cleared his throat. "I can't do anything with the CCTV recordings surrounding Powell Antique Acquisitions. I've tried every filter, every trick in the book, but they show nothing but white noise and blur. The police said they have no idea what's wrong with them, but that they've been like that for years. They've checked everything, even changed the cameras and the wiring a couple of times, but they just can't make them work again. They've given up. Nothing ever happens in that neighbourhood, anyway, they said."

"So, you've got nothing?" Connor couldn't believe that. There had to be more. Isa wouldn't have called him otherwise. Though, from the look on her face, he wasn't going to like it.

"Not from those cameras, no." She pushed a folder towards him.

He grabbed it and opened it. It was a surveillance report. On Jason. He turned it towards Isa. "What's this?"

"Just read it."

Connor narrowed his eyes but did as she told and read the complete file. Numbness sank into him with every page he read. He dropped into the nearest chair. "No. This can't be."

"I'm sorry, Connor. Everything fits. His height, the shoe print, the dates of his trips abroad."

It was all in front of him, but he couldn't believe it—didn't want to believe it. "But he was at my place the night of the break-in."

She sighed. "CCTV shows him arriving around eleven and leaving a little before six, and there were no glitches in the recordings. I admit, we're a bit stuck on how he pulled that one off. But, Connor, it doesn't negate the evidence. We found the shoes in a gym bag in the boot of his car. It's him."

She put her hand over his. "We checked all Jason's trips for the last two years. He's clever, I'll give you that. All the flights he booked coincide with A-Watch picking up artefacts. Turns out, it was never Jason who checked in." She handed Connor a picture of an athlete who could have easily been mistaken for Jason from a distance. "Meet the Jason Powell who runs the triathlons. We're still trying to track him down, but we don't have much to go on yet. We don't even know whether his name really is Jason Powell or whether it's an alias."

No. He refused to believe Jason could do this. Not the Jason he knew... Connor hung his head and closed his eyes. Did he really know Jason?

"That's not all. Francis here has been a busy bee."

Connor looked up just in time to see her nudge Francis, who was watching him warily. "Come on. Out with it," he said. "I'm not going to bite your head off for doing your work." What he really wanted to do was scream. They had to be wrong. They had to be.

"I...er..." Francis cleared his throat. "It took a lot of zigging and zagging and a lot of waiting, but I found our hacker. The hacker broke into our system from fifty-one Carlton Close."

Jason's antique shop. "It doesn't make sense. If he's so clever, why break in from his own shop?"

"He thought he was untouchable," Isa said. "And he was. Until he suffered a power outage early this morning. Unlike the farm, the antique shop doesn't have its own generators."

The farm? What did it have to do... Oh. "The antique shop is shielded?"

"Yes. At least, it's the only explanation we have for now. If the computer shop next door hadn't suffered a short that left the whole neighbourhood without power for two hours, we'd be none the wiser. It was dumb luck that Francis was working on tracking him at the same time."

Connor couldn't wrap his head around what this all meant. He browsed the file again, looking for something that showed they were wrong. "There's a mention of a woman in here, a redhead."

Isa showed him a photo of Jason and a redheaded woman standing next to him. Connor didn't like the cold expression in her eyes one bit. "Who is she?" Something about her seemed familiar somehow.

Isa pushed another file over to him, keeping her fingers on it and preventing him from grabbing it. Connor glared at her and she let go. Before he could open it, she spoke.

"Her name is Alicia Powell."

"He has a sister overseas."

"It's not his sister," Isa said. She shook her head when Connor opened his mouth. "She's his wife, has been for the past four years. Though she rarely goes by Powell. Her maiden name is McAllister. She authenticates antiques and used to work at auction houses in and around London."

"Married?" Connor stared at the redhead. His stomach turned. There was no denying the overwhelming evidence.

Anger welled up deep inside him, and he clenched his fists. "I was set up."

He threw the photos on the table and closed his eyes to regain some sense of balance. A calming warmth came through the connection, but it didn't soothe Connor the way Noah no doubt hoped it would. He wanted to pace, wanted to hit something, wanted to run. Instead, he grabbed the armrests of the chair so tight his knuckles turned white.

A hand on his arm made him look up. Isa sat in the chair next to him, watching him with sad eyes. "I'm sorry. If I hadn't set you up with him... He seemed so eager to meet you."

For a moment Connor just stared at her. Then he hung his head and sighed. "That's rubbish, Isa, and you know it." His voice sounded rough, and he cleared his throat. "This isn't your fault. He planned this. He played me...us." Met someone, his arse. He was bloody married. "I want to watch his interrogation."

"You can't, Connor. We haven't brought him in."

"Why not?"

"We need him. We don't have enough leads on where the Westland Group stashed all their possessions. We're hoping he'll lead us to them."

"He's under surveillance, right?"

"Actually, we put a bug in the shoes."

Connor narrowed his eyes. "You think he won't figure that out?"

"The bag is still in his car, and he hasn't ditched it, as far as we can tell."

"I don't like this."

"I know. I'm sorry."

Connor waved her apology away. Jason had played her as expertly as he had Connor. He looked at the photograph again. He felt like he should know the redhead. Noah! Noah had mentioned a redhead at the auction, the one who had cut his arm. Connor jumped up, only to find his path blocked by Isa.

"Where are you going?" she asked, crossing her arms.

She must think he was going to confront Jason. He couldn't deny he wanted to, but it wouldn't achieve anything, aside from venting his anger.

He showed her the photo. "I need to show this to Noah. If they are connected to the Westland Group, this could be the redhead who cut his arm at the auction."

Isa's eyes widened as she nodded and stepped aside. "Call me as soon as you know."

NOAH DIDN'T KNOW WHAT TO THINK WHEN CONNOR STRODE INTO the shop and motioned to follow him into the hall. Connor told Stembridge, lounging against the wall, to leave the two of them alone. He took something out of his trouser pocket, a folded piece of paper or a photo.

"You mentioned a redhead at the auction."

Noah shuddered and rubbed his arm.

Connor showed him half of the photo. Noah froze at the sight of her familiar red hair. The cold expression in her eyes shook him as much in the photo as it had at the auction. He swallowed against the lump in his throat.

"So, it *is* her?"

Connor no doubt sensed his reaction, but Connor's voice interrupting his thoughts helped Noah take some distance. It was over and done with, no matter how well his body remembered his wounds. "Have you caught her?"

Connor grimaced. "No. But we're keeping an eye on them."

*Them?* Noah had to be missing something. "Who is she?"

Connor folded the paper back so the photo was whole and stared at it, broadcasting the same anger Noah had sensed earlier. "She's his wife," he spat as he showed Noah the photo again.

Noah recognised the blond curls even before Connor had spoken. Jason. "His wife?" He didn't understand why Connor was so angry. They'd broken up, hadn't they?

Slowly, it dawned on Noah that Connor's anger wasn't all directed at Jason. He was angry at himself.

"He dated me to steal from Primrose." Connor hunched his shoulders. "He stole my ID, broke into the Eastworth building..." He swallowed. "They've been married for four years. She cut your arm, but he... We think he's the one who abducted you."

Noah studied the photo. He remembered her so clearly, but he only knew Jason from Connor's memories. "Why?" Somehow Noah couldn't imagine the curly blond as the man who had ordered his bouncers to cut him.

Connor snorted. It sounded lost. "I didn't see it coming. I should've seen it coming."

Noah wanted to hold Connor, but he wasn't sure Connor wanted him to.

"They found you because of me. He must have seen the file on you Isa gave me the day Primrose picked you up. I took it home, and he was there—"

"Stop." Noah sensed the truth in that, but ignored it. He wrapped his arms around Connor. "I was rescued because of you," he countered.

Connor's emotions were all over the place, but when he took a shuddering breath and leaned his head on Noah's shoulder, he seemed to relax. "I know it's not my fault. Or Isa's fault. He planned it. He played us. I know that. But I can't stop thinking I should have known, should have done something to prevent this."

Noah held Connor tight. "Why do you think you should have known?"

"He was too perfect. That's always a sign, isn't it?"

Noah was about to answer when there was a knock on the door.

"Come in."

Stembridge entered. "Agent Smith? Lieutenant Tallis has been trying to reach you. You're needed back at Primrose. ASAP!"

Isa and Agent Jimenez had gone off radar while trailing Boyd Penwell, a member of the Westland Group, and hadn't been heard from since. Connor tried not to think of what his team would find when they reached their SUV. It hadn't moved in over an hour, and Isa's last check-in had been five minutes before that.

His team consisted of Tallis and Diana Stembridge, who'd been pulled off Noah's protection detail because no one else was available on such short notice. Connor cursed the Westland Group for keeping their teams so occupied.

Back up was being arranged, off-duty agents were being called in, and, with luck, they wouldn't be far behind. For now, it was just the three of them, and that had to be enough.

"Their SUV should be around the corner." Connor didn't need to say it—Stembridge saw the GPS just fine—but he felt better for it, having something to do.

Stembridge was Isa's height, though not as wiry, with dark ringlets tucked behind her ear. She seemed very much at ease behind the wheel of the SUV, and not afraid to ignore speed limits, either.

They found Isa's SUV abandoned on a long stretch of road

in the middle of nowhere. Connor jumped out first. The doors stood wide open, and the vehicle had been emptied out. He cursed when he found the crushed commlinks and the keys on the street. "We'll never find them this way."

His mobile rang, once. He frowned and fished it out of his trouser pocket. Relief flooded him. "Isa sent me a text message."

"What does it say?" Tallis asked.

"Windmill train tower," he read out loud, trying to figure out what Isa meant. At least she was alive and had access to her phone. Connor hoped the same applied to Jimenez.

Stembridge grabbed the laptop from their SUV and put a map of the area on-screen. "She's giving us directions!"

"Not many windmills around here," Connor said, looking at the screen. "I know there's one there, but nowhere near a train crossing or station."

Stembridge put a dot on the map where she thought they'd find a windmill, and another one to indicate where they were now.

"Tower," he mumbled. "The only tower I remember is a water tower. Unless she meant castles."

"I think the water tower is our biggest chance," Tallis said. "If Agent Griffin had meant a castle, she would have said so."

Connor agreed. He studied the map and pointed at a spot to the south, close to the direction they had come from. He narrowed his eyes and traced a line back from the water tower to where they were now. "There *is* a train crossing there..." He zoomed in. "Right. There's a narrow path leading from where we'll find the windmill to the street leading to the train crossing and the tower."

"I suggest we take this one, it'll get us there quicker," Stembridge said, pointing to a parallel road.

"Right. Back in the car," Tallis said as she closed the doors of the abandoned SUV and locked it.

They'd barely turned onto the road leading to the train crossing when Connor's phone rang again. "Train church stop white van," he read aloud, while Tallis checked the map.

Stembridge took them past the train crossing in no time, and they already saw the tower in the distance. There were several churches, but not a train crossing in sight unless they followed the road they were on and veered back towards the tracks they'd already crossed.

"She didn't type crossing, though," Connor said as Stembridge and Tallis argued over where to go next. He pointed out a set of tracks that they'd come close to once or twice, but wouldn't cross. "This road leads directly to Marrow and Marrow Church."

With no alternative, Stembridge turned onto the road Connor pointed out. His tried to still his trembling hands when they finally reached Marrow Church. It was a large, decorative medieval church, smack in the middle of the town, surrounded by houses that didn't look much younger than the church. A white van and a large black BMW were parked near it, blocking the narrow street.

"Not very secluded," Stembridge said.

Tallis scoffed. "Who'd suspect alien artefacts in a church?"

"Or underneath it." Connor pointed at the windows close to the ground.

"We'd better park out of sight." Tallis activated her commlink and asked after their back up.

Stembridge found a parking space out of sight around the corner.

"The closest team is at least half an hour away," Tallis said as she rang off. "I prefer to wait, seeing as Agent Griffin is still alive. We'll need to do some recon, find the entrances, scan the building for alien artefacts." It was clear from the tone of her voice that Tallis didn't think the scan would turn up anything.

Crawled into the back of the SUV, Connor raided the weapons cache for tranqs. The three of them got out of the car and circled the church separately, marking the entrances and listening for any noises coming from the inside. Not much chance of that with those thick walls. With luck, Stembridge would pick something up with the scanner.

Connor found a small window leading into the cellar that seemed fairly easy to open. He crouched down. It was latched on the inside, but he wriggled his hand into the gap and released it. After pulling the window open, he stuck his head inside, and listened.

Faint footsteps, but no chatter. A nasty stench, though.

Connor stared down into the chute and realised he'd just broken into a medieval toilet.

# 23

"Fifteen minutes before back up arrives," Tallis said after contacting Primrose again. "I told them we're going in. They'll let us know when they arrive. Turn your commlinks on."

The scanner hadn't picked up anything inside the church, which they'd expected, but it had found traces outside. Minute traces, but traces nevertheless. Enough to stop pussyfooting around, as Tallis called it, and take action. They had to get their people out of there.

Connor led them to the window. He stuck his head inside and listened. It seemed quiet. He ignored the stench as he crawled through first, and while the others climbed in, carefully opened the door to peek out into a long, empty corridor. Still no footsteps, but soft chatter came from his left.

They slipped into the corridor and turned left, towards the sounds. They tried a couple of the doors they encountered, all to rooms being used as storage and causing the scanner to light up like a Christmas tree.

Suddenly, Tallis hushed them as footsteps approached. They ducked into the nearest room and pressed themselves against the wall behind the door, tranqs ready in case someone opened it.

There were at least two suspects, talking in low voices as they passed without pausing.

Soon the sound of their footsteps faded, and the agents eased out of their hiding place, proceeding along the corridor without checking the rest of the rooms. Connor kept an ear out for the suspects.

They reached the end of the corridor, which veered off to the left. Tallis tried the door to their right. "More storage. If anything happens, we'll hide in here."

Connor nodded, inching towards the corridor on the left, which led to a large room filled with bookshelves stacked with books. Old, dusty books, some of which looked like they hadn't been touched in years. Connor couldn't help but think Noah would love browsing those books. He was tempted to take a photo.

This wasn't the best room to be caught in. Their only advantage was that it was badly lit—to preserve the books, maybe.

They crept along the bookshelves, trying to stick to the shadows as much as possible, an ear open to all interruptions, but it stayed quiet.

"Where did they go?" Connor asked, fearing they had walked straight into a trap. "They couldn't have been the only ones here, could they?" Were they in the wrong church? No. They'd found traces of alien material. Isa and Jimenez had to be here. But where?

Tallis shook her head. "I don't know. It's odd we haven't run into more of them."

She took the lead as they entered another corridor, darker than the first, the only light coming from narrow windows in the outside wall. They stuck to the shadows again, crouching when they came close to the outside wall.

Three doors, two on the left, one at the end of the corridor. The first one was a small kitchen with reasonably modern appliances that looked used. The second turned out to be a sparsely furnished bedroom. The book on the night table and the shirt hanging next to the wardrobe made it clear someone had slept here recently.

The sound of footsteps echoed through the corridor as they reached the door at the end, making it hard to pinpoint where they were coming from. Tallis motioned Connor and Stembridge to stay in the shadows as she pressed herself against the wall and eased the door ahead open for a peek.

She held up two fingers, but indicated she wasn't sure. Connor had no doubt there would be more, including the ones who had passed them earlier.

Tallis crouched and crawled through the opening as the suspects behind them closed the distance between them. Stembridge went next, and Connor followed closely behind her. He joined them behind a large, solid pew out of sight of the door.

Tallis pointed to the other side of the room just as someone across the room called out, "Hurry up, people. Stop wasting time!"

Connor jerked, and he crouched even lower, tranq ready. He glanced at Tallis, who peeked around the pew. She shook her head when she caught his eye, and waved a hand in front of her eyes. No clear view. Got it.

He gestured he'd try, but the door they'd crawled through slammed open and several suspects entered the room. He waited for them to pass, and took a quick look. Two blokes, he signalled as he leaned forward to get a better view. He couldn't see the front of the room clearly, either, but there were at least four more. All blokes. That made six, maybe more.

The two new arrivals joined the conversation, but, aside from the occasional curse, Connor couldn't make out much of what was said. Neither could Stembridge and Tallis, judging from their expressions. There was nothing to do but wait for the backup.

A pained groan from the other side of their pew startled them. Connor lost his balance and fell back. His heart pounded in his throat as he righted himself.

With one eye on the mob across the room, he glanced past the pew. He couldn't believe their luck. It was Isa! And Jimenez lay on the floor in front of her. Connor couldn't see Jimenez's face, but he seemed out cold. With the way Isa twitched, she should be coming to any moment. Neither wore a vest or jacket, and their hands and feet were bound with rope. He crawled back behind the pew when Isa groaned again, loud enough to alert the blokes across the room.

"Sounds like she's waking up, boss," a deep voice boomed through the room.

The three of them ducked as low as possible as the suspects approached Isa.

"Is she tied up good?"

"Yes, boss. Knots are tight as possible, she can't move much."

"What about him?"

"Still out. Kev hit him pretty hard."

A concussion for Jimenez, at the very least.

"Right, keep an eye on them. Come get me when she's awake."

That was good news. One bloke they could deal with.

"Gabe, did you call the mistress and tell her we lost our tail?"

"Lost, boss?" The one closest to them asked. Connor didn't think he was the brightest of the bunch.

"You wanna explain to her we're holding Primrose personnel?"

"No, boss." He actually sounded scared.

Connor wouldn't be surprised if the mistress was Alicia

Powell, Jason's redhead.

"Then stop wasting my time, you eejit. Just keep an eye on them and get me when she wakes."

"Yes, boss."

"The rest of you, start packing!"

SLOWLY, THE CHATTER IN THE DISTANCE FADED, AND EEJIT SEEMED to be the only one left.

Tallis exchanged glances with Stembridge, pointed at her tranq and then at Eejit. Stembridge nodded and crawled around the pew. A gasp, the beginning of a curse, and silence. Tallis and Connor glanced over the pew where Stembridge had cushioned Eejit's fall. She dragged him behind the pew and cuffed his hands.

With a nod to Tallis, Connor checked on Isa. She had a large bruise on the right side of her face, but no other visible wounds. Connor put his fingers to her neck and checked her pulse when she opened her eyes.

"Connor?"

He cringed. Too loud. He put a finger to his lips and pointed to the front. Those blokes could return any time.

"You got my message, then?" she mouthed.

He nodded.

Isa threw him a weak smile, raised her bound hands and pointed at Jimenez.

Connor glanced down at Jimenez and winced at the darkening bruise covering his olive temple. They'd hit him harder than Isa. His eyes were closed and his mouth hung open.

"Unconscious," he mouthed as he fished is pocket knife from his trouser pocket.

He helped her sit up and cut the ropes around her wrists and ankles. She stood, pale and wobbly, holding on to Connor's hand and the back of the pew. She spotted Stembridge and Tallis and blinked.

She glanced at the front of the room. No one was there.

"Where are the rest?" she whispered. "Did you catch those Westland guys?"

Connor shook his head.

"Backup is five minutes out," Tallis interrupted them, her voice low. "We need to move."

"We need to secure their stash. If they manage to—"

"Five minutes, Agent Griffin. We'll have plenty of agents then. Our first priority is getting you and Jimenez out safe."

Leaning heavily on the pew, Isa opened her mouth and shut it again. She nodded, but seemed none too happy. Connor understood, even if he didn't think those Westland guys, as Isa had called them, would be able to get all their wares out in five minutes.

Stembridge picked up Jimenez in a fireman's carry. "We could head for the library. It's close, has enough shadow. They might not expect us to hide there."

Connor shook his head. "I don't think we have enough time to reach it. Not with him. We should try the bedroom."

Tallis seemed to consider that. "It might be one of the first places they would look."

"All the other rooms are too far away. Besides, the bedroom door can be locked."

"Bedroom it is. Let's hope they're busy packing for a little while longer."

Stembridge, carrying Jimenez, went first. Connor moved to follow her, supporting Isa, but Tallis stopped him when Stembridge stumbled. She sprinted around them and grabbed the hem of Stembridge's vest to keep her upright. She glanced over her shoulder at Connor, who waved her on.

"We're right behind you," he told her.

They'd almost made it through the door when a voice echoed behind them.

"Who the fuck're you? Boss! There's more of them."

Connor barely had time to push Isa into the corridor. The suspect took a shot at them, and bits of stone from the wall landed on him.

Sinking to his knees, he took a deep breath. He could do this. He aimed his tranq, shot at the suspect, and dived into the corridor.

More voices joined the shooter as Connor rolled to a stand. He pushed the heavy wooden door shut and looked for a latch or something, but the door couldn't be locked. Bugger.

Connor sank to the floor with his back against the door, planting his heels into the ridges of uneven stone floor to give himself purchase. The door shuddered as several bullets hit it.

"What happened?" Tallis asked through the commlink. "Where are you?"

"One of them came back," Connor replied. "We need something to block the door."

Someone rammed into the door, trying to force it open. Connor braced himself. He couldn't hold them off for long. Isa hoisted herself up on her feet and shuffled over to him, putting her hands against the door to help him keep it shut. She looked pale, but when Connor told her to sit down, she ignored him.

Stembridge came running with something looking like a broom in her hand. She tried to clamp it between the door handle and the floor, but it kept sliding away. She threw the broom away and joined Connor on the floor.

The three of them barely held it when the suspects rammed against it again. The shocks reverberated through Connor's back.

"Where is that bloody back up?" he yelled at the same time

as the sound of running echoed through the corridor, approaching fast.

"They're coming, Connor. Hold on," Tallis replied.

Connor cursed as the door connected with his back again. Despite their best effort, it cracked open, barely an inch, but they had a hard time closing it again, no matter how hard they pushed.

One inch became two as a handful of agents came running towards them.

"Need some help, Smith?"

He had never been so happy to see Simpson.

Connor and Stembridge pushed hard against the door when one of the agents gently pulled Isa away.

Time froze as the door opened another inch. A shot echoed through the corridor. Connor's ears rang, and his heart broke as Isa crumpled to the floor as if in slow motion. He launched himself forward and caught her in his arms. One of his hands came away bloody.

"No!" he screamed as he cradled her against his chest.

Agents stepped around them, tranqs aimed at the door. Gunfire and shouts filled the corridor, but all Connor saw was Isa's pale face, and the blood seeping through her white shirt.

This couldn't be happening. *Keep your head,* Connor admonished himself, *she needs you.* He rucked up her reddening shirt, not bothering to undo the buttons. The entry wound at the bottom edge of her bra was too close to the heart. Far too close. Connor struggled to get out of his vest and jacket. They only carried small sterile gauze pads and adhesive tape in their vests, which were useless for stopping a bleeding like this. He ripped his shirt off, sending buttons flying, and pressed it to the wound. Isa moaned in pain.

"I'm sorry," Connor whispered.

"It's not that bad," Isa whispered back, sounding out of breath. "It doesn't hurt much."

Someone knelt next to them. Elliott, carrying a first aid kit. Connor giggled; a terrible, desperate sound he was unable to stop. He didn't think it was going to help.

"Connor?"

He flinched. Isa's face was so pale.

"Tell Mum not to worry, okay?"

Connor couldn't speak. He held her hand as Elliott cut away her shirt and ignored the blood soaking through his own. It was too close.

"Connor?"

"Yes," he whispered. "I'll tell your mum. You're going to be all right."

Isa smiled at him, and Connor tried to smile back as she closed her eyes.

Noah locked the door and sagged against the counter. It hadn't been this busy in weeks, and he was knackered.

"Want me to finish cataloguing these books, Noah?"

He shook his head. "Go home, Lily. I'll sort this out in the morning."

"If you're sure."

"Of course I am."

Lily put on her bright red coat and gave Noah a quick hug. "Have a good night, Noah. See you tomorrow."

"Thank you. Enjoy your evening."

She walked through the back of the shop into the hall and chatted with Agent Nicol, a young, muscular man with spiky russet hair. They went outside together. Noah shook his head. Of course Lily would strike up a friendship with his keepers. She was too friendly for her own good, sometimes.

Noah made a final round, straightening books that had

been browsed, and checking if all the display cases were locked. Returning to the counter, he turned off the computer. It was an old, sturdy thing, but it did the job Noah had bought it for.

As he dimmed the light in the shop, a sudden rush of panic and sorrow shot through the connection. Noah grabbed for the counter to keep steady and took deep breaths. An image of Isa lying on the floor, blood soaking her shirt filled his mind, followed by more despair and pain. A pain so deep, Noah's stomach turned. All Noah could do was let Connor's emotions flow through him, be an outlet for his grief. No soothing Noah sent his way would lessen Connor's pain of knowing Isa wasn't going to make it.

Noah closed his eyes. His chest ached for Connor for losing his best friend. Noah would have liked to have become more acquainted with the vibrant young woman who played such an important role in Connor's life. She deserved more.

He entered the hall, surprised to see it empty. Agent Nicol was probably still talking to Lily outside, though he couldn't see them through the glass. Tempted as he was, Noah didn't go outside to ask the agent for news about Connor. Instead he climbed the stairs and went into the kitchen, where he made sandwiches on auto pilot. He ate them much the same way.

Connor's emotions didn't let up. They echoed through his mind, still so full of sorrow. It was draining.

He dumped the dishes into the sink, leaving them for the morning, and took the stairs to his bedroom. Yet, once he lay in bed, he found no relaxation. He grabbed a book from his night stand and read. Maybe that would settle him.

He'd not even read five pages when a sound between a popping balloon and bad fireworks echoed through the hall. He put the book away.

"Agent Nicol?"

No reaction.

He was about to call out again when the bottom set of stairs creaked. It was barely audible, but in a house as quiet as this one, every sound counted. It couldn't be Nicol. For one, none of the agents ascended his stairs this quietly. Secondly, none of them pretended not to hear him, either. If anything, they were too attentive at times.

Whoever was coming up the stairs didn't want Noah to know. And Noah had just given away his position by calling out.

Where *was* Agent Nicol? Why hadn't he answered? Had the intruder taken him out? Oh, no. Lily! What if she had still been with him?

First things first. He got out of bed and looked around. He had nothing to defend himself with, aside from some heavy tomes.

A loud creak broke the near silence. Noah's heart skipped a beat. The intruder had reached the living room floor. Noah needed to hide, and he needed to do it now.

Under the bed was out of the question—too low, and the intruder would look there first—and his wardrobe was too narrow for him to fit into. There was only one spot where they might not look, and he might fit with a bit of wriggling.

He grabbed his mobile and, keeping an eye on the stairs, shuffled quietly into his bathroom. He closed the door. He didn't lock it, though he wanted to. It would be too obvious, a clear sign he was in here.

It took little effort to take the panel off the side of the bath, and it made less noise than he expected. He crawled into the maintenance space underneath the bathtub and closed the panel.

A floor below, the intruder was rummaging in the kitchen, dropping things to the floor. Cutlery. Or his cookbooks.

Heart pounding in his throat, Noah opened his mobile. He

pressed the button for Connor's number, but stopped the call before it started dialling. Calling Connor meant talking, and talking meant the intruder could hear him. A text message would have to do. Noah kept it short and hoped Connor would receive the message in time.

It would be grand if the intruder gave up and assumed Noah wasn't home, but he doubted it would be that simple. He tried to find the most comfortable position, and waited.

# 24

CONNOR SLUMPED AGAINST THE DOOR OF THE MEDICAL ROOM Isa had been put in, the flat-line sound ringing in his ears. This couldn't be happening.

"Come on, Connor, you need to clean up."

Connor blinked. Francis stood next to him. He shook his head but still let Francis drag him away. "I..." He couldn't say it.

"I know." Francis said, dragging him into the nearest shower cubicle.

Francis helped him undress, did all the work, really, because Connor couldn't even take off his own jacket. He vaguely remembered Simpson putting it on him in the SUV on their way here.

Connor stared at his hands, which were still bright red with blood. Isa's blood. His eyes stung, but blinking only resulted in blurring his vision. It made all the red seem that much more daunting. He lowered his hands so he didn't have to look at them anymore.

"Lift your foot," Francis' voice came from somewhere below.

He complied, and Francis took his shoe, trousers, and pants off.

"Other foot."

Connor frowned and stood there, not moving. Francis sighed and tapped against his right leg. He lifted it up.

When Francis finally pushed him into the cubicle, Connor let the warm water soak him, arms held tightly to his sides, and let the tears blurring his eyes dribble down his cheeks as he closed them. The touch of something coarse made him jump, but Francis' soft voice stopped him from backing away.

"I'm only going to wash the blood off, that's all."

Connor nodded, or at least, he thought he did.

The coarse material of the towel felt slightly scratchy on his skin, but he tried to block it out, tried to block everything out, everything but the water.

Water was healing, wasn't it? That's what his mother had always said when she'd prepared a bath for him when he was little. He still remembered the oils she'd put in—could still smell them. Peppermint was her favourite, but Connor had always preferred her more smoky fragrances, like cypress, and she'd gladly indulged him.

The memory of his mother faded as a citrusy scent entered his nose He gagged. Standard Primrose cleaning product. He hated it. He'd never minded citrus much before, but now it made him want to hurl, made him want to throw things. Now, every time he smelled citrus, it would make him remember Isa lying dead in the medical room.

Funny, intelligent, free-spirited Isa. His colleague, his confidante, and his best, best friend. She gave so much and asked so little.

The warm water disappeared, and Connor was left shivering until a large towel was wrapped around him.

"Can you dry yourself?" Francis asked.

Connor frowned and moved the towel to his hair. Why wouldn't he be able to dry himself? By the time he was finished, he was losing the haze he'd been moving around in and became more aware. He wasn't sure it was a good thing, since all he could think of was Isa, lying on the floor, asking him to tell her mother she was all right as she was dying.

"Stop thinking."

He couldn't. He'd lost his best friend. He couldn't not think of her. "I need to call her mother."

"Lieutenant Matthews is taking care of that."

Connor wondered what her cover story would be. Shot by a thief, probably. It was part of their job, writing cover stories, his and Isa's. They tried to make the victims come out as heroic as possible. These families had no idea what their children, parents, or siblings were up to during work hours. Being told they died in action was shock enough.

Francis handed him clothes he must have retrieved from Connor's office. Connor dressed slowly.

"Lieutenant Tallis arranged for a taxi," Francis said, holding up Connor's trousers. "She wants me to take you home."

Connor shook his head. "No, not yet, I need to see Isa." He needed to see her one last time, now that the fog in his head had faded.

"Only if you promise me you'll let me take you home after."

The promise was easily made. Connor finished dressing himself and followed Francis to Isa's room.

In the dimmed light, she looked so peaceful. As if she had slipped away in her sleep. Connor put his hand over hers, whispering an apology and a wish—something from an old poem his mother had taught him a long time ago. Isa deserved better than this.

With one last glance, Connor exited the room and closed the door behind him. "Let's go."

They were barely out of the building when Connor's phone buzzed. He tried ignoring it, but it was as if the sound awoke something within him. He became aware of emotions that were not his own. Fear. And it was coming through the connection. He fished the mobile out of his trouser pocket.

"It's from Noah," he said as he opened the message. For a moment he couldn't breathe. He read the message again. "Noah's in danger."

When the taxi came around the corner, Connor sprinted towards it and jumped in. He gave the cabbie Noah's address and told him to hurry, ignoring Francis running along, calling for the cabbie to stop.

"Keep driving," Connor said. He had no time to waste, and Francis wasn't a field agent. It would be dangerous for him to tag along.

THE TRIP TOOK FAR TOO LONG. CONNOR PUSHED THE CABBIE TO GO faster, to overtake the car in front of him, to step on it, afraid to be too late. Noah's message hadn't given him much to go on. He was lucky the cabbie hadn't dumped him somewhere along the way.

He apologised for being rude when they reached Noah's, shoved some random notes and coins at the cabbie, and ran up to Noah's flat.

From the outside, nothing seemed wrong. The lights were on and the front door was locked. Connor grabbed his keys and opened it. He pushed against it, but something was in the way and wouldn't give. He pushed again, harder this time, and hoped it wasn't Noah.

It wasn't. It was Agent Nicol, often called Beacon because of the way his red hair lit up in the light. Connor knelt next to him and checked his pulse. He sighed in relief when he felt one, faint, but regular. A quick search revealed the reason for his unconsciousness: a small dart in the left shoulder. Drugged. Nicol's commlink and phone lay cracked on the floor.

Connor dragged Nicol into a corner next to the stairs. Not exactly hidden, but not in plain sight, at least. He took his jacket off, and cushioned Nicol's head with it.

"You'll be all right," he whispered as he grabbed Nicol's tranq and took the safety off.

Keeping an eye on the stairs, Connor reached out through the connection in an attempt to locate Noah. *Tell me where you are.* It was worth a try, right?

A chill came through the connection, but no answer. Where in Noah's flat would it be cold? An image entered his mind. Noah's bath.

*Where's the intruder?* If they weren't close to finding Noah, Connor had more time to find him. Connor received confusion from Noah, sort of a mental head shake. Noah didn't know.

He'd have to start from the bottom up.

He toed his shoes off and made his way up, one step at a time, skipping the ones he knew creaked. No footsteps, no chatter coming from any of the rooms. If anything, it was too quiet.

At the top of the stairs, Connor ducked into the kitchen. Empty. He tiptoed back into the hall, pressing himself against the wall, and inched his way through the living room—empty—the library—empty—and the cloak room. No surprise there, it was empty. Where was the intruder?

As Connor grabbed his mobile to call for back up, something fell upstairs. *The bedrooms.* Connor climbed the stairs, willing the intruder to not be in the hall.

He was only halfway up when a loud crash echoed through the house, and Connor lost all caution. He sped up the stairs, forgetting the creaking top step, and raced into the first bedroom. No one. From behind a wardrobe, Connor looked into the hall, but there was no movement. He tried to pick up sounds, anything to tell him where he should be looking, but it had gone quiet again.

One bedroom to the right, a bedroom and bathroom to the left. Connor didn't know where to go next until he sensed Noah's heart racing. The intruder was getting close.

"I'm coming," he whispered as he sprinted towards the left bedroom—Noah's bedroom, closest to the bathroom—and ducked inside. Next to the bed stood a small, wiry bloke dressed in black, gun pointed at Connor as if he'd been waiting for him.

Connor stumbled backwards as a sudden spike of pain erupted in his chest, followed by another. Fighting the pain, he squeezed the trigger, but he was already falling. He banged against the doorpost and let go of his tranq to grab hold of it, trying to keep himself upright. He pushed one hand against his chest in an attempt to stop the pain, but when he tried to breathe, he ended up coughing, which only caused more pain.

Connor's knees buckled from under him and the room went dark.

"Noah," he screamed, as the wiry bloke brushed passed him, but all that came out was a hoarse whisper.

Noah's anguish followed him into the darkness.

When Connor's questions came through the connection, Noah had no idea how long it had been since he'd sent the text message. It had gone eerily quiet after the ruckus in the kitchen, and he kept waiting for that tell-tale creak from the top step of the stairs.

His mobile slid to the tiled floor with a soft clunk. He held his breath, but there was no sign the intruder had heard it.

There was a crash that Noah couldn't place. Not the kitchen, but somewhere downstairs. His leg started to cramp. He managed to push his foot out, having little room to play with, but it did nothing to alleviate the cramp. With luck, Connor would find him soon.

He doubted he could stay in this strained position long. He would, he had no choice, but he didn't think he'd be able to crawl out by himself if he had to stay here much longer.

Another crash, and this time, Noah knew exactly where. His bedroom, the room next to the bathroom.

Then the top step creaked. His body tensed in reaction. He wanted it to be Connor, though he feared it was a second intruder.

"I'm coming," Connor's voice echoed through his head. He must have sensed Noah's tension.

Resting his head on his arms, Noah waited, paying attention to the noise coming from his room.

He sensed the shot before he heard it. He gasped in pain as his chest burnt, and his mind was a mess of impressions and emotions that made it hard to think. It took a while to grasp it wasn't him who was shot, but Connor.

*No!* Noah bit his lip to keep from crying out. Connor was in so much pain. Balling his fists, Noah screamed for Connor through the connection, as the connection faded. He pressed his cheek against the cold floor and reached out to Connor, seizing that tiny, fading thread between them and desperately willing him to hold on. The thread flared to life at his touch, tugging at him. Energy flowed through the connection, from him into Connor. After the first shock, Noah didn't question it, didn't try to direct it—he just let it happen.

It wasn't enough. He was running out of energy, and it wasn't enough. Connor wouldn't make it.

No! He couldn't lose Connor.

As the connection faded again, and Connor's last breath whispered away, Noah reached for the only source of energy he had left.

Even if Noah could never go home again, his storage had been his connection to his past, his kin, had been his duty, his life, and his reason for being. But what did he have left if he let Connor die?

It took his remaining energy to dissolve his storage and push the freed burst of pure energy through the connection. It wouldn't be enough to heal Connor completely, but it would at least repair the worst of the internal damage. It would give Connor a chance to pull through.

Sensing Connor twitch, sensing him take that first breath, Noah's heart soared. He had succeeded.

Someone called his name, but he couldn't move, couldn't even lift a finger, and when he tried to call out, his voice refused to work.

He had nothing left, but knowing Connor would live made it worth it.

EMPTY. DIFFERENT. NOAH COULDN'T DESCRIBE IT, BUT HE'D changed. His body had changed. He'd lost his storage—sacrificed it. Even though he had given up on going home, losing the one thing that connected him to his kin hurt. It left him...empty.

The odd thing was that he hadn't lost the information. He remembered all of it and could access it as if his storage were still working. How could the information still be there when he'd destroyed his storage?

Noah stared at the glass of water and plate of sandwiches

in front of him. Food and drink to replenish his energy. Doctor Quiggins had fussed over him when he'd been brought in, certain he'd been wounded, too. Apparently, he'd looked pretty bad when they'd finally got him out from under his bathtub.

Severe exhaustion had been her final diagnosis, and once again Noah had been set up with a diet of food and water... and rest, plenty of rest. Again. Still, seeing as he could barely stay awake longer than an hour at a time the past two days, he had to admit he needed it.

A weak flutter of unease coursed through the connection, Noah answered it with calmness and warmth. The first time he'd woken at Primrose, he hadn't sensed Connor at all. He'd been convinced he'd destroyed the connection along with his storage. He'd been wrong. The connection had survived. Noah sensed it growing stronger every hour, despite Connor still being unconscious.

"Mr. Jones?"

Noah faced Doctor Quiggins. "Blood pressure again?"

"Exactly. Besides, now that you've gained some strength and you've been awake for a couple of hours, I'd like to run some tests."

He'd half expected to be interviewed already. He had so much to tell. He'd tried talking to Doctor Quiggins about healing Connor a few times, because she kept muttering about missing something and not understanding why Connor was still unconscious. Yet, she was always preoccupied when she visited him and didn't seem to hear what Noah had to say.

It was still hard to believe his healing had worked. Doctor Quiggins hadn't been very forthcoming when he'd asked, but he'd picked that up from chatter in the hall outside his room. Though she'd had to operate to remove the bullets, Doctor Quiggins had found no internal injuries, only healing tissue surrounding the wounds and the bullets, including scar tissue on Connor's right lung.

Bullets. Not one, but two bullets had been retrieved. All Noah remembered was Connor being shot, sensing him dying through the connection. It had never occurred to him that Connor might have been shot more than once.

While Doctor Quiggins worried about Connor still being unconscious, Noah saw no reason to fret. Not with the connection growing and Connor gaining strength. He needed rest, like Noah had. He'd wake up when he was ready for it.

"Mr. Jones? Did you understand the question?"

What question? Oh, right, tests. "Yes. Go ahead." If that answered the questions they weren't asking, then fine, they could do their tests.

"Good," Doctor Quiggins said as she lowered his bed.

The electrode pads felt cold against his skin, but Noah didn't much care. The doctor's face gave nothing away as she took his pulse and blood pressure. She also took a couple of vials of blood from him.

It wasn't until she ran a full body scan—twice—that her expression changed. At first, Noah assumed something was wrong with the machine, but Doctor Quiggins barely checked the machine at all. Instead she seemed confused by the printouts. It had to be his missing storage. "Something wrong, Doctor?"

"Your scans don't match."

Of course they didn't. "It's the dermis, isn't it?"

She looked at him. "How do you know?"

Noah stared at his hands and took a deep breath. As he explained what had happened from the time of the break-in to the moment Connor was shot, the pain Connor suffered echoed through his body. He shuddered.

"I felt his pain, felt him slipping away, and my essence reacted by transferring energy from me to him. But it wasn't enough." He explained what he'd done to save Connor. Saying it out loud brought back his own pain, at losing his storage, at the thought of losing Connor. By the time he'd finished, he was shaking and craved to see Connor.

"You're the reason I didn't find any internal injuries? You healed Connor?"

Noah glanced up at the awe in Doctor Quiggins' voice. That was not what he'd expected. "Yes."

"He died?"

"Only for a moment," Noah said. He didn't like to think about it.

"I'm not sure I understand all of what you told me, but at this point, all I can do is thank you. Without you, Connor wouldn't have made it."

Noah grew still.

Doctor Quiggins rose and squeezed his shoulder. "I hope you'll allow me to ask questions later. When we can focus on the science of it." She threw him an apologetic smile. "It's too fresh, now. I understand that, but I won't apologise for being intrigued."

He hadn't expected her not to be. "When I'm not so tired."

"Works for me. Until then…I'll keep this between the two of us."

If that meant no interviews or interrogations, Noah would be eternally grateful.

# 25

Soft, whispering voices filled the room around Connor. He couldn't understand what they were saying; he couldn't focus long enough to eavesdrop. They drifted in and out, left and right. A soothing sensation flowed through him, and it made Connor smile. Noah was still there.

"Connor?"

Noah? Noah. He remembered. He'd gone to Noah's. He remembered pain, and falling, and being shot. And he remembered Isa. Holding her. Missing her.

"I think he's waking up."

Connor let Noah's voice wash over him. Some pain had faded now. The light beyond was too bright for him, and his lids too heavy. The same applied to the rest of his body. Everything was so heavy. Warmth flowed through his left hand. Someone held it.

He licked his lips. They were dry. He was thirsty.

"I'll get the nurse."

Francis. Francis was here as well. That meant he had to be at Primrose.

He blinked and tried opening his eyes. The light was still too bright.

"Turn the lights down," Noah said.

The next time Connor opened his eyes, the light had been dimmed.

"Hey," Noah said, his voice laced with worry.

"Hey," Connor replied, but no sound came out.

Noah put an ice chip against his lips. Cold and soothing, but Connor didn't talk again—instead, he focussed on the connection, and Noah was there, welcoming, soothing, worried–

Something wasn't right. Noah felt different. What had happened? He clenched and unclenched his fists, trying to remember. Pain, pressure, not enough air, and falling, trying to save Noah. Floating, surrounded by warmth. He could breathe again, the pain faded, leaving him drained and heavy.

And aware.

Noah had saved him, healed him, but he shouldn't have done that. It cost too much. He shouldn't have had to give up part of himself. Noah could have died.

"You *did* die," Noah blurted out, his voice echoing the pain he broadcast through the connection.

Connor tried his voice and failed. He took the ice chip, but as he opened his mouth to try again, the nurse came in. She took his vitals, gave him another ice chip, and asked him silly questions, like who the head of Primrose was. Connor gave short, croaky answers that seemed to satisfy her.

"Good to have you back, Agent Smith." She wrote on his chart and handed Noah a cup of water. "Small sips. Don't drink it all at once."

Noah held the cup to Connor's mouth, but one sip wasn't enough. It barely wet his lips, so he took another and another, until Noah took the cup away.

"You can have more later."

Connor let his head sink back into the pillow. "I'm sorry," he said, though he wasn't sure what for.

Noah squeezed his hand. "You're here now. You're alive, that's what counts."

Because of Noah. Connor couldn't express what that meant to him. The one thing that linked Noah to his species, his kin, destroyed to save him. It weighed heavily on Connor's heart. Surely, he wasn't worth that much.

"You were slipping away from me," Noah whispered, bringing Connor's hand to his cheek. "I couldn't bear to lose you."

"But to give up your storage for me." Connor shook his head.

"I still remember everything."

That stopped Connor short. "You do?"

Noah nodded.

Connor closed his eyes. The interrogation reports mentioned Noah couldn't use the brain as a storage during his transformation because it had too many functions of its own. Not then…but he was human now. "It's in your brain."

"Yes. That's what Agent Zabrowski and Doctor Quiggins came up with as well. The information on my storage transferred to, no, *turned into* memories because I frequently replayed it." Noah swallowed, and Connor sensed his sadness. "It helped me hope, helped me remember whenever I got… homesick,"

"I'm glad you didn't lose them." Connor yawned.

"You should go to sleep," Noah said.

Connor shook his head. There were things he wanted to know, like, "How long?"

"Five days."

He'd been here for five days already? "Who?"

It wasn't Noah who answered. "John Taylor, small time crook," Francis said.

Connor opened his eyes again and clenched his fist. "Working for Jason?"

Francis shook his head. "No. He worked for Edward Allen, something Taylor only too readily admitted when Parker interrogated him. Unfortunately for him, we don't do deals."

Connor's anger lingered. It didn't make Jason any less guilty of hurting Noah.

"That's not all. Security footage of Mr. Jones' shop shows Taylor in the shop shortly after we incarcerated Allen." Francis approached Noah and showed him a photo. "He was seen giving you a card."

Noah frowned. "I remember. He seemed very interested in a specific book, but he wouldn't look at me directly. The card is in my desk at the shop. Carter, I think his name was."

"His mother's maiden name." A loud beeping made Francis jump. "That's me," he said as he grabbed his phone. "Yes, Lieutenant? Of course, I'll be up in a second."

He fidgeted with his phone and couldn't seem to look at Connor. "I have to go. Lieutenant Matthews... It's only temporary."

Connor thought of Isa—of lounging on her comfy sofa, laughing at her anecdotes, and groaning at her matchmaking ideas. For a moment, he imagined her walking through the door, smiling, teasing.

There was only Francis.

Connor ignored the ache in his chest. "I understand. Go do your job."

"Yes, sir." Francis threw them a smile that didn't quite reach his eyes. "I'll be back later."

Connor kept his eyes on the door—torn between missing Isa and feeling happy for Francis over the promotion, however temporary it was—until tiredness won out.

Noah kissed his cheek. Connor turned towards him, eyes closed, and Noah took the invitation and pressed his lips against Connor's. "Go to sleep. I'll be here when you wake up."

Connor brought Noah's fingers to his lips and let himself drift off.

CONNOR TOUCHED THE CASKET AND GLANCED AT THE PICTURE OF Isa, smiling and carefree on her last birthday. "Goodbye, Isa. Wreak havoc up there."

He grabbed Noah's hand and walked out of the sombre room and into a beautifully designed garden filled with vibrant green trees and flowers in soothing colours. A light breeze whooshed past his cheek as the sun warmed his tear-stained face. Perfect day for a funeral.

Too perfect. Isa would be pissed. She'd always said she wanted thunderstorms to ring her out. Then again, the day had just begun.

"Connor."

Isa's mother entered the garden through the large glass double doors.

Maggie Griffin—an older version of Isa, with her long auburn hair and piercing cognac-brown eyes—seemed frail and shattered, leaning on the arm of her lover, Justin, as they approached.

Connor wanted to run away. Anything to stop his heart breaking all over again. Noah's hand in the small of his back kept him in place. Kept him safe. He clutched Isa's remembrance card tighter in his left hand, and reached out with the other one.

Maggie grabbed it and pulled him into a fierce hug.

"I'm so sorry," Connor whispered, "I—"

"Shh," Maggie said. "I knew her job was dangerous. Always off chasing burglars, nothing good could ever come of that." She stepped back and smiled despite her sorrow. "But

Isa loved her job, and she was good at it."

Across the garden, Matthews and Tallis stood with their heads bowed together. Connor crossed his fingers for nothing to come up today. He squeezed Maggie's hand, and smiled the warmest smile he'd managed since Isa died. "She did, and she was."

He had nothing left to say. Isa *had* been good at her job. She'd worked at Primrose a lot longer than he had. It wasn't hard to admit that she was—had been—a better field agent than he would ever be.

The soft piano sounds of *"L'après midi"* by Yann Tiersen came through the speakers. Connor closed his eyes for a moment and let the music grab his heart.

"She really loved that song, didn't she?" Maggie asked.

He nodded. Every now and then Isa had insisted on playing the DVD of the French film—*Amélie* something—that featured the song, and then proceeded to talk through all of it. Connor barely remembered what the film had been about, but he remembered Isa's chatter word for word.

"It reminded her of your holiday to France," he told Maggie.

"She loved Paris," Maggie said, dabbing at her eyes with a small handkerchief. "Until I met Yves, of course."

Boyfriend number five, the painter.

"He always tried to get Isa to pose for him."

Naked.

Maggie giggled. It sounded heart-breaking. "I can't believe she lectured me when I chased Mitch off with a baseball bat, when she nearly castrated Yves."

Connor leaned into Noah as Maggie told Justin the story. Isa had thought Justin was too clingy for her mother, but there was something in the way he gazed at her that told Connor he might be perfect for her.

*Your mum will be all right.* "I miss you, girl."

As he looked up, a flash of lightning burst through the clouds, and he smiled. Isa might just get her thunderstorm.

SHADOWING JASON HAD FINALLY PAID OFF. THE WESTLAND GROUP was holding another auction—in Milridge, the Westland Group's headquarters of all places.

Connor sat in the SUV, listening to some interesting and less interesting conversations going on in the stately home they were surveying across the street.

Connor sensed Noah's unease at him being out here. Despite all they'd been through, Noah didn't quite grasp that Connor was a fully trained field agent. He might have joined Primrose as a researcher, and his job description might say PA, but he was a capable field agent, one who had scored high on all his tests. Tallis expected nothing less from her PA.

He let Noah know he was all right, as if Noah couldn't sense that anyway, and focussed on the conversation again.

Apparently, they were waiting for a delivery of some alien species Jason had caught. They were all very excited about it. Connor gritted his teeth as he heard Jason's voice loud and clear.

"It took me a while to find out it doesn't react well to most foods, but it likes grass and leaves. It plucks the grass with its front paws before stuffing it into its mouth."

Simpson, listening in as well, asked, "Any idea what species that might be?"

Connor shook his head. "Not a clue. Let's just hope it'll be all right until we make a move."

A lorry drove up to the mansion, and Jason got out. Four bulky blokes unloaded a large crate and carried it up the stairs and through the front door. Jason followed them inside.

Simpson touched his commlink. "Attention! Everyone in position."

Connor barely heard anything over the exited chittering when the crate was brought in, but the woman announcing the auction was about to begin was loud enough.

He took the headphones off, got out of the SUV, and joined team Bravo. He checked his tranq, and let Abernathy lead. He'd do best as last man.

They crawled along a long row of hedges, sheltered from the view of both the windows along the side *and* the street, where another, taller, hedge surrounded the grounds.

The grass was damp under their hands and knees, but they didn't dare walk since the inner hedges were only so high. Somewhere at the far end of the immense garden dogs barked, but they were locked in a kennel. They'd been recorded barking at birds, though, so with any luck, no one in the house would be alarmed by it.

They reached the back of the house without a hitch. Even the wide stairs leading to a large balcony, which could be seen from several neighbouring houses, posed no problems. They all milled around the curtained balcony doors.

"Bravo in position," Connor announced through the commlink.

"Charlie in position," Agent Groom, Charlie's leader, replied.

It took a minute or two before Simpson finally said, "Alpha in position. Go."

Connor nodded to Forente and Ipsen, who kicked the doors in. Weapons ready, they all streamed into the large, elegant room, ordering the occupants to freeze. The attendees complied, but only until one of the woman screamed. Despite the weapons pointed at them, the crowd scattered. Chairs tumbled and tables were shoved out of the way, making it harder for Connor and his team to keep the attendees from fleeing. It was a mess.

When Simpson and his team entered through the front hall, most of the attendees moved back towards Connor's team. By using the tables as crush barriers, they finally herded the crowd into one corner.

Somewhere behind Connor, heavy footsteps thundered on wooden steps, and team Charlie moved into the room from the wine cellar to catch stragglers.

"Cellar's clear," Groom said.

That was a relief, at least. Connor had feared to find a mess like they had at the farm.

Connor and Abernathy left the herding to the other two teams and took their team to inspect the crate that held the alien.

"Do we open it or take it out like this?" Abernathy asked.

"Like this. Whatever's in there might be drugged or might not be. We don't want to risk it lashing out at us."

Ipsen, Briers, Forente, and Quadeer each grabbed a corner and lifted it up.

"Whatever's in here is either very small or abnormally light," Briers said, blowing his sleek, in-dire-need-of-a-haircut fringe out of his eyes. "This thing barely weighs anything."

It was a tight fit through the high double doors into the hall, and the Bravo agents only just managed not to bang it into anything as they carried it outside. Still no sound from inside the crate. The creature had better be as alive as Jason had said.

As Connor and Abernathy joined the other teams, a blond head of curls disappeared down the stairs into the wine cellar. Connor cursed and sprinted across the room, hell-bent on catching Jason himself.

"Powell is escaping," he said to whoever was listening. "I'm going after him."

"Need help?" Simpson asked.

"Send someone around the outside to the back garden."

"Will do. Go get him!"

Connor sprinted down the stairs, listening for footsteps, or any sound to tell him where Jason was headed. A door slammed as he landed on the wine cellar floor, hard enough to rattle a number of the bottles. There was only one other exit, on the far end. Connor hurried towards it, zigzagging around barrels haphazardly placed in the open space. The back door slammed closed as Connor reached it. He threw it open.

"Powell made it outside."

When he exited the back door, Jason disappeared around the corner of the house.

Connor took a deep breath and raced after him, rounding the corner in time to watch Jason barrel into Kelp. Jason jumped over him without losing much speed.

Kelp hit his head against the wall, but Connor couldn't risk Jason escaping, and called it in instead of stopping to check the agent out.

He pushed himself to increase his pace. One last burst brought him close enough to fling himself towards Jason. Connor tackled him, losing his tranq as he hit the ground, hard.

Out of breath, he brushed aside the ugly twinge in his shoulder and straddled Jason to keep him from rolling away.

"You do not have to say anything, but it may harm your defence if you do not mention, when questioned, something you later rely on in court. Anything you *do* say may, and will, be given in evidence." Connor rattled off the lines while Jason bucked under him, trying to throw him off.

He grabbed his handcuffs, but lost them when Jason kicked his legs out. When he made a grab for them, a sudden right hook threw him off balance, and he slid sideways. Jason struggled to his feet and ran.

Connor wasn't about to let him go. Ignoring his poor sore body and impending headache, he picked up the handcuffs and jumped after Jason. He was a better runner than Connor had expected, considering he wasn't the one actually competing in those triathlons.

Connor pushed himself to the limit, giving it his all for the satisfaction of forcing Jason to the ground a second time.

This time, Connor had the handcuffs out as he straddled him, wheezing and coughing, and wasted no time fastening Jason's wrists behind his back. He took a deep breath, and repeated the arrest protocol in a clear, clipped voice. He roughly pulled Jason to his feet as he rose, gave him a quick pat down, and forced him to walk in front of him.

"What the hell are you doing here, playing the hero?" Jason asked, sounding genuinely puzzled.

"My job."

Jason stopped and looked at him over his shoulder. "Your job? You're just a PA."

Connor couldn't help but grin at the disbelief in Jason's face. "Yes, well," he said with a shrug. "Being a PA at Primrose isn't exactly a run of the mill job. It's not all about serving coffee and typing reports, you know."

Someone snickered behind him, and he turned around. Simpson, Groom, Briers, and Abernathy tried to hold in their laughter.

"We secured all of them, sir," Simpson said. Connor had no doubt he threw in the *sir* just for Jason's benefit.

He suppressed a smile. "Well done. I guess this one is the last of the lot then?"

"Indeed. Shall we take this one off your hands, sir?"

"No, thank you." The satisfaction of marching Jason to the SUV was all his. He pushed Jason out in front of him. "Move!"

Jason did, but slowly, looking around as if contemplating how to get away.

"Don't bother. You won't get far."

Jason snorted, but Connor ignored it. He merely asked Briers for his tranq and pushed it into Jason's back as an incentive.

Connor's injuries were catching up with him, and he sensed Noah's worry as he delivered his ex-lover to the SUV. The moment Jason stepped into the SUV and Briers took over, Connor rolled his shoulders, wincing at the twinge, and finally smiled.

Briers secured Jason into his seat, right next to his wife. The couple barely acknowledged each other, instead chose to waste what little time they'd have together by throwing Connor nasty looks.

Connor just smiled at them. Job done. Time to go home.

Through the connection, Noah's relief embraced him.

# Epilogue

SITTING CROSS-LEGGED IN FRONT OF THE POLYCARBONATE cell, Noah watched the Narf settle in a collection of blankets. The rose-coloured, bipedal, hedgehog-like creature with spongy spines looked a lot healthier than it had when he'd first met it. It was young, barely mature, if at all. He had no idea what its actual name was, so the poor thing would have to live with the name Primrose had given it. Connor had warned him Primrose wasn't very original when naming things. Given that they'd called it a Narf because of the sounds it made, Noah agreed with him.

Connor's boss, Lieutenant Tallis, had requested him to write up what he knew about these Narfs.

Easier said than done.

Most of Noah's knowledge consisted of impressions that weren't easily translated into speech or description. Still, he'd written a decent report, nevertheless. He at least knew where their planet was and what they lived on.

The Narf uttered something as it watched Noah, but though he understood its confusion, Noah had yet to decipher what it was trying to say. Spoken language would always be his weak point, and, as far as he knew, the Narfs had no written language. Still, the Narf didn't give up, so Noah would come back until he understood.

Because of his wealth of knowledge—her words, not his—Lieutenant Tallis had offered him a job at Primrose. He'd declined, of course. He wasn't eager to let Primrose have access to his knowledge. Contrary to what he'd expected, she had taken it in stride and offered him an advisor's contract instead—one that gave him far more control over what knowledge to share and what not.

"Just tell us what we need to know to keep them alive," she had requested.

He wouldn't even have to come in if he didn't want to, even though the contract stipulated he'd have unlimited access to their on-site holding facilities. They were willing to contact him by email, instead.

Noah had accepted the terms. Only, he *had* to come in, *had* to see how the creatures were doing, were being treated. Which was better than he had expected. He was also becoming more and more curious about the alien islands Connor had told him about. Connor was still negotiating access rights for him.

About Connor... Noah smiled and turned to face the entrance.

It didn't take long for Connor to appear. "Hey," he said as he sat down next to Noah. "You've been down here for a long time."

Noah grabbed Connor's hand and pulled it into his lap. "Someone had to keep this little one company. Its confused, has no idea where it is, and its lonely." Eating well, at least. The grass Jason mentioned it ate had sliced its tender palate. It had been far too sharp. Noah had no doubt it had only eaten it because it resembled something edible on its own planet. It was happily munching on lettuce and cabbage now. Not ideal, but the best they could do. "How did it go?"

"Quick and efficient. You won't believe the setup he had

down there. Cells—empty, thank God. Storage rooms with a variety of alien artefacts, and this large room spanning two floors..." Connor paused when Noah shuddered. "That was the room he kept you in, wasn't it?"

"I think so." It had to be. The ceilings had been very high, and the creepy butler had been looking up at Jason, as if he'd stood on an upper level. Noah swallowed against the memory of being cut. He pushed it down and sent Connor an image of what he had seen.

"Yes, that's it."

Connor leaned against Noah, resting his head on Noah's shoulder. "The building will be demolished."

*Just like that?* Noah didn't ask. He was just glad no other creature would be tortured there ever again.

They sat watching the Narf preen itself, trying to make itself comfortable in the bundle of blankets.

"That reminds me. I got you permission to see the Noren lift off in their repaired pod."

The Noren pod had been recovered from the auction. Noah may not have had any information on the Noren, but his technical knowledge was advanced enough to help the Primrose engineers with the repairs.

The Narf rolled over, dragging a blanket over itself. It was small enough to be mistaken for a pet, but Noah knew better. He'd seen their tree houses, far more elaborate than humans would believe them capable of.

"What's going to happen to it? Are you sending it to one of those islands?"

"Not for a while. It needs to be acclimatised first. We need to know whether it can survive on its own, for instance."

Sounded reasonable enough, though Noah thought the little Narf would do just fine. "Am I the only one not living in captivity?"

"As far as I know, yes. Though, who knows what's out

there? I mean, it took us long enough to find you."

"You wouldn't have, if this connection between us hadn't happened."

Connor froze.

Noah wrapped it around Connor and pulled him closer. "I have no regrets."

Connor's head shot up. "But if—"

Noah pressed his lips against Connor's to stop him from talking, and Connor fell quiet.

"Primrose was bound to discover me some day. It might have taken them another hundred years, but it was inevitable," he said, leaning his forehead against Connor's. "After Dafydd, I never thought I'd ever experience such a connection again, and nothing, absolutely nothing, will ever make me regret us."

Connor pulled him to his feet and dragged him into the corridor. He pressed Noah against the wall just outside the door—a camera blind spot—and claimed his mouth in a demanding kiss that left him breathless, and very turned on.

"Let's go home," Connor whispered against his lips.

Connor hadn't spent a single night in his own flat since the shooting, but this was the first time he'd called Noah's place home. Noah doubted Connor had even realised it. He smiled. Home sounded good.

Connor pressed his body closer.

Home sounded great. Noah gave Connor's cheek a quick peck.

"Yes, let's go home."

# Bonus Scenes

# The Origin of Primrose

## The sea serpent in Orkney

From *The Orcadian*, November 11, 1905
http://www.orkneyjar.com/folklore/shapinsay1905.htm

AN ARTICLE IN THE ORCADIAN IN NOVEMBER 1905 IS WHAT started it all for Primrose—an organisation tasked with monitoring and tracking aliens and alien technology.

Founder Captain Alfred McCulloch's grandfather—a ninety-year-old retired fisherman from Kirkwall who refused to move out of his house, much to Alfred's mother's dismay—read the article out loud during evening coffee in front of the fire, mocking his 'colleagues' for being taken in so easily by the so-called spotted sea serpent.

Alfred had moved in with his grandfather after a car accident that cost Alfred his commission and the full use of his left shoulder and leg. After months of recuperation, he could walk a couple of miles a day without too much pain.

When he'd set out in his grandfather's old fishing boat—another thing his grandfather refused to do, sell the boat—during the summer of 1906, he'd forgotten all about the spotted sea serpent, at least until he found himself facing it, bobbing near the coast, as he rounded a small uninhabited island.

Alfred remembered the article then, and his grandfather's mirth and mocking, once he got past his frozen state.

*"The body is described as massive as that of horse, covered with a scaly surface, and spotted. It was the eyes of the monster, however, that attracted most attention. These are said to have been as large as a bowl, and had a most fascinating attraction for the beholder."* – from the article in the Orcadian

The monster didn't attack him, didn't even come closer. It merely watched him, and followed Alfred's every move. The eyes were fascinating, indeed. The monster was big, it was quiet, and the eyes had a look in them that reminded Alfred of the child-like joy he had seen in his nieces and nephews. It was hard to fear a creature that looked at him like that.

Alfred sat in his boat for a while, watching the monster watch him, wondering what he should do. In the end he went with saying, "Hullo."

The monster shrieked and dove underwater, leaving Alfred clutching his chest. It was the start of a strange sort of peek-a-boo game that would last for hours. Finally, after Alfred decided he would have to be the one to end the game, the monster surprised Alfred by flopping up onto the beach, stretching its paws out in the warm sand—Alfred had expected flippers—and making a noise that Alfred chose to interpret as an invitation to join it.

Almost twelve years later, Alfred had gathered three more alien creatures on the small island. He also opened Primrose's first office in Kinnon, far from his beloved Kirkwall, and gathered a decent staff around him, all eager to find more alien creatures inhabiting the Earth.

Today, in 2012, Primrose has offices all over the world. Primrose also has a number of islands which serve as harbours for the non-hostile aliens Primrose hasn't been able to send back to their homes.

The small island north of Scotland is still in use today. Both Alfred and the Shapinsay sea monster are buried there.

# A Day in the Life of...

## Agent Ornella Amato.

PrIMROSE IS NOT QUITE A REGULAR COMPANY RUNNING NOT quite regular hours. While for some departments, like Administration, the basic hours run from nine to five, departments like Security regularly call their field teams out of bed in the middle of the night to hunt down A-watch alerts. A-watch being Primrose's alien substance detection system.

One of those teams is team Alpha, one of the two teams under direct command of Chief Security Lieutenant Natalie Tallis and her personal assistant Connor Smith.

Italian born Ornella Amato is a member of team Alpha. Born and raised in Cremona, Italy, Ornella started out working for the Primrose office north of Milan, but after a whirlwind romance with an English intern, she moved to England to be with him. By the time the intern left Primrose, *and* her, Ornella had become a valued member of team Alpha, and decided to stay.

To show how hectic a field team Agent's day may be, Ornella gives us a little glimpse into a day of her life, by letting us read an entry from her own, private diary.

06:15 - Called out of bed to check up on an A-watch alert. I can't believe we have an early call again. Yesterday it was three am. Can't wait until we're off call and I can sleep in until eight.

06:31 - In SUV on our way to Eggleby. Dennis Kelp's turn to arrange breakfast to go. Can't say I like dry doughnuts very much, but it's better than the home made soup he brought last time.
Gregory Warren looks hung over and a little green in the face. You'd think, after being on this team for two years now, he'd know better than to go clubbing when on call. Friday or no Friday.

07:45 - Arrived at the outer edge of Eggleby. Only barely getting light out. Area is deserted, seems like an old factory of some sort. Nothing to see from here.

08:50 - In SUV, back to Primrose. Check up—including hour long detailed search of the factory, top to bottom—was a bust. No artefact in sight. Not the first time this has happened.

10:04 - Debriefing by our team leader, Travis Simpson, in canteen with a warm lunch. All except Warren, who disappeared into the loo the minute we arrived, and is toying with a glass of water.

11:17 - Run over in corridor by escaped walrus like creature. No idea what it was secreting from its pores, but my jacket was drenched in orangy goo. Had to take clothes to Cleaning and grab a clean set out of my locker—last set. Filled out replacement request and put it in the mailbox near the entrance.

Sent a text to Agent Smith about having cell four checked for faulty latches... again. The stupid thing keeps breaking. And yet they keep putting creatures in cell four. Hopefully he'll scare Maintenance into finally doing a decent job of repairing it.

11:28 - Barely dressed and we have another call. Alien sighting, called in by old biddy from Leybridge.

11:43 - Arrived to quite a sight. Front garden completely demolished. If owner and neighbours hadn't seen something large and black rooting around, you'd think they were doing a garden renovation, the hard way.

12:25 - Caught the bastard. Fast bugger for its size. It managed to outrun us several times, until it reached the river. Who knew such a big fella would be so scared of a bit of water. The thing didn't even reach our knees. Still managed to put up quite a fight, though. No serious wounds, its claws weren't sharp, though it had a real mean left hook. Bryan Xiang's cheek's already starting to go blue. The rest of us came off with mere scratches. Only Quinn Flanigan got away unscathed, seeing as he was driving the SUV. I need to get me a licence.
Clean up crew is going to have a difficult time explaining this one away. Too many clever witnesses. Can't wait to read the report and see what they came up with. A small bear, maybe?

12:44 - Black monster in lock up—Kelp only dared calling it blackie once, before Simpson cuffed him. Once we got it tranq'd, it was easy to get in the SUV. A bit of a tight ride on the way back, with the thing being stuffed in the back seat. I spotted a repair man in cell four. Agent Smith works fast.

13:00 - Got a TIG treatment (tetanus immunoglobulin) in Medical, again, and had a quick shower.

14:57 - I knew I shouldn't have made a comment about it looking to be a quiet afternoon. Another sighting. And just when I was beating Warren at Halo. Probably won't get another chance any time soon.

15:02 - Ran into Stephanie Young from team Delta. I was about to comment on the blue streaks in her hair, when I noticed it wasn't a dye job. Not sure what it was, but it would probably be hell to get it out.

15:30 - Arrived at site. Nothing suspicious at first sight. Simpson is talking to the man who called it in.

15:35 - And we're on our way to Gelling—A-watch alert— leaving Kelp, Warren and Simpson to chase the "small ferret-like" thing that apparently chewed through his stainless steel fence.

16:23 - And Bingo. When we arrived I thought it would be another dud, but we actually managed to find it, albeit buried underground. No idea what it is—we know better than to touch it—but it looked like a mediaeval torture apparatus. Safely sealed it in a container.

16:45 - Picked up rest of the team, including one ferret-like creature in non-metallic crate. Two successful catches in little over an hour. Not bad at all. Though Kelp suffered a nasty bite from the ferret. Good thing he already had a tetanus shot earlier.

17:30 - Delivered both packages and went to the canteen for dinner. Warren's finally eating something. Kelp's been recounting their ferret-catching tale, wildly gesturing with his bandaged hand, while Simpson keeps rolling his eyes.

19:05 - Nothing for a while, so I decided to hit the gym for a nice run on the treadmill. If nothing hits us before eight, I'm going home. Fingers crossed.

20:13 - On train home, texting with Teddy. He keeps pushing me to move in with him, but I'm glad I have my own flat to come home to when I'm on call. Couldn't stand to wake him up at god-awful hours and unable to say more than, "Have to go."

20:40 - Hot chocolate and a classic Who, fourth doctor. Love the fake aliens. Though some are closer to creatures we've come across than the makers could have ever thought.

21:34 - On train back into Primrose. Another alien sighting

21:45 - On our way to Greyson's Woods, joined by Young to replace Xiang, who's down with a migraine.

00:26 - Combed out the forest, twice, it feels. Gathered plenty of traces for Research, but no alien anywhere. Scanners didn't pick up anything in the trees either. Whatever was here had long gone, or was too clever to let us and our scanners catch it.

01:30 - Just noticed a text from Teddy, time-stamped 23:58, wishing me sweet dreams. Maybe I should see if he's free for lunch tomorrow.

01:45 - Dropped off home, since my place was en-route to Primrose. I'm not holding my breath to get a good night's sleep, and I'm tempted to just veg out in front of the telly, but...

# From the Desk of...

## Connor Smith.

**A**S MUCH AS Connor TRIES TO KEEP HIS DESK IN ORDER, paper work keeps piling up. We unearthed these internal memos from the bottom drawer of his desk.

**From: R. Holloway – Research**
**To: C. Smith – Security**
**Subject:** Magical earrings?

Connor,

Attached you'll find a copy of my report on the magical earrings team Alpha found last week. Memo **P111051509S1537 / 15-05-2011**.

The research was...interesting to say the least. Many of our female researchers eagerly offered to test them out. Unfortunately, we had to destroy the earrings to find out what caused the headless look. I've boxed the pieces and sent them to Archives, along with the report.

Sincerely,
Rupert Holloway

PS: Thank you for the photo of Agent Amato walking around headless.

**From:** I. Griffin - Security
**To:** C. Smith - Security
**Subject:** Glowing rocks

Connor,

Remember that A-watch alert I told you about yesterday? Where we found those fluorescent rocks? Anyway, Jimenez forgot to put gloves on before he touched them, and apparently the rocks give off some sort of residue. No idea what it is, I haven't had the results from Research back yet, but it's STILL on his hands.

He's tried to wash it off several times already, but every time we turned off the lights in the locker room, his hands would light up like crazy. And not just his hands. Everything he touches lights up in the dark. He won't be forgetting his gloves anytime soon.

Maintenance is none too happy about it either.

Isa
*ROFL*

PS: I'm gagging for ice cream. Want to hit the park during lunch?

# Acknowledgements

A big thanks to:

All those who've been asking when this book would be re-released. It's here!!
My critters—Cleon, Don, Jennifer, Kaje, and Lou—for helping me iron out the kinks,
Lou Harper, for the ever so gorgeous cover design, and bringing Noah and Connor to life
J.R. Frontera, for editing my revised manuscript, and correcting my past perfects… ;),
Kiki Clark, for getting me through blurb hell.
You rock!
To SMP, Nathie, April, and Tush for all their hard work in making the first edition happen. I haven't forgotten,
Jarsto, Dorinde, and Jasper, for putting up with me asking the strangest questions—mostly out of context,
My husband and kids, for supporting me.

# About Blaine

BLAINE D. ARDEN IS A PURPLE-HAIRED, FORTY-SOMETHING author of queer romance mixed with fantasy, magic, and suspense who sings her way through life in platform boots.

Born and raised in Zutphen, the Netherlands, Blaine spent many hours of her sheltered youth reading, day dreaming, making up stories and acting them out with her Barbies. After seeing the film *"An Early Frost"* as a teen in the mid-eighties, an idealistic Blaine wanted to do away with the negativity surrounding homosexuality and strove to show the world how beautiful love between men could be. *Our Difference Is Our Strength*, is Blaine's motto, and her stories are often set in worlds where gender fluidity and sexual diversity are accepted as is.

Blaine is an EPIC Award winning author and her sci-fi romance *"Aliens, Smith and Jones"* received an Honourable Mention in the Best Gay Sci-Fi/Fantasy category of the Rainbow Awards 2012.

For more information visit: https://blainedarden.com

# Also by Blaine

The Fifth Son

<u>Tales of the Forest Series</u>
A Triad in Three Acts (The Complete Forester Trilogy)
The Forester (Forester Triad Act One – single release)
Lost and Found (Forester Triad Act Two – single release)
Full Circle (Forester Triad Act Three – single release)
Oren's Right

<u>Short Stories</u>
A Time Traveler's Valentine
Click Your Heels

<u>Anthologies</u>
IMPACT – Queer Sci Fi's Fifth Annual Flash Fiction Contest

<u>Freebies</u>
check https://blainedarden.com/books/freebies/

# The Fifth Son

**A PRINCE WITHOUT POWER**

In a land where magic is commonplace, Prince Llyskel has none. He can't command spells, he has never been taught to fight, and as the fifth son of the King, he will never rule. Everyone believes he's a weakling, most of all himself.

Powerlessness is Llyskel's problem—and his pleasure. In his secret fantasies, the prince dreams of nothing more than finding himself helpless at another man's hands… particularly the hands of Captain Ariv of the Guards.

Then Ariv makes Llyskel's dream a reality, and as the powerless prince surrenders to the soldier's desire, he finds his own true strength at last. But a web of royal politics is closing around Llyskel, threatening to tear him from his lover, and it will take all his newfound courage to escape…

# The Forester

A Tales of the Forest Short

*"Your Path is muddy, Kelnaht, but don't think avoiding the puddles will make it easier to travel."*

Kelnaht, a cloud elf, is a truth seeker caught between love and faith when a murder committed ten days before Solstice reveals an illicit affair between two tree elves he desires more than he can admit. Kelnaht's former lover Ianys once betrayed him, and the shunned forester Taruif is not allowed to talk to anyone but the guide, their spiritual pathfinder.

When Taruif turns out to be the only witness to the crime, Kelnaht must suppress his forbidden feelings or face the ire of the elders. Ianys is terrified the tribe will blame Taruif for the crime, and despite their painful history, Kelnaht tries to keep his impulsive ex-lover from sacrificing his freedom for an impossible love. If Taruif and Ianys' affair becomes known, Ianys will lose his daughter.

Kelnaht finds himself yearning to claim both Taruif and Ianys at the coming Solstice and turns to the guide, who gives him only cryptic advice. It is up to Kelnaht to prove Taruif's innocence and find a path free of puddles and mud for all three of them.